The Bai

By Charlie Wade

The Bailout

Copyright - 2011 Charlie Wade

Cover by Steven Miscandlon

For Karen

Chapter 1

They came in the dead of night.

A noise downstairs: wood crunching as it split. The front door smashed against the wall. Heavy footsteps climbed the stairs.

Rob had been waiting. He knew this was coming. For the last year he'd barely slept. Jumping at every noise, he was more than ready.

The footsteps reached the landing. Rob had planned this many times. Every night he'd change the plan, make it stronger. He had enough time to get out of bed, open the window and jump into the garden. He'd run away over fences and gardens to escape.

But now he could only concentrate on breathing. That once natural action needed all his attention. Heavy boots moved across the landing towards the bedroom but all thoughts of escape had vanished. Instead, he pulled the quilt tighter and waited. Breathing in then out.

The footsteps stopped. The bedroom door smashed against the wall. Black-uniformed, faceless men charged in. The red laser dots of their assault rifles scanned the room, searching. The dots merged to one large, pulsing blob on the duvet, just below his face.

He had no time to notice the cold as the duvet was pulled from him. Tiny shards of metal pierced his skin and though they hurt, it didn't feel like being shot. Then, the Taser pumped ten thousand volts through the wires.

His body jumped, contorting at angles as the electricity pulsed. He was helpless, couldn't resist. Arms and legs flailed uncontrollably, the pain searing through his head and heart unlike anything he'd felt before. He tried to scream but no words came.

The pain stopped but his body felt useless, like it was just a dream.

Within a second hands covered his body, moving him onto his front. His arms were twisted behind and something was placed over his head.

It felt like a plastic bag. He was going to suffocate.

He opened his mouth and sucked. Relief as breath hit his lungs. The taste of plastic from the mask was bitter and stale. He imagined the mouth hole giving him air. His life belonged in the hands of those tying him.

Something was pushed up his legs then rolled round his waist. His arms pulled up, he could hear metal clasps strapping leather together. A straitjacket. It was pulled tight, maybe too tight, before the final strap clasped. Rough, tight shoes were forced onto his feet, the clang of metal told him the shoes were chained together.

Their entry had been quick, they were well trained. None of them spoke, but he felt no anger. They were probably as scared as he was. Maybe more scared. They had to do this; they had no choice.

Four sets of hands wrapped round his stomach and legs and picked him up. Roughly the hands carried him downstairs. The cold night bit into him as they went outside.

He heard a metal door swing open in front. A lorry, it had to be. That's what they used.

The hands disappeared from his body. He wasn't falling but flying. They'd thrown him forward. For a second, just a split second, he was floating. With legs clasped together and hands behind his back, Rob knew he'd be unable to break the fall. Stiffening, he braced as best he could.

Landing face and arms first, the blackness of the lorry floor became more intense before he lost consciousness.

He woke to the screech of worn brakes.

Now upright, his arms were high in the air and fastened to something on the wall. Murmurs came from nearby and he could almost taste fear in the air. There were others in the lorry. He had no doubt they were the same as him.

The lorry moved on, accelerating hard and swinging him around until it reached top speed. Now gently swaying, Rob assumed they'd stopped at a checkpoint. One of many set up since the silent occupation. A chugging drone in the background, at first unrecognisable, was the engine. Contrary to the adverts, biomass diesel didn't make for a quieter or smoother ride.

Though the plastic hood had eyeholes, he could only see darkness. Moving his head, he tried to look towards the rear: no light from the door. He daren't move his hands or legs. Though the hood was skin tight, he imagined it slipping if he struggled. The mouthpiece could move. His breathing hole would disappear.

5

He should have run. Waiting for the inevitable was a poor plan. Others had fled. There were rumours of a camp in the Scottish Highlands with over a thousand people. They were supposedly safe. But what life did they have? Foraging in the forests? At least they had a life.

"Is anyone else here?" said a man to Rob's left side. His voice broken with fear.

Rob waited. He assumed the others were waiting for the same reason: there might be a guard with them. He didn't speak again. The chugging engine reigned for half a minute before a gruff, Yorkshire accent replied, "Yes, keep it down."

His heart beating fast, Rob said, "And me."

Another voice, from further away in the opposite direction to the engine said, "Yeah."

No one else spoke.

Who were these people? Rob knew they had plenty in common besides their incarceration. They were like him. They'd annoyed someone. Annoyed the new government.

As the lorry picked up speed, Rob's swaying reached a rhythm. His companions quiet, he tried to pinpoint where this had gone wrong.

The credit crunch four years ago was just the start. Small in comparison to now. Banks collapsing and being bailed out was a fairy story people told their kids these days. It was the start of all this.

Rob noticed the smell of diesel fade as a heavier, damp smell seeped through the lorry's sides. The smell of trees, of countryside. A smell he'd forgotten existed. Rob had no idea how long they'd been travelling or how long he'd passed out. He knew exactly where they were headed: The Isle of Wight.

The first voice spoke again, "How far is it?"

Again, a pause while the others waited. "Another hour or so 'till coast, I think," said the Yorkshire man. The furthest away grunted approval.

Rob knew he should be scared. He should be thinking of what was coming, but he couldn't. He'd been scared too long. He'd lived this moment over and over. In a way he felt happy. It was ridiculous, but the waiting was over. All he could do was think back to better times.

He'd always enjoyed his job at the local paper. His days filled with reporting raffles, school closures and minor acts of violence. He was as scared as everyone else when the banks failed. Though largely unreported in his paper, the real cause of the crash interested the journo in him. He spent his evenings reading broadsheet papers, watching finance channels and scouring the internet for dubious websites claiming to have seen it coming.

The gentle rock turned to a large jolt. The lorry must have cornered too fast. One of the others cried out, most likely the scared one. They were all scared, but that one in particular sounded terrified.

He was building mental pictures of the others. The Yorkshire man a lean ex-coal miner in his fifties. Pock marked face, evil to his enemies but kind to his friends. The nearer one, the scaredy cat, would be a rounded, timid man, probably an office worker.

He sighed. The country's problems were easy to pinpoint with hindsight. Back in the day though, the world had apparently changed. Everyone became convinced house prices could rise forever. No one thought it could end. Boom became larger boom as more money was borrowed to continue climbing the infinite ladder. Of course the wrong people were lent money, it was the only way to keep the boom booming.

They'd been wrong. They hadn't created a new world, they'd just forgotten parts of the old one. The comedown was quick. In the space of two years, Rob witnessed many friends and colleagues lose their homes, savings, pensions and sanity. The government bailout never really worked, it just slowed the collapse. Three years later the banks were in trouble again. This time, there was nothing the government could do to bail them out. The UK wasn't alone. Banks were collapsing all over the world. Ironically, the losers were those with money in the banks: the people who'd not previously borrowed.

"We're slowing down," said the Yorkshire man.
"Oh god," said the scared one.

"Shush," said the far away man. Rob had yet to build a picture of him, but suspected he just melted into the background. The type people forgot was there. Probably an accountant or architect.

The lorry screeched to a halt, Rob swayed heavily to his left, struggling to keep pace with the breathing hole. The gush of air from the brakes and the engine's dying throbs told him this was more than a checkpoint.

Chapter 2

"Where are we?" asked Scaredy.

"Shush," said the Yorkshire man.

Rob wondered more about his companions. What had they done to annoy the powers? Was it the same as him? He also didn't know their names, but until he found out, the Yorkshire man would have to be Yorkie.

Both the lorry's front doors opened. The sound was clear, the back of the lorry acting like a loudspeaker. A car or van pulled up behind them with people exiting. Then nothing as footsteps walked away.

Rob thought that things had really got worse during the second round of bank collapses. Whole countries failed the way Iceland did years before. First Greece and Ireland then Portugal and Italy. Spain was the big one. The world changed when that crashed. The European Union collapsed trying to bail it out, which in turn bankrupted Germany, France and Britain. All they could do was print money. They printed it by the bucketful.

Footsteps approached. The voice with the footsteps was both female and annoyed. Rob sensed he wasn't alone in grimacing at her tirade of screams, shouts and swear words. It would only annoy them more. Remembering his own capture and crashing fall to the back of the van, he sympathised with what she was letting herself in for.

The back doors opening and the inevitable crash and squeal of pain were followed by silence as footsteps climbed in. Rob guessed from the dragging, rustling and metal on metal noise that she too was being strung up. Soon, the sound of boots hitting tarmac and the door being closed removed the tiny rays of light inside the lorry.

A minute later, the lorry chugged into life, pulled away and accelerated hard.

The printed money kick-start to Europe was too late. People had lost confidence in money itself. The game was over. Queues formed at all banks and soon they were collapsing daily. Anyone with money in the bank lost most of it. Three emergency bank holidays were called to stem the tide. When they reopened, the money had vanished. Those who'd hoarded cash watched as prices inflated beyond belief and calculators. The rest of the world ignored pleas for help. They couldn't help. They had the same problem.

"Are you okay, love?" said Yorkie.

"Yeah." Her voice low, mumbled. "This is it, isn't it?"

"Keep it down," said Scaredy.

"It's probably best to whisper," said Yorkie.

"I can't believe this, it happened so quickly. I thought I was safe."

"We all did," said Yorkie. "We all did."

With the lorry nearing full speed, the engine's noise made talking difficult. The pain in Rob's stomach, from having his arms stretched, seemed to increase with every mile. With the pain also came the urge to wee. The gentle swaying and lack of distraction increased the pressure on his bladder.

The bailout, the final one that actually worked, eventually came. Not from America or Europe but a Far East Consortium. Not capable of growing enough food to feed its people, Britain needed the bailout more than other western countries. Of course, people were worried about the Consortium. Was there a hidden agenda? Why were they doing it? But, beggars couldn't be choosers, and in two years they'd become more than beggars.

Rob noticed the van sway more; he assumed they'd left a main road and were on a minor one. According to Yorkie they were nearly there. Crunch time was approaching.

The next sway and curve came faster. Rob knew something was wrong as the tyres squealed, struggling to grip the road. The sense of motion became confused as the lorry's rear skidded sideways. Wheels left the road. The van flipped onto its side. The screeching sound of metal on tarmac continued for seconds before stopping.

Everything was quiet.

Scaredy broke it. "What happened?"

Rob waited for someone else to reply, but no one did.

Being handcuffed to the roof in a toppled lorry had benefits, Rob's hands were now chest high and though he couldn't see, he could feel the strap holding his cuffs to the van.

Feeling the fallen Yorkie at his feet, Rob knew he was at a disadvantage as his hand grips were further across and lower than his own. Rob shifted to give him more room.

"Everyone okay?" asked the quiet one. Rob had forgotten the bloke was with them.

The cries of yes came. Scaredy added, "What happened?"

"Shush," said Yorkie. "Try to free your hands."

Rob twisted and pulled at the strap connecting the handcuffs to the roof. By touch he reckoned the chain around the handcuffs was hooked into the roof by a wing nut. The nut loosened quickly, though with cuffed hands it was awkward to twist. Rob thanked god the cable ties had been removed and replaced with handcuffs.

He thought of the driver and guard. Surely they'd come and catch them? Were they inviting death by trying to escape? Or trying to escape from death?

"Haven't heard the guards move," said Yorkie.

Rob tried to shift again, Yorkie sounded very near his legs. "If this was a crash, they'd have been thrown around."

Rob thought being tied to the ceiling could have saved them. Ironically, he imagined it would make train and bus travel safer if replicated.

"There's a wing nut at the end of the chain round our handcuffs," said the girl. "It turns clockwise."

Rob felt guilty for not sharing that information, he'd just assumed everyone had realised. His wing nut fell to the floor, hitting Yorkie on the way.

"Sorry."

"Don't apologise, get yourself free."

Raising his hands to his head, he felt the zip that held him in the plastic hood. His shaking fingers and thumbs hacked at the zip, pulling it down. Finally his face was free. He took a deep breath of stale, biodiesel-fumed air. It was the sweetest breath he could remember taking.

Rob bent to help Yorkie. Unzipping his hood, Rob was able to pull Yorkie's zip further than his own. Though detached from the van, the handcuffs still restricted movement.

"Come on, let's get the door open," said Yorkie as he stood up.

Walking to the rear, Scaredy pleaded for help. Rob guessed he was making heavy weather of the wing nut.

"You'll be alright," Yorkie muttered.

Passing by Quiety, who was helping the girl with her hood, they stopped at the rear door. The toppling had partially crushed the corner, letting in rays of moonlight. Rob watched Yorkie grab the edge of the door and pull. He joined him and after a few attempts the door gave.

Yorkie jumped and Rob followed. The full moon shone between the trees, lighting the tarmac as they walked round the lorry. The air, heavy with the musk of wet trees, was being replaced by the stench of spilt diesel and burnt rubber. Rob saw the shredded, almost disintegrated tyre on the ground. Like a sacrificial lamb, that tyre might have saved them.

Reaching the cab, Yorkie paused and poked his head round. Avidly watching him, Rob saw a smile grow on the face of the fifty-something's lips. The mental character he'd built of Yorkie was spot on. About five ten high, Yorkie was built like the proverbial outside toilet. Powerful cheek bones bore a few scars. Though he'd certainly take no shit, Rob was convinced he'd die for those he cared for.

"Come on," said Yorkie. He edged round the corner towards the cab.

The cab was badly crushed, the driver's side taking the full impact. With the passenger side now facing up, Rob saw Yorkie peer over the top and inside.

Sneaking round the front, Rob looked in the shattered windscreen. Through the shards of ice-like, cracked glass, the driver was slumped in the corner, his neck contorted at right angles to his body. Lying half on top of him was the passenger. He moved slowly with his eyes closed, clearly alive but in pain.

Rob was surprised to see Yorkie pull himself up to the lorry door and dive in. The surprise became horror as Yorkie smashed the still barely alive passenger round the face. Using his cuffed hands together, the punches were more slaps but they were still harder than Rob had seen before. Yorkie finished by strangling the last drops of breath from his body. He both gained and lost respect for Yorkie in a few seconds.

Stunned, he watched Yorkie kick out the remains of the windscreen. Staying as one piece, it peeled out like skin on custard. Helping it on its way, Rob avoided Yorkie's gaze.

"Had to be done, lad. They've got guns here and radios. It was him or us."

Forcing himself to meet Yorkie's eyes, Rob nodded. "Any keys?"

"Just looking." He rifled through the dead men's pockets, eventually finding and chucking them to Rob.

After Yorkie crawled from the cab, Rob unlocked his handcuffs. When Yorkie had returned the favour, Rob watched him reach back into the cab and pull out a small machine gun, a pistol, some ammo and a water bottle.

"Come on, lad," said Yorkie, handing him the pistol. "We need to get out of here."

Walking to the lorry's rear, the others were unzipping each other's helmets. As Yorkie unlocked their handcuffs, Rob leant against the lorry, nervously holding the pistol away from himself.

Chapter 3

When he'd worked for the newspaper, Rob had had access to information not seen by everyone. The real cost of taking the bailout was clear to him. Freedom was gradually withdrawn, internet access cut, and the press censored. Almost every week a new proclamation appeared, whether restricting travel, increasing working hours or multiplying police and army numbers. After months with no stability, riots and little food, the public were easily bought. It amazed him what rights the public swapped for three meals a day.

The clearances came. Rob kept a diary and found other sympathisers. Some said the huge numbers of displaced people were sent to work camps. Gypsies, travellers, tramps and other non-productive groups were sent to camps in mid-Wales. The idle, the long-term sick and the scroungers were taken to Norfolk. Similarly, the elderly who couldn't support themselves were sent to Hastings and Eastbourne.

The first of the clearances was also the largest: political prisoners. Hundreds of thousands had been moved so far. Their destination: The Isle of Wight.

As the five assembled in the moonlight, their collective crime wasn't clear. Dissenters, radicals, rebels. Whatever and however people referred to them, Rob knew that's what they were. They looked such an odd combination. Harmless. But what did a dissenter actually look like?

Scaredy stood out the most. It wasn't obvious what he could have done to annoy the overlords. He looked so innocent, how could he offend anyone? His beard stubble added years to him, yet he was only early-thirties. Though his size dwarfed the others, he looked like a gentle and scared giant. He was tall, at least six foot six, but he also had the look of someone who'd lost a lot of weight rapidly. The flimsy rations couldn't have been easy on him. Rob immediately changed his nickname to Large Lad.

The girl, mid-twenties, was prettier than Rob had imagined. Petite, her face had a redness, an intensity that matched her long hair. Rob looked at her eyes. Green. Deep green, they seemed to reflect the moon. He had to force himself to look away from her, he was staring and her left hook looked as feisty as her will.

Quiet Man blended in amongst the trees. Quiety was fairly tall, well set and seriously bald. He seemed happy enough leaning back, just out of the main group. Happy in the shadows.

The five stood like young school children. All of them barely able to believe the gift they'd been given. Freedom had somehow hijacked their capture. Rob had been convinced this had been the end. Somehow they'd been given a second chance.

The clearances had never been explained and no one talked about them. Fear over the next meal had changed people. Previously aggressive people became subservient. No one spoke against the new regime. Certain theories about the clearances appeared on the few radical websites that hadn't been closed down. They said the camps were the main demand of those supplying the money and food. Why wasn't clear. No one knew who they were. Even the documents and proclamations Rob saw which gave clear indications of what could or couldn't be reported didn't explain why. They had a strong work ethic. Everyone had to do something productive. They carried no one.

Rob knew friends who'd left the country for Europe by boat. Though the ports and ferries were restricted, passage could be bought for food or gold. When they arrived in Europe, most discovered it wasn't worth it. At least food was guaranteed in Britain.

With the crashes came unemployment on an unimaginable scale. The Consortium utilised the cheap labour well. Builders made prisons to house the many new criminals and labour camps for the clearances. Others ploughed fields the old way, by hand, or dug for coal in re-opened mines. The biggest use of the newly unemployed middle class was the police, the special police and the army. These were paid a good wage in New Sterling, the new currency linked to the Chinese Yuan, and given the best food and housing.

Though free, Rob's relief was short lived. He was a stranger, miles from home. The choice was clear. Hop through the hedgerows or face certain death along the road. He'd no idea if the lorry had reported the accident. Even if they hadn't, someone would eventually drive by. Whatever time it was, it was still night-time curfew and they were wearing prison-coloured partial straitjackets.

Rob looked to the others for ideas. The girl was looking at her feet, intimidation glowing from her. He supposed she must feel more alone being the only woman. The Large Lad stood still, looking round. Looking as lost as Rob felt.

Yorkie spoke first, "Come on, let's get off the road."

Trees lined either side of the road. Rob's sense of direction was non-existent. "Which way?" He shrugged his shoulders.

He watched Yorkie look round, though he seemed to look through all of them, searching for something to give him direction. Pausing, he gazed at the stars.

"I think that way," chipped in Quiety, who again had melted into the background.

Rob and Large Lad looked at Yorkie for confirmation.

Yorkie nodded. "Aye. That way."

The newest arrival hadn't acquired a nickname. Rob thought she deserved something better than just, 'The Girl.' She spoke quietly, a shadow of her former rage. "This is the New Forest. The road leads to a town. There are miles of forest and scrub. We can hide there?" She shrugged her shoulders, unsure if it was enough of a plan.

Rob saw Yorkie smile. "Aye, we head to the woods. Make some ground before they realise we're gone."

The trees grew thicker, becoming dense woodland. Night time was no friend to forest walking. Large Lad cut himself on a sharp branch within seconds, Quiety bought up the rear in his own uncomplicated way, while Yorkie and the girl led.

The occasional chatter of, "Mind that branch," was joined by, "Where's the moon gone?" and Large Lad's, "My feet are killing me."

After fifteen minutes walking, Yorkie said to the girl, "What's your name, duck?"

"Sam."

"I'm Pat," said Yorkie.

Rob had been expecting an older, more regionalised name, maybe Jeremiah or Ebenezer. He was mildly disappointed. The girl looked every inch a Sam.

Just keeping up with the leaders, Rob said, "I'm Rob." Yorkie turned and nodded. Sam didn't.

"Richard," said Large Lad, again spoiling another of Rob's thoughts.

Quiety didn't speak and no one thought to ask his name. Rob checked two minutes later to make sure he was still behind. He was.

The silence of another five minutes walking was broken. Sam said to Pat, "Where do you come from?"

Rob was struggling to keep up with the leaders. There was something about that girl. Something about the way the moonlight flickered off her eyes. Now was not the time to be doing anything about it. He reckoned he'd no chance anyway. All the same, though, there was something about her. He needed to know more.

"I come from Essex," said Yorkie, killing off the coal mining vision. "I moved there ten years ago. I'm from Doncaster originally." The coal mining vision stood at the side-lines, waiting to be substituted back on.

"I'm from Southampton," she said. "Born and bred. I didn't believe this day would actually come."

Rob knew he should be making conversation with the other two. Leave Yorkie and Sam alone. But that was easier thought than done. He should at least make an effort.

"You alright mate?" he asked Richard.

"Yeah." He panted. "Can we stop for a bit, I've got a stitch?"

"York..." Rob stopped and restarted. "Pat, can we stop a minute?" Noticing Sam's shoulders drop and silent huff, he guessed she disagreed. Pat, on the other hand, called a ten minute break.

Sitting in a crude circle on the dew soaked ground, they got their breath back. Rob heard Yorkie estimate they'd walked two miles. Rob just hoped they weren't walking in circles. Any minute now they'd see the upturned lorry and an army of soldiers waiting.

Sam was attempting to explain to Yorkie how big the forest was. It sounded larger than he thought. There were apparently few villages or identifying features to look for. Lots of open space with the odd town and village dotted round. She was very vague though.

Rob knew they were all thinking the same thing: exactly where were they walking to? Rob thought of asking, but knew it was pointless.

"Is that gun loaded?" asked Large Lad.

Rob looked at the pistol he'd laid on the ground. It was facing away from himself, through a gap between Large Lad and Quiety. "Dunno. I haven't unloaded it."

"Is the safety on?" asked Quiety. They looked at him. His voice felt like a stranger's.

"I don't even know what a safety is," said Rob. "I've never fired a gun."

Noticing Quiety and Large Lad move further from the pistol's aim, Rob instinctively drew back. The cold lump of steel he'd been carrying for the past few miles, waving around, pushing branches with and even, he remembered, scratching his itchy arm with, had now become an item of respect and danger.

Quiety stood and approached the pistol. Rob noticed Yorkie stop talking to Sam and take in the quiet man. Picking it up by the barrel, Rob saw Quiety open the chamber and look in the compartments.

"Six bullets. The safety is on." Quiety pointed a withered finger at a hook near the trigger. "You need to slide that up before you can shoot."

"Have you shot a gun before, umm," asked Yorkie. His confused face said he'd either forgotten Quiety's name or just didn't know it.

"Yeah, twenty years in the Air Force. Most of the time I flew helicopters, didn't see a lot of actual combat."

"You should carry this, not me." Rob realised he'd said that with too much enthusiasm. The lump of metal had become a murder machine and he wanted nothing more to do with it.

Quiety held it up and away from the group. Twisting it from side to side, Rob guessed he was getting a feel for the weight. This wasn't the first gun he'd held.

Rob would later wonder why an ex-military man had been lumped together with them. The government and Consortium had been good to them. Ex-military personnel were treated with respect and given the best of what few jobs were available. Those they couldn't employ elsewhere had been re-recruited into the military. Whatever was in Quiety's past had annoyed someone high up.

Yorkie stood and stretched his legs. "Come on lads, better get going. We don't know what lead we've got."

Large Lad stood with a sigh and the creak of unused bones. Rob knew he'd find this the toughest. He wasn't exactly built for speed. The nervousness in his voice hadn't carried over since their escape. His confidence seemed to be growing. Rob hoped it wasn't short lived.

They walked for another hour but at a much slower pace. When the first glimpses of daylight broke, Yorkie stopped. Up ahead he'd spied a break in the forest. Miles of plains stood in front.

"Any ideas, Sam?"

"Sorry, no. I've been trying to think of the villages and towns, but my mind's blank. If we're walking north-west we should have come across the Bournemouth road by now. I can't remember though. They picked me up at Southampton and they always get the ferry at Lymington. I thought we'd gone through Lyndhurst, maybe not. Sorry, not much help, am I?"

Rob guessed that was the problem with maps. You rely on them so much you forget what your country actually looks like. One thing he did know, wherever they were and with daylight approaching, open ground was a bad idea. He didn't need Yorkie to tell him that.

"Can we make it over these plains before dawn?" asked Yorkie. He wasn't addressing any of them. It wasn't a question.

Rob thought he wanted them to say yes. Looking hard, he could see the forest continued in the distance. Guessing how far was impossible. There didn't seem to be any roads crossing but that wasn't the point. A helicopter would pick them out like pips in a melon. Surely they'd be after them by now?

"I say we follow the trees north," said Sam.

She pointed the way she thought was north. A quick look where the sun was rising showed she was right. Yorkie nodded and sat down for a breather. Rob and the others joined his lead. The only sounds were occasional bird song and their heavy breathing.

None of them was in great shape. Rob hadn't worked out in years. His local gym had closed when money became useless. Yorkie was trim, though definitely past his prime. His need to sit down worried Rob. Maybe he was feeling the strain? Quiety looked in fair shape, but didn't look used to long walks after little sleep. Due to his height, Large Lad was carrying a lot of weight on thin, badly fed legs. Sam, well, though Rob had noticed her skinny figure, he guessed it was from lack of food rather than exercise. Noticing her again, the morning sun caught her hair, revealing a depth of colours making up the red. Looking down to her face, he caught her eyes, looking back at him. How long had she been watching him watching her? Looking away, he thought he saw her smile.

"What's your story, Rob?" asked Quiety, to all their surprise.

He turned to Quiety. "Small town Journalist. I live." He paused. "I lived in Basingstoke and worked for the Basingstoke Bugle for thirteen years." Looking round, he saw them staring, not unfriendly, just curious and interested. "It's a small local paper. I can't really call myself a journalist. Small stories, who's had their shed broken into, lost dogs, who's been caught fighting after closing time. Boring stuff really. We used to make some of it up or re-use stuff in really quiet weeks."

Taking another look round, they really were listening avidly. They all had a normal story similar to his. Maybe hearing someone else's took you back to better times?

"When the banks first went pop, I did a series of stories about local businesses and house prices, you know the effects it was having. That's one of the reasons I'm here I guess. I should have stuck to dogs that say sausages and the Mayor's new haircut." Looking round, he received the approval he wanted for his half joke. "Anyway, I kept reading about finance and banks and politics. And I wrote more and more complex articles. I tried to keep it easy to understand; explain to everyone how the banks and the City had killed their money. I won an award for a piece I wrote. They republished it in the Times too."

His claim to fame got an approving nod from Yorkie.

"I had a battle with the editor and publishers over some of it. They didn't like the truth, or my version of the truth. Some of it was toned down; who to blame was never fully explained." He sighed before continuing. "After the first bailouts, I went back to writing about fetes and cats stuck up trees. But I kept reading. I kept writing as well and tried to get more articles published in the big, real papers. Had a few little articles printed but they thought the crisis was over and they'd moved onto the next thing."

"Then, when the second crash, the real crash came, well I was more than ready. My editor changed almost overnight, I guessed it was pressure from the publishers and owners, but the work I was writing was really toned down. As the currency crashed and the food riots started, it became plain old censorship and propaganda. I'd send off my piece, and it'd come back with half of it missing. But over that next year, as the Consortium arrived and the food returned, everything changed. You all know that. There was so much crap, so many lies being broadcast that I had to do something."

Looking up, he realised there were all still looking. Was he over milking this? He was a second rate reporter, not Bruce Willis saving a burning skyscraper. Large Lad's breathing had calmed and Yorkie had regained some of his colour and was standing up. Rob guessed that was as far as his story went. Shame, he hadn't got to the good part.

Yorkie handed round the water bottle. One mouthful each, he clearly told them. Despite walking for so long, Rob wasn't thirsty and the others weren't either. The dew filled, damp forest seemed to filter water through them as they walked. As they stood, Large Lad made his way towards Rob. When they set off the groups had changed. Rob and Large Lad were at the rear while Quiety had joined the leading pair.

The conversation wilted as they trudged on, tiredness affecting them. They needed shelter and a chance to sleep the day off so they could walk again at night. Exhaustion was catching up. The others were as optimistic as Rob that a deserted house, full of water, food and shelter would appear any second. It was just round the next tree.

Chapter 4

After another mile, daylight had brightened the sky. Though the forest remained thick, they could still see the plains. Occasional glimpses of conversation from the lead group hit Rob. They weren't saying anything profound or even interesting, just idle walking chit-chat.

Beside a particularly dense piece of woodland, just at the plain's northerly point, Yorkie stopped them. "We should rest."

Rob saw the colour had drained from his face. He didn't look well. None of them looked well, but something wasn't right. He thought the others knew it too. Large Lad had sat down immediately and was removing a shoe. Quiety took a good look at Yorkie then turned to Rob, shrugging.

As Rob sat beside Large Lad, whose rough shoe seemed over-worn and hole-filled, Sam sat the other side of him with Yorkie and Quiety opposite. Yorkie lay back against a tree and fiddled with his digital watch, no doubt setting an alarm.

Within minutes Large Lad was snoring, Sam was yawning heavily and Yorkie's colour had returned though his eyes were closed. Rob was exhausted but had never felt so alive and awake. A nod from Quiety suggested he was too.

Rob flicked his head, suggesting they moved while the others slept. Quiety bought the gun and they sat beside a large tree, roughly fifteen yards from the others.

"You think we'll make it?" asked Rob.

Quiety's headshake and shoulder shrug was the only reply Rob needed. The real question was did they know where they were going? It was a race against time, the prize for winning, a few hours freedom.

"I'm surprised they haven't found us," said Quiety.

Rob nodded. "Why are you here then?"

Quiety laughed. "Principles. They shouldn't be allowed, principles. Cause more wars, broken marriages and deaths than religion. Actually, principles are probably not allowed anymore are they? I was either a hero, foolish or brave. I haven't worked out which."

Rob waited a few seconds, listening to the birdsong in between Large Lad's snores.

"I was a hero once. Iraq war. The first one, obviously. Four marines got separated and cornered. They were running out of ammo; it was a bad fire fight in this little town. Anyway I had to fly a sortie in, take out a few mortars and drop off some ammo. There were mortars and bullets flying everywhere. Scared witless I was. I lost the gunner, you know the one who sits behind the pilot firing a machine gun? Lucky shot by some Iraqi."

Rob nodded.

"My co-pilot took the gun. God knows how but we took out one of the mortars. I kind of sensed a lull in the fire, so instead of dropping the ammo, I ordered the co-pilot to drop the ladder instead. I hovered low and ordered them to climb up. We saved all four of them. No doubt we saved their lives. The fresh ammo wouldn't have lasted, they were regrouping you see? That's why the lull."

"Anyway, I got a bollocking for ignoring orders, but me and the co-pilot also got a bravery medal. Outstanding service to the British Empire. Now look at me."

Quiety was taking time over his words, scratching at his arm and playing with a stick. Rob avoided eye contact as he seemed tearful. He'd no idea where Quiety's story was going, but he knew there was a reason to go back so far.

"Left the RAF ten years ago. Good pension. House in Devon on the coast, all paid for. I thought that was it for me. Just me and the wife pottering round. Kids had left home. I did a bit of work driving for a local firm. We were happy. Then it all went to shit."

Rob noticed Sam stand and stretch. She'd maybe got twenty minutes' sleep. It probably wasn't enough but she looked like she'd survive on it. Mouthing the word toilet, she walked off into the woods.

When she was out of sight, Quiety continued, "We weren't as badly hit as most. Owned our own house, little debts, government pension. Obviously when the house fell in value, my wife Bren was worried. But as I pointed out, everyone else's house was falling too. The banks failing wiped out some of our savings, obviously the insured bit was safe, but like many, we had a lot more than that. What we ended up with was worthless after the second crash. Never thought a bank would lose all its money. It just doesn't happen, does it?"

"When the money printing started and the food ran out, I got a call. The RAF recalled me. Bren didn't want me to go. Hell, I didn't want to go. But, with the troops still in Afghanistan and back in Iraq they wanted to bolster reserves. It wasn't obvious why at first. My job's always been to protect Britain and its citizens. That's what I always fought for."

Sam had finished her business and was walking towards them. Sitting cross legged to the side of Quiety, she was visibly shaking.

"You cold?" Quiety asked.

She nodded.

"If I had a coat, I'd share it." He shuffled over and placed a fatherly arm round her shoulders. Though the morning sun was strengthening, the trees blocked its heat. Sam seemed comfortable enough in his arms and seemed to make the most of stealing his warmth.

"Are the others still asleep?" asked Rob. It was a stupid question, Richard's snores could probably be heard in Bristol and Yorkie's eyes were firmly shut.

Sam nodded but avoided eye contact. "I think I got a bit, but don't really feel tired."

"We didn't either."

"What you talking about?"

"Qu..." Rob stopped.

Shit. What was his name? He couldn't call him Quiety. "Just you know, about his experiences." He pointed at Quiety to clarify and felt himself go red.

"What have I missed?"

Quiety recapped his build up. Sam listened intently, but pulled away from his arm half way through, when it was obvious she'd warmed up. As Quiety explained about his recall, Rob nipped off for a toilet break. He should have done it during Quiety's recap, but he was enjoying hearing his gentle voice.

Finding a solid tree, Rob relieved himself, realising in the process just how tired he actually was. Sitting down he was wide awake, but now, after the smallest of movements, lethargy had hit hard.

24

Walking back to Quiety and Sam, Rob lay stomach down on the floor. Quiety was talking about his house and wife. He seemed more comfortable and chatty talking to Sam, but he quickly finished his side-tracked story for Rob's benefit.

"All better now?" he asked.

Rob nodded and yawned. "Yeah."

"So I became a reserve pilot. I thought I'd be standby for home protection or maybe even flying the air-sea rescue copters, but I soon realised what was happening. You have to understand this, all my flying had been to protect Britain. Protect the citizens. So when I was asked to do *that,* well I couldn't. We were flying armoured gun copters. We were supposed to quell riots, protect the food convoys and public buildings from pilferers. They ordered me to fire..."

His pause was noticeable. Sam put her hand on his shoulder. Taking a deep breath he continued, "Fire on a crowd of rioters. These starving people, just like us, were just trying to get food. It could have been any of us. I said no, I won't do it. They ordered me to do it. Eventually they said they'd put me and Bren in prison if I didn't. I had to."

Rob shared an uncomfortable pause with Sam as they took in what he was saying. Rob knew that wasn't the end of the story. Quiety wouldn't be here if he was part of the Consortium's machine.

"I took to the air and although I fired, I missed them all. I made sure of that. I gave one or two a few scares, but I never hurt anyone. I did scare them off though. A few days later I said my eyesight was going and asked to be moved to ground control, you know fixing, refuelling, cooking that sort of thing. They agreed. But that's only half the story isn't it?"

"I ended up chief cook and bottle washer for the pilots. They all looked down their noses at me. I think sometimes they wished they'd thought of bad eyesight first. The other lads never lasted long: killing your own makes you crack. Mental breakdowns, suicides, one of them had to be shot by another pilot after going on a killing spree round the base. Fucking cruel world we live in. Fucking cruel."

Though drifting in and out of sleep, Rob couldn't believe what Quiety had been through. It made journalism seem as dangerous as peeling potatoes. However, it still didn't explain why he was here. Thinking brought exhaustion nearer: he was too tired to listen anymore. With one final yawn, Rob caught the sleep he'd been looking for.

While Rob slept, Quiety continued talking to Sam about the RAF and his family. After what seemed like just a few minutes, Yorkie's alarm went off.

A freshened and healthier looking Yorkie nudged Rob awake. Through bleary eyes, Rob saw the rest of them talking. They must have let him catch a few extra minutes. He felt refreshed after his sleep. He couldn't remember the last time he'd slept so well.

What was more surprising, as he re-joined the others, was they hadn't been captured. Yorkie's digital watch said it was nine in the morning. Six or seven hours since the accident, and no one had found them. Maybe they walked so far their searchers had a lot of ground to cover? Recapture was inevitable but would take time.

Either way, the group was buzzing. They looked more than ready for walking, though Rob wondered just how rested Quiety and Sam were. Richard the Large Lad looked a stone lighter already, his tall frame more gaunt and stringy than before.

"Here, take a sip." Yorkie handed Rob the nearly empty water bottle. Though thirsty, Rob knew as the icy water hit his stomach it was food he needed. They all needed it. They'd have to eat today and not just foraged berries. Wherever they were headed they needed energy and Rob knew the body would only supply a certain amount.

"Ready?" Yorkie asked.

Rob nodded.

They walked again in two groups, Quiety, Sam and Yorkie up front, while Rob was left with Richard again.

Heading along the top of the clearing, which spread across the horizon, they plodded on. Ahead of him, Sam told Yorkie more about the New Forest, but she didn't appear to remember any more than last night. Rob knew their only hope was to keep moving; keep heading north and west to the temporary safety of the Welsh hills.

Yorkie was setting a slower pace than the previous night. Rob wondered if he was feeling alright, the speed he fell asleep was disturbing. Large Lad seemed less inclined to walk into trees during daylight. Rob noticed a glasses ridge on the middle of his nose, and suspected poor eyesight the cause of his frequent accidents.

The first stop came after two hours. None of them was tired such was the slow pace, though sore legs were a problem. The edge of the clearing could easily be seen. Also what looked like a road ran near the clearing, north to south.

"Everyone okay?" asked Quiety.

"Apart from the hunger and dead feet, fine," said Large Lad. He seemed to mean it humorously but his natural sarcasm gave a different tone.

The others grunted; considering the alternative a bit of starvation and sore feet were a small price to pay.

Sitting in a rough circle, their collective gazes met Sam. She realised it was her turn. "Well," she started, "I guess I'm here because I'm a gobby cow." She paused. "Seriously, I do have a bit of a temper so it's not surprising I've annoyed people."

"I worked for an Estate Agent. Before you start hating me, I wasn't an Estate Agent myself. I just answered the phone, booked viewings. I was like a trainee. It was so much fun at first. I mean house prices were just going up and up. Everyone was making money from it and the bonuses were unreal. For a twenty year old it was crazy money."

"Anyway, Gary, my manager, had this plan. Buy-to-Let was the new thing. Everyone was doing it. You basically got a valuation on your home, one that said it was worth more than the mortgage, then you used that equity as a deposit for another mortgage and bought somewhere to rent out. No money changed hands. All the fees and charges were added to the new mortgage. The rent you got from letting the flat paid just a bit more than the interest only loan, but, and this is the but, as the property increased in value it gave you more equity. Everyone was doing it. It just couldn't go wrong. It was like free money."

Yorkie looked like he had something to say, but didn't have the heart to interrupt. However much Rob enjoyed hearing and watching her speak, Sam had just dropped massively in his estimation. He'd always considered Estate Agents barely human. How could she be one?

"After a few years of price rises, some people had ten apartments and houses without paying a penny. It really was just a money making machine. Everybody was paper millionaires. I was too young for a mortgage. Though the banks were chucking money around, they drew the line at a twenty one year old who'd only been working a year. But then, my boss had this plan."

Stretching her legs, she moved onto her left side. The still dew wet grass was uncomfortable, especially when dressed in half a straitjacket.

"He'd become friendly with this mortgage advisor. They'd got chatting and came up with a plan. Self-Certification it was called. Basically, you lied. You wrote down on a piece of paper I earn x and sign it and they believed you. Problem was, you weren't supposed to use them for Buy-to-Lets. Just for home owners. It was meant for builders and self-employed; people who couldn't prove their income. But everyone was doing it."

"I wanted my own place to live in. I know I was only twenty odd, but living at home was a nightmare. Plus I saw all this money flying around and got suckered into wanting some. Makes me sound selfish, but everyone was doing it and prices were going up so much, I couldn't see how I was ever going to own a house. Born in the wrong generation, that's what we were. No one my age was ever going to be able to buy a house. We'd spend forever living with our parents or renting off their friends."

"Anyway, that's where my boss helped. We had a house and a flat come in. The flat was new build in a popular area, but the house was old. In need of modernisation, god how many times have I typed that? An old lady who owned the house was moving to a nursing home. She didn't have any family you see, except a son in Australia. So what my boss did was set up this new company. He offered her a bit under market price, not a huge amount under, just ten percent. She still had enough to pay her fees and live happily. But it was this new company that bought the house, not me. Then, the day after it was sold, I bought the house off the company for way over market price, twenty percent more. We split the profit fifty-fifty. I used some of it to modernise the place and the rest I put down as a deposit on a buy to let apartment. The advisor sorted the mortgages out. We didn't just bend the truth: there were blatant lies. That was that. I had a house and a flat, two huge mortgages, but enough coming in to pay off the interest. I was on the ladder."

"And then." She paused. "Northern Rock went pop and prices started to fall."

A long silence was broken by Yorkie suggesting they head off. As Rob stood and joined Richard the Large, he knew that despite what Sam had done, ripping off an old lady, mortgage fraud and possible tax evasion, it wasn't enough to be sent to the Isle of Wight. Like himself and the others, something else had happened. She'd done something else. Broken one of the new laws.

Chapter 5

After the government accepted the Consortium's offer of help, most old laws were left intact. A few minor ones were repealed or in some cases tightened, but the new laws caused the most concern. Most people were apprehensive, and the new laws unanimously passed overnight only made it worse. Everything changed. Night time curfews were introduced to stop the food riots. Food and energy were rationed.

For Rob, the power of detention was the biggest worry. Sentences were increased for petty crimes and the already full prisons became as overcrowded as Victorian times. Everything on a police state checklist was being ticked.

With the currency destroyed, New Sterling was quickly accepted as the new currency. Pegged to the Chinese Yuan, the runaway inflation of food and fuel prices halted overnight. Rob always thought that fixed prices enforced by law had more to do with the halt in inflation than any perceived stability. Either way a loaf of bread cost the equivalent of a week's work, and that was if you could find anywhere selling it.

Unemployment hadn't stopped rising at ten million. Work projects to utilise the unemployed were started. Prisons, work camps and food production were given priority with the workers paid just enough to buy food. The repossessed houses owned by the failed banks reverted to the government. The pick of these went to the new police officers. Recruited in secret, these officers, along with their new army counterparts, formed the strong arm that exerted the changes.

Rob sometimes thought he was dreaming. Most of the time, he wished he was.

Before moving off, Rob walked over to Sam. She watched him approach and left a gap between her and Yorkie to meet him. For their first contact, other than the occasional smile and sigh, Rob tried to be casual. "You alright?"

"Yeah."

"Sort of helps doesn't it? Talking, I mean."

She nodded and followed Yorkie and Quiety, hanging a few yards behind though still in front of Rob and Richard. Rob half considered catching her up. Though miles and worlds apart, they were the closest in age.

Settling beside Richard, they continued walking just inside the forest towards the road. As they neared it, the heavier Richard's breathing got.

Over the hour it took to reach the road, Rob moved ahead of Large Lad, with Sam slowly dropping back. After only sleeping for half an hour, she'd lost most of her colourful looks and charm. Bin-liner sized bags hung from her green eyes and her skin, once fresh was glazed in a sheen of sweat and forest dew. Rob caught up, noticing her smile the nearer he got. He finally spoke, asking how often she'd been to the New Forest.

"We used to come here when I was young. During the summer holidays all the family would come and play cricket and football. There was a clearing, similar to this." She paused. Her eyes welling up she added, "Sorry, getting out of breath."

Rob nodded. "Not quite the same in terms of scenery, but we used to go to Basingstoke Municipal Gardens. We'd have a picnic when it wasn't raining. We also played football and that. Happy days."

Sneaking another look at her, he could see tears being held back. Maybe that was enough nostalgia for now.

The road that bisected their path approached. Yorkie raised a hand, slowing them. "We'll break here. Try and work out how to cross this thing."

"What's the time?" asked Quiety, who Rob thought needed a new nickname.

"Twelve."

"Count how many cars in the next quarter hour? Should give us an idea."

"Good idea, Dave," said Yorkie.

Dave - so that was Quiety's name. Rob wondered both how Yorkie had found that out, and also whether he'd remember it longer than a minute.

Sitting down, Rob left a respectful distance between himself and Sam, which Richard the Large promptly sat in. Shifting further towards Dave, and further from Richard and his split shoes which didn't smell too fresh, Rob sat cross-legged and toyed with a few blades of grass.

"Guess it's my turn," said Richard.

As they turned, his face went dark red, not just from lack of breath. "You heard of quants?"

They collectively shrugged their shoulders. Rob had heard of them, but he didn't want to spoil the story.

"We were the masters of the universe apparently. Created a new age. Created a crock of shit in reality."

Sweeping his longish hair back, he continued. "I was always into computers, just seemed to click with them. I suppose I understood their language."

This didn't surprise Rob, nor it seemed, the others. As harmless as he was, he had computer geek written all over him.

"Straight from school in the eighties I worked in a bank. A junior at first on the mainframes that powered cash point machines. You wouldn't believe it, but that digital watch you're wearing now." He pointed at Yorkie. "That's more powerful than the first cash point machine network. Crazy, eh?"

"In the nineties they set up a computerised trading division. I was chosen to work on it. At first it was nothing complex, just a huge database and we configured reports to look at trades to pick up anomalies. It looked at indexes to spot trading patterns. Eventually we'd created this automated trading system. It worked too. I'm not saying it had Nostradamus like foresight, but it actually traded correctly more times than not."

"We were given huge bonuses then given another job: quantifying risks in loans. A few American banks were already doing it and were making a fortune selling the loans on so the bank wanted in. That was how it started. We wrote the software, based on parameters given, that priced risk into mortgages. It enabled people to trade them. The people buying knew, or thought they knew, how risky they were. It was a huge success. Even the riskiest mortgage on a collapsing house could be spliced and added together with safe ones and sold as a risk free investment."

He paused, looked at his feet and sighed. "Until house prices started to fall."

Rob wasn't the only one who knew what came next. Yorkie stood up, forcing a break in Richard's story. Again, Rob knew there was something else, something bad enough to land him here. Okay he was responsible for writing the software, but he'd just been doing a job. He couldn't have known it would backfire so catastrophically.

"One car's gone by in fifteen minutes," said the now quite talkative Dave.

Yorkie pondered this. "Mmm. I think we have to do it. A show of hands?"

All of them nodded.

"All those who want to cross the road, raise your hand."

They all raised a hand.

"Okay," said Yorkie. "Now how do we do it? All together or one by one?"

The considered view was one by one, however Richard disagreed. "I know you might think my analysis is questionable." He laughed alone at his joke. "But if we all go together it takes less time, so there's less chance of a car coming and less chance of being seen."

Yorkie nodded, having followed the logic.

"The only question is, if one of us gets caught, the rest may escape. If we all go together, the chance of us all being caught increases."

The cheeky imp deep inside Rob wanted to suggest they send out Richard first as a decoy, but they were in this together. As much as his feet whiffed, he was one of them. They'd stick together, they were in agreement. Deep down he knew they'd eventually get caught anyway.

The plan was clear, if not very good. They'd just run the fifty yards between them and the road. If they heard a car coming they'd stop and hide. If they saw a car while crossing the road, they'd carry on running.

"Three, two one," counted Yorkie, "Go."

It was obvious before they'd got ten yards, that Sam and Rob would be the fastest with Richard bringing up the rear. Careering across the road, they looked in both directions.

Nothing.

Falling in a heap, twenty yards across the other side, they waited.

Finally, Yorkie stood and led them again, settling for roughly north west as their path. Rob walked beside Richard, while Sam had moved back to the leading group.

They kept moving for three hours, crossing occasional tracks, rivers and moving ever deeper into the forest. The regular groans from their stomachs became a talking point, Quiety had been declared the winner after one particularly long rumble. As the mid afternoon heat grew and the water bottle emptied, fatigue set in. Rob, Quiety, Sam, Yorkie and Richard needed food, drink, toilet paper, cigarettes and some foot cream respectively.

The railway line crossing their path came as a surprise.

"Of course the railway," said Sam. "That road we crossed a few hours back must have been the Beaulieu road."

"Are we near Beaulieu?" asked Rob.

"Not anymore. We must have been near when the van crashed."

Rob was unsure if the rest of them knew how lucky they'd been. Though there was no documentation, Beaulieu was thought to be a temporary holding place before the final transfer to the Isle of Wight.

"Where does the railway go?" asked Yorkie.

"Ashurst in the North and Brockenhurst the other way. We used to get the train to Bournemouth."

"Any idea how to cross the line?"

"It's electrified, I know that. Some kid got killed doing graffiti near Southampton once. There are a few bridges and little holes that go under the line."

"Tunnels, you mean," said Richard.

"Whatever." She smiled.

"Okay," said Yorkie. "I say we have a break then follow it West and South."

"There's a row of cottages somewhere," Sam continued. "But, I don't know where, could be either way."

"A cottage would be good," said Quiety. "Warm bed, soup on the stove, bath, clean clothes..."

"Plus unhappy occupants," Rob interrupted.

"I was dreaming pal, that's all. A man needs to dream,"

"Come on lads and lassie, quit your bickering." Yorkie moved from the railway line and sat behind some trees. "There's stories to be told and I believe it's my turn."

"My tale starts later than yours. I weren't a banker or stock broker or what have you. I were just a miner. That's all. When there weren't no mines left, thanks to the milk snatcher, I got on me bike and found work in Essex. Part of Joyce's family lived there. The last fifteen years I've been gardening, handymanning, and done the occasional bit a building work."

"We never had much money, so the banks going under didn't matter. But when all the neighbours and Joyce's sister lost their houses and cars, well, you can't avoid it can you?"

"After that day, you know Black Monday, when the pound collapsed, well I got angry. It was so quick, wasn't it? We had to pay the price for others' mistakes." Seeing Richards face drop, Yorkie clarified, "You was a foot soldier mate. None of this is your fault, don't think it is."

"Anyway them bank holidays, when the banks collapsed, they got me angry. All the supermarkets and shops closed didn't they, and the lorry drivers refused to deliver food. After that the state of emergency." Yorkie frowned and looked into the distance.

"There was rioting on the streets of Basildon, not that you'd've known the difference on a Saturday night. But everyone was at it: looting shops, burning cars. Obviously, I joined in. We had a good stock of tinned peaches and pasta and that, but if everyone else was helping themselves to food, I wasn't going to stand by and do nowt."

"Was like old days, you know fighting the police. Except, they were well tooled up. Not like the Miners Strike. All they had then were dustbin lids and a baton. Now they've got pepper sprays, proper shields, stab-proof vests, even them Taser things. And there were so many of em. Along with the Army and Specials." He looked at Quiety and shrugged his shoulders.

"Well, pretty soon the curfew was working, but by then a few of me mates and my brother in law had had enough. After all we'd done for this country we felt let down. How could they have let this happen? Some of the lads were just out for a fight really, but one or two were more organised. We kept in touch after the riots ended, had secret meetings and that. What we wanted to do was change things,

35

make them the way they used to be. I'm sure up and down the country there's loads like us."

"After the bailout came and the curfews worked, well, we did the odd bit of civil disorder, looting and what have you. Gotta say, I ain't proud of some of the things we did. When everyone's drinking from the same stream, you don't piss in it do you?"

He turned to Sam. "Sorry love, forgot you were here."

She shrugged her shoulders.

"One day there was this food lorry. Full of canned chicken stew all the way from China. One of the lads followed the route and they went the same way each week. Straight from the docks to one of those supply centres in the Midlands. The plan was we'd highjack it. The Basildon Bovver Boys we called ourselves. Freedom Fighters. Look at me, I'm too old to be a pissing Freedom Fighter. Even if I weren't, what good was hijacking twelve tons of chicken stew ever gonna do?"

"It went wrong, obviously. We messed up. The driver got badly hurt too, that wasn't supposed to happen. I was supposed to be driving the lorry, but the driver threw the key into a ditch after we stopped it. Instead of scarpering, we messed around trying to hotwire it. That's when the police got us."

"I've just spent a year on remand in that new prison in Stoke. Then two days ago, they came for me. Said they were moving me. When I was in the back of the lorry and shackled to the ceiling, I clicked where I was going."

Yorkie had done a good job of quieting and depressing them all. Rob's romantic vision of Yorkie the loveable coalminer had faded, replaced by a second rate Neanderthal Wolfie Smith. 'Power t'people,' he imagined him saying.

Rob knew they'd all made a stand against the system, but stealing canned chicken stew? Surely there were better targets. Chinese canned chicken stew was a large part of Rob's and everyone else's diet since rationing. God only knew what part of the chicken it came from; it didn't taste anything like chicken, but it was omnipresent. Everywhere you went it was the only food on sale.

If Rob was being generous, he supposed the can of stew represented the heart of the Consortium's repression. The only food not on ration, its consumption was practically law in itself. No one knew where China was getting all the chickens from, but the cans

36

occupied over half of most supermarkets' floor space. Recipes to
liven up the stew were broadcast on television. Ready, Steady,
Chicken Stew was a popular programme featuring once in demand
celebrities who looked nervously at the theatre wings during filming.
The whole nation of sixty million was surviving on Consortium stew
of questionable provenance.

"What were you gonna do with the lorry?" asked Sam. Rob
thought she had a point. What did you do with twelve tons of canned
stew?

"We hadn't really got a plan for disposing, like, but one of the
lads owned a garage. Because there was no petrol, his garage was
always empty. We was going to park in it there for a bit. Another lad
had a plan to use a big hosepipe or muck spreader, we'd go round to
the council building or police station and spray it with stew. Course
the roadblocks and armed police would've made it impossible. But
just imagine what it would have looked like. Just imagine how much
that would have cheered everyone up."

His head full of a bunch of fifty year olds going round the
country, muck spreading their way to victory, Rob smiled. "We'd
better head off."

"Aye," agreed Yorkie, standing up.

As much as he'd hated chicken stew, Rob knew he was close to
killing for just a spoonful of it. With thirst and hunger had come
lethargy, headaches and heavy legs. He knew they couldn't continue
walking forever. Surely another day was all they'd manage without
water?

Richard would be the first, Rob thought. How long could he
continue? With every mile he looked paler and paler. Sure he had
reserves to eat into, but he was also unfit. How long before he
collapsed?

As the afternoon heat faded into the cloudy sky, the gang's
pace slowed. A blackberry bush brought some relief as they helped
themselves to its fruit. Quiety warned them to be careful and not
overdo it. "Getting the skwits won't be pleasant," he'd said.

In the brief pause around the blackberry bush, Rob pulled
Yorkie to one side. "These cottages, if we find them what do we
do?"

"I was wondering the same thing."

"We need food and water." Rob knew he was stating the obvious.

"Aye. It could get messy though. We don't hurt no one."

Rob agreed and moved from the bush. His stomach complained more than ever after the dozen or so berries hit its waiting acid. Behind him he heard Richard run then sick up his newly acquired food. So long without food seemed to have unsettled not just his own stomach.

Seeing Quiety go after him, Rob watched Sam and Yorkie pick the rest of the blackberries by tearing off whole branches. The berry stains mixed with blood on Yorkie's hands as he cut himself several times.

Having returned with a once again empty stomach, Richard gingerly ate a few berries and picked some more. The once full bush now lay plucked and ruined, as if devastated by a tornado.

Falling back in line, Richard beside him, Rob began the slow trudge towards what he hoped was a mystery cottage. Their speed now barely a baby's crawl, they once more followed the railway line.

Chapter 6

They came across the cottages suddenly. Despite walking near the railway for hours, not a single train passed. The cutbacks and electricity blackouts had shut most of the railway network, only troop and food movements being regular carriage.

The cottages were from another age. Victorian or Edwardian, they sat back from the line; their overgrown back gardens no doubt once full of flowers, cabbages and carrots for the railway workers that inhabited them.

Though they looked long deserted, Yorkie still led them slowly. Briefly signalling to Rob for them to go first; the others would wait with the pistol toting Quiety. This close up, Rob could tell just how much the past day had taken from Yorkie. Drained of his colour, his eyes seemed like icy glass. Estimating his age was difficult, everyone between the age of forty and sixty looked the same to Rob, but if he had to guess, the top end of fifty had to be near.

Scouting through the trees towards the low fence of the first cottage, the pair inched forward. Rob noticed the front garden was as overgrown as the back and a few roof tiles were missing. The structure looked sound though. Sam would say it was in need of modernisation.

Reaching the fence, they crouched behind, peeking over. Three cottages: the far one looked the most recently inhabited judging by grass length, but the curtains that hadn't fallen down were drawn. No cars were parked nearby, no obvious parking places that hadn't overgrown and most importantly, no sound.

Seeing Yorkie's nod, Rob sneaked past the disintegrated gate and towards the door. The buzz and rush from his over-pumping heart felt like he was ten again, playing a game of soldiers.

At the front door, with Yorkie traipsing towards him, gun in hand, Rob tried the handle. Surely it wouldn't just open? The handle creaked as it turned and though the door was wedged in the jamb, the lock had been ripped out. Someone else had been here, that was clear. Whether they were still around wasn't clear.

Wondering why his gun-less self was in the lead, Rob opened the door and gazed into the room. The smell of decay and damp rushed past. The room, a small living room cum kitchen with a solitary flight of stairs, had seen better days. A very mouldy sofa and two armchairs sat round the fireplace with a solid wood table filling the kitchen. Every item of homeliness or value had been taken. Only a few old envelopes and a newspaper lay on the table. An ancient range set in the corner of the kitchen was caked in rust.

Walking in with Yorkie behind, Rob nodded at the stairs, Yorkie nodded back and took a step onto them. The groaning of warped wood would have woken anyone within a mile. Yorkie stopped as they listened. The only noise he heard was birds taking flight outside.

As Yorkie creaked and groaned up the stairs, Rob went to the kitchen dresser. Opening a drawer, the stench of a long dead mouse wafted out. The cupboard was bare, but not as bare as Mrs Hubbard's unless she'd started serving Chinese chicken stew. Five faded but full cans lay at the back of the cupboard. Whoever had stripped the house had baulked at the chickeny goodness they contained.

Yorkie creaked down the stairs, shaking his head with a smile. Leaving the house, they caught the others' attention, Yorkie making an okay signal with his thumb and forefinger. As they traipsed towards the cottage, Yorkie made another signal, the shush one with his forefinger held to his lips. They understood and walked quietly inside the cottage. Rob did consider miming, 'There's five cans of chicken stew in the cupboard,' but life was too short. Besides, they'd find them in seconds.

The second cottage was as deserted and pilfered as the first. Rob helped himself to an old saucepan and a few mugs sporting a probable new species of mould. Leaving them by the front door, he headed for the last cottage.

The front garden had once been well tended. Borders gave way to a gravel path with now defunct flower beds lining it to the door. The grass long and the flowers either seeded or wilted, the pair crouched crab-like towards the front door. A gentle breeze rocked the bushes as they approached.

Rob headed left, towards a partially un-curtained window as Yorkie guarded the door. Poking his head up and gazing in, Rob wasn't surprised to see a gutted cottage similar to the others. Turning to Yorkie, he nodded.

Yorkie understood his signal and pushed the door open. Joining him inside, Rob looked round. More recently decorated than its counterparts, this one had been modernised. The fireplace replaced by new tiling and a woodstove heater, the floors stripped back to cold, bare wood and the original range restored to its decades ago state.

The newly fitted kitchen cupboards were bare. Someone had spent a lot of money fixing the place up, most likely borrowed money. Wherever the inhabitants had cleared off to, they'd taken anything that could be sold and left only the worthless, unsellable thing behind: the house itself.

Rob took the upstairs, Yorkie still didn't look right to him. They were all lacking food and energy, but he seemed over exhausted.

The upstairs bedroom was well decorated if too pink for Rob. Like the others, it'd been ransacked. A quick glance in the newly built walk in wardrobe, gave a solitary pile of old clothes. Whether the remains of a charity bag or tramp's off casts, Rob wasn't sure. They looked more comfortable and less conspicuous than straitjackets. The bathroom was pinker, but someone had pulled up the floorboards to compensate. All copper piping had been stripped out. The basin and bath would be useless. Towards the back of a cabinet were a few near-empty bottles of shower gel and some haemorrhoid cream. Rob took the shower gel, leaving the cream for some future pilferer.

Taking his loot downstairs, Yorkie was sitting on the floor, waiting.

"Sit down, lad."

Rob sat opposite. He'd known him less than twenty four hours, but knew something was wrong. It was written all over his face. Shivering, Rob looked in his nearly closed eyes. "What is it?"

"I'm not very well, lad. Diabetes."

"Shit." It explained a lot. No insulin and a lot of exercise wasn't a good idea. Rob knew little about diabetes apart from the usual, if you don't get insulin, you'll die. He suspected he was about to learn more.

"There weren't no insulin in the lorry cab, I thought there might have been. I guess they were going to get a doctor to look us over wherever we ended up."

Rob wondered if they were kidding themselves about the Isle of Wight. Maybe the camp didn't even exist. Perhaps they were just going to be murdered as many had already been. Remembering the lorry and the driver Yorkie had killed, there was so little paperwork. Just their names, serial numbers and old National Insurance numbers.

"What can I do?" asked Rob.

"Don't worry about me, lad. There's nothing you can do. After you all get some rest, you're going to leave me."

"No..."

"Shut up. Just shut it and listen. One of you needs to be strong about this and lead the rest to safety, wherever the fuck that is. It's got to be you. Dave's too old and a bit quiet. Richard's not a born leader. It's you. When the time comes, if I don't pop it before, you've got to be strong. The rest'll need it."

"There must be some way. You can't expect us to just run."

"There isn't. Without insulin I'm not capable of walking. I'll get worse then slip into a coma. You won't be able to save me. You don't want to see it either. None of you do. You've all got a chance of freedom without me."

Rob had been scared for a year but nothing until now had bought him to tears. Wiping a tear from his cheek, he bit his tongue to stop him howling like a banshee.

"And stop crying you big wet lass." Yorkie smiled. "I've had a good life you know. I ain't exactly looking forward to a life on the run, and well, my body won't last, will it? I know my time's up. I meant what I said, you've got to be the strong one. You lot can make it if you keep going and be lucky. You've got to convince them to leave me. Now, finish your blubbering and we'll get back."

Rob turned and wiped his eyes clear. After waiting a minute to de-panderise his eyes, they returned to the first cottage.

All eyes were on Rob as he walked in, the pile of clothes the reason, his red eyes what he thought was the reason. Tossing them on the floor, he sat between Sam and quiet Dave. Richard was standing, trying to get a can of chicken stew open by hitting it against the range.

"There's a pan and some mouldy cups outside," said Rob. Though not appealing in any way, their eyes nonetheless lit up.

"Sam wants to light a fire, heat the water up," said Quiety. "I said no because of the smoke?" He looked at Yorkie for guidance. Rob realised just how hard this was going to be.

"Fire's maybe not a good idea. Does the water even run?"

Richard left the half mangled can and turned the kitchen tap on. Chugging away, it eventually spat a chunk of black gunk before dark smelly water trickled out.

"Might want to let that run a bit." He returned to his can.

"There's a bath upstairs and next door. If you can get it running," said Yorkie.

"You can go first if you want, Richard," said Quiety.

Rob turned away trying not to laugh, but caught Sam's smirk and eyes on the way. Apparently he wasn't the only one who'd noticed Richard's feet.

"Uh, yeah okay." He looked confused, the half mangled can of stew still in his hand.

Sam sorted the smelly clothes into three piles, two t-shirts, one very large shirt with collar and two smallish pairs of trousers. "I take it there's no washing machine?"

Rob smiled. "They'd probably disintegrate. They might keep us warm or give us some cover. We look conspicuous in these."

Handing Richard a bottle of shower gel as he made for the stairs, Rob said, "No singing."

Richard nodded, took the large shirt Sam held up and climbed the stairs which creaked and moaned under his steps.

As Quiety resumed trying to open the can, Rob walked to the kitchen window. The grass and weeds nearly six feet in places, it hid the cottage well from prying eyes on any passing train. Behind, he heard Sam ask Yorkie if he was okay. Spotting a decrepit shed in the back garden, he tried the back door. As he heard Yorkie reply he was fine, just tired, he opened the door and walked into the jungle that was once a thriving allotment come flower garden.

Stooping to keep low, Rob waded through the long grass. A multitude of bees and butterflies disturbed from their busy lives, fluttered and buzzed round. The shed's door was both padlocked and hanging off its hinges, though rust rather than a break in was to blame. Inside, a long-deserted bird's nest lay on the top shelf. Every cobweb within a ten mile radius seemed to have moved to the shed.

Wiping the slimy string from his face, he searched the work table and tool box beneath.

Various jars once filled with turps and paintbrushes lay empty. A tin of wood preservative sat next to the jars, amongst the dust and dead flies. The tool box revealed a small collection of snails, both dead and alive, and also a pair of pliers that hadn't quite seized. A small, unopened pack of nails and a drill bit, possibly three eighths, completed his haul.

Rob re-entered the back door just as Sam was leaving the front.

"She's gone next door for a bath," said Quiety. Despite mangling the can, he hadn't gained entry.

"Here." Rob handed him the pliers, nails and drill bit. "Might help."

"Ta."

Yorkie now lay on the mouldy carpet, eyes shut. His regular breathing suggested he was not only still alive, but also asleep.

"Think he's knackered," said Quiety, hammering a nail into the can.

"Mmm."

As the groaning floorboards above revealed every movement Richard made, Rob grabbed one of the other cans of Chinese liquid chicken, trying to pierce it with the drill bit and a rotting lump of floorboard.

After ten minutes of wrestling, Quiety and Rob had opened the cans of foul smelling stew. From the noises above, it appeared Richard was out of the bath. A minute ago they'd heard him say, "Argh. No towel," and chuckled to themselves.

Rob and Quiety sat in near silence as Richard bounded down the stairs in his new shirt and old straitjacket bottoms, shortly followed by the damp looking Sam coming through the front door wearing very large jeans and a 'Rock Forever' t-shirt.

"You didn't search next door very well, did you?" In her hands were half a jar of instant coffee and an old packet of solidified sugar.

"Is there more food?" asked Richard.

"No. Nice shirt."

"Yeah. You look great yourself."

"Whatever." She stuck her tongue out at him.

"Keep it down a bit," said Rob, "Yor ... Pat's asleep."

Richard nodded. "We can eat the sugar if we get hungry I suppose."

Sugar.

The whole diabetes thing confused Rob. But he knew if someone had an attack, you gave them chocolate, or sugar. Maybe if Yorkie crunched his way through half the packet, there might be some hope? It probably wasn't that simple, but it must help. From Yorkie's mood, he was resigned to ending his days here. It wasn't a fitting end to a Basildon Bovver Boy. He wondered exactly what he should tell the others. Remembering his words, he needed to be in charge and keep an eye on everyone. He had to be the one they turned to. He knew he wasn't qualified for anything like that.

"I think we should keep the sugar for now," he said. "You never know what's coming."

He couldn't give up on Yorkie. Without him that guard may have reported them. They'd have been caught by now for sure. It was Yorkie's brutal punching that'd given them this chance. He wasn't going to leave him.

Chapter 7

After suggesting to Richard and Sam they have less than half a can of the soupy goodness, Rob headed for the bathroom, with Quiety popping next door.

Halfway up the stairs, Richard said, "Oh, the toilet doesn't flush. Sorry."

Rob shook his head and wondered what surprise he'd been left. Despite the cold water, Rob enjoyed the bath. The water, a reddy brown colour, was soon freshened with a squirt of shower gel. Sore wasn't a strong enough word to describe his feet. Blistered, swollen and red, they ached first from the freezing water but after washing the pain was different, like they needed two days rest before moving again.

He dressed in the mystery trousers, which he'd favoured over a t-shirt as the rough straitjacket trousers had rubbed his legs. Ruffling his washed hair in the broken mirror, he soaked his straitjacket trousers in fresh, or nearly fresh, water. Though annoyed at having to reuse his pants, given the state of both the new trousers and the straitjacket ones, there was no way he was going without.

"Better?" asked Sam, as he walked down stairs.

"Yeah. I'll stick these out back to dry."

"Good idea," she said, "we might need them later."

"I just left mine upstairs," said Richard.

I noticed, Rob didn't say. "Just give them a quick rinse."

As Richard clumped up the stairs again, Rob turned to Sam and whispered, "Has he woken yet?"

She shook her head. "Is he alright?" She screwed up her face, expecting to be hit with a bombshell.

Rob half shook his head. "I'll explain later, when the others are here. Just don't let him." He pointed upstairs, at the clumping Large Lad. "Don't let him eat that sugar."

She nodded. Though a self-confessed gobby cow, she'd so far said little on their predicament. Like the rest, she seemed to be holding back, trying to put it out of her mind. Like a volcano about to erupt, Rob knew it would only take something small to release the pressure. Yorkie's sugar was that little thing.

The sobs came, her face twisting and contorting. Rob instinctively put his arms round her and squeezed. Since he'd first seen her, he'd imagined a smell of freshly cut petals and hay meadows, but her actual aroma of freshly washed skin and shower gel was offset by the musty, year old clothes.

Sam continued to cry in his arms, Richard, who'd returned downstairs, avoided them and rushed outside with his wet straitjacket.

"Come on, it's okay. Let it out." Though a cliché, he carried on nonetheless. His head was full of clichés fighting each other to be said. He wanted to say something original, something memorable and poignant, but nothing was coming. "Get it all out now." Most of the tears having now been cried, she sniffed a snotty tear back into her throat.

"Listen, this is important," he whispered, moving his face closer. "I'm going to need help later when Pat wakes up." His mouth now almost touching her neck and wet hair. "I'm going to need that gobby girl to help me, not the sobby one. Come on, let it out now. Let it all out." Feeling his own eyes well up, he pulled her closer. His half bearded cheek caught the smooth skin on her neck.

He could have stayed there all night holding her, despite her smelly t-shirt, but she pulled away. Still close and face to face, her bleary eyes stared at his. The first fragment of a smile appeared between her reddened cheeks. He felt his head move towards her, felt his lips reach out, stretching for hers, then...

"I think I've blocked the toilet," said Quiety, barging in through the front door.

Both pulled away. The tears were gone, a smile taking its place.

"Too much information," said Sam.

"Sorry. Where's Richard?"

"Outside. Go and get him, Rob."

Rob immediately got up and went to the door. Outside, he wondered just how her royal gobbiness had got him to jump so quickly so soon. Nothing had actually happened, just a near miss. Seeing Richard beside a tree, he walked over.

It wasn't just any tree. The nearer he got, the more appley its fruit became. "God knows how this survived," said Richard, spitting chunks of apple as he spoke. "Bit sour, but who gives a shit."

You probably will later, Rob thought. The apple tree had somehow overcome two years of non-pruning in order to keep its fruit available. Taking a bite of one himself, he admitted it was sour, but after a few chomps you barely noticed. His stomach growled on receiving its second small gift in nearly twenty four hours. The best part, two-fifths of a can of chicken stew, was still to come. This was like a starter or aperitif.

"Found anything else?"

"Nah. I've picked most of them, we can take them with us."

Pausing until Richard looked at him, Rob said, "Pat's ill you know."

"Really? He didn't look well earlier. Is it bad?"

"Yeah, come back inside mate. We need to work out what to do before he wakes up."

Walking in with a handful of apples, Rob picked up a can of stew. The one he picked was half full, someone had had more than their share. It could have been either Richard or Sam, but he wasn't going to make a deal of it. He drank a small amount, occasionally getting a small chunk of potato, carrot or a piece of white, meat-like chicken. Warm it was a foul thin liquid. Cold, it was worse; gloopy, stringy and salty.

By the look on Quiety's face, it was obvious Sam had already spoken. As Rob sat next to her, she grabbed an apple.

"He's diabetic," said Rob. He'd meant to start with a flowing introduction, like one of his column fillers from the paper, but his mind was blank. "He told me not to tell you. He needs insulin. He also said we were to leave him, just go without him when we wake up tomorrow. I can't do it. I really think the rest of you should go now. You could get miles away, find freedom. They must be close to us now. Waiting here's just asking for trouble." He sighed. "There's no point us all being captured, is there? We're on the run, we can't forget that. I'll stay here, look after him. With that sugar, he might regain some energy, we might be able to move in a day or two."

He paused, looking at them following his every word. "Either stay here the night and go tomorrow morning or go now. Just leave me a few apples and the sugar."

Quiety placed a hand on his shoulder. "Rob, stop. I think we know all what we're going to do."

It didn't seem to be going to plan. Deep down Rob hoped they'd refuse and either stay and help or find some way of moving him. He also knew this was risking capture for all of them.

He shook his head. "You really need to think about this. The slower we are the higher the chance of getting caught. You don't have to decide now. If anyone wants to leave, go. No one will think the worse of anyone."

Rob looked at them all, his eyes resting on Richard. If any of them were going to baulk and run, he was odds on favourite. "I used to give great piggybacks when I was young," he said. "I'm sure I still could now."

Sam grabbed Richard's hand and squeezed it.

Quiety looked at the sleeping Yorkie, then back to Rob. "Nice speech and that, Rob, but we're all in this together, aren't we? If anyone wants to go they should stand up and go, now."

They all sat still. If anything, Rob thought they slumped further towards the ground.

"Settled then," said Quiety. "I think we ought to wake him. I don't know much about diabetes, but if he's in a coma we need to know. If he's asleep, we're not going to know, are we?"

"Fucking hell these are sour," said Sam having bitten into the apple.

Richard laughed. "Few more bites and it'll go away."

"Is that sugar any use to him?" Rob asked Quiety.

"I think so. Got to watch we don't overload him, but I'm sure it'll help."

"The curtains," shouted Sam. "Of course."

Looking at Richard, Rob knew he wasn't the only one to not understand Sam.

"A stretcher? Put them together, take a corner each. No need for piggy backs. Okay, they're a bit dusty but they should work. We could do with them anyway for sleeping under or for putting down on wet ground or whatever."

Rob had to admit it was a good idea.

"We could make a little carrying sack too, for the apples and cans."

Yeah alright, Rob thought, don't get too clever.

"What we need to decide," said Quiety, "is when we're going to leave. The longer we stay the more chance of being found. I don't

49

know if we're better off walking now and catching a few hours in the night, or sleeping and leaving in the morning?"

Unable to believe they were actually looking at him for the decision, Rob's mind went blank. Mess up here and lives were at risk. How did he become the leader anyway? Looking back at the dozing Yorkie, he remembered how.

"Okay. When they come after us, it's either on foot or helicopter. They're not going to bother driving round, not with all these trees. Those infra red things, Qu... Dave, can they see inside cottages?"

"They see heat sources. In a very dense forest or in a very thick stone house they might miss us. But they are very effective."

"Okay. Dogs. If they use sniffer dogs, then we need to keep running or walking to escape. Surely if they had dogs, they'd have picked us up by now? We've not exactly been moving fast, have we?"

They nodded agreement.

"Now, these dogs will have soldiers with them. We've got two guns, not much ammo, but we've got cover here, haven't we?"

Again, they nodded. Again they waited for his decision, putting their lives in his hands.

He paused and sighed. "I can't decide. We need to all agree. Our lives are at stake here."

Silence. Rob knew they were exhausted. A good night's sleep could be had here. It was covered and comfortable, there was running water, though it wasn't very appetising. However, giving anyone eight hours to catch up wasn't a good idea.

"I vote we stay here," said Sam.

They agreed with her. For a decision no-one wanted the blame for, Rob was pretty sure they'd have agreed either way.

"You must be exhausted, Dave, you didn't sleep earlier, did you?"

"Yeah suppose I'm a bit tired." His face told a different story.

"It's five o'clock now," said Rob, squinting to look at Yorkie's watch. "Why don't you all get some sleep? I'll wake two of you about midnight, you can take over the watch."

Keeping watch was one thing, but what if they were found? Rob thought it probably better to die in your sleep than face whoever was chasing them. As losing battles go this was the biggest. A quick death seemed more appealing than a life running.

"What about Pat?" asked Sam.

"I'll wake him when you've all dropped off. I'll persuade him to eat sugar."

"Don't think I could sleep without knowing if he's alright."

Again they agreed with her. Rob was impressed with how well she was leading without being too bossy. He could only imagine how forceful she could be if she tried.

It was agreed that Quiety would wake him while Rob, Sam and Richard pulled down the curtains and got things ready for their night's sleep. Though the recently renovated cottage seemed more comfortable and had the only remaining unspoiled, though unflushable, toilet, they'd decided to stay where they were. Anyone arriving would look first in the renovated cottage: that may give a few vital seconds.

The dusty, moth eaten curtains literally fell from the rails. A few carpets also pulled up easily. Though Rob had initial doubts about sitting on carpets that were home to all sorts of bugs, it was just an extra bit of comfort. It also got them higher off the damp floor.

Half way through their plundering of the last cottage, Richard nipped off into the woods. Due to the lack of toilet facilities, they'd agreed to relieve themselves outside, especially as the apples seemed to be quick working.

The few minutes Rob was alone with Sam were in near silence. They'd come so close earlier to getting closer. Now he was as embarrassed as he knew she was. It was hardly the right time or place. He considered bringing the subject up, apologising even, but couldn't. Leaving the house, with their booty of curtains, they made eye contact.

Smiling she said, "Sorry for blabbing like that." Her face grew as red as her hair.

He shrugged his shoulders. "Don't apologise. This takes getting used to, doesn't it?"

She smiled again and led him back to the end cottage.

Yorkie was sitting as they entered. Gingerly taking a few sips of chicken stew, he nodded at them though avoided Rob's eyes. His cheeks almost devoid of colour, he attempted to stand.

"Need toilet."

"You're probably better off outside, we've had some toilet issues," said Sam.

Though woozy he found his feet and with the help of the walls, he plodded into the front garden.

"He's annoyed with you," said Quiety to Rob.

Rob shrugged his shoulders. "I couldn't leave him, could I?"

Feeling Sam's hand on his shoulder, he turned. "Ignore the old sod. We'd have all done the same."

"Did you ask if sugar would help?"

"He just turned his nose up. Said we'd be better having it, give us energy."

"Stubborn old git," said Sam.

As Yorkie and Richard returned, Sam shared out the six small curtains. Sitting in a rough circle, Quiety, Richard and Sam settled down for what they hoped wouldn't be their last sleep.

Sitting with Yorkie on one side and the nearly asleep Sam on the other, Rob caught Yorkie's eye. "Sorry. I couldn't do it."

Yorkie shrugged his shoulders. "You're fools risking capture by helping me."

"Maybe, maybe not."

"Shush," said Sam. Richard giggled.

One by one the three fell asleep. With only Yorkie left, who wasn't talking to him, Rob settled himself in for a boring few hours of listening to snoring.

Ten minutes of silence was all he could bare. "Are you going to eat the sugar then?" he asked Yorkie.

"Don't seem worth it. Don't know how much longer I can walk. If it gives me another day, what happens when it runs out?"

"We'll have found something else by then. You can't give up. What would the other Basildon Bovver Boys say?"

Yorkie half laughed. "You shouldn't have told these. You've made it harder. We're supposed to be running for our lives and you go and bring saving some old fool into it."

Rob shrugged. He tried to explain that it was a case of living with yourself for your actions, however long you actually lived. He felt, after his long winded rambling speech, that he'd got the point over. Yorkie certainly had no reply.

Reaching over for the rock hard lump of sugar and the pliers, Rob said. "Here. Have a mouthful and go to sleep."

After smashing a small handful, Yorkie swallowed and sucked it, his face contorting as he chewed the lumps a thousand flies had landed on.

Giving Rob his watch before he lay back down, Yorkie whispered, "See you in the morning."

I hope so, Rob thought.

Chapter 8

The hours passed, leaving Rob little to think of but their near capture, the smell of Sam's neck and Yorkie's diabetes. At eleven he went to the toilet. Now stood just outside the front door to try and stop himself falling asleep, he heard one of them stirring.

As heavy footsteps approached the front door, Rob knew who their owner was. Nearly scaring the life out of Richard, Rob whispered sorry. After a quick trip to the woods, Richard returned, his face and stomach looking thinner than five hours ago.

"I'll cover now," he said. "You look exhausted mate."

Rob couldn't disagree. A couple of hours sleep in two days plus a lot of exercise had had the required effect. "Thanks. I would have woken you in another hour."

"I've never slept well anyway. All those years playing computer games and coding at night, I've just kind of lived without it. I'll tell you what, my feet are killing me."

Rob laughed. "Yeah, know what you mean. Walked further today than I have all year."

"Go on, Rob. Get some sleep. Is Pat okay? Did he say much?"

"A little. I got the message over that we're not leaving him. I made him eat some of that sugar. It looked disgusting, I was worried for a while it might poison him."

Richard smiled. "Go on, you need sleep. I'll wake everyone at six."

Rob nodded, handed him Yorkie's watch and walked to his curtain.

Though initially worried that sleep wouldn't come through over tiredness, it eventually crashed through.

"Rob wake up, mate," were the first words he heard on a new day. The first face he saw, Sam's, caused a sleepy, involuntary smile.

Second by second, his mind whirred through the reasons this good looking girl was waking him as he lay under a cobwebby curtain in a deserted cottage. Reality soon caught up. As he rubbed his eyes, Quiety shoved half a can of watered down, cold chicken stew in his hand.

"Breakfast in bed, eh?" said Yorkie.

"Can't think of anything I'd rather eat."

It occurred to him that Yorkie was standing. He looked fresher, more with it than last night, though still pale. The sugar must have worked.

Sam sat beside Rob, partially leaning on him. "He's eaten a lot of sugar," she whispered. "We hid it in his stew."

Winking at her, Rob drank his. Foul as it was, it stopped his stomach complaining.

Looking round, he saw the curtains had been wrapped around into sacks and tied up with pelmets or straitjackets. Their quarry of chicken stew, apples, old empty cans and the water bottle arranged in each of them. It reminded Rob of a camping trip he'd been on years ago with his brother. Though they had beans then, not chicken stew. And proper rucksacks, not curtains.

While he came round, they filled him in on the morning's events. They'd been awake for a few hours. After getting ready to leave, they decided to give Rob more sleep. Using the third can of stew, they'd watered it down between the five of them.

Munching on an apple, Rob put his shoes back on, his swollen feet barely fitting inside. "Which way, then?"

Not a single train had passed all night. It seemed obvious to cross the tracks, though the electrification worried Rob. It was obvious which rail was the live one, and they all reckoned it was turned off, but it didn't seem worth the risk. They had enough on their plates without dealing with the 5:55 from Bognor.

Leaving the cottages to their future decay, they continued. As daylight grew stronger, they walked beside the railway and the old path that once led cars to the cottages. The walking groups were much the same as before, except Sam joined Rob and Richard. The road split from the railway after a quarter mile, giving them the chance to re-enter the forest for cover as they walked west.

Feet still tired from the previous day made hard work of the first hour. Carrying their little curtain sacks like an eccentric Dick Whittington appreciation society, they trundled along in silence.

After his encounter with Sam the previous afternoon, Rob wanted to talk to her alone. He'd no idea what to say, he just felt, possibly wrongly, that they'd come so close that it needed sorting out. Leaning against him earlier had been more than just a friendly thing, he was sure of it. They needed to be on their own. He needed to know. With Richard beside them, the time or opportunity wouldn't arrive.

They arrived after an hour at a small tunnel, or hole under the tracks as Richard reminded Sam, which was barely wide enough for a modern tractor. Agreeing to follow the new track, they walked under.

"Stop here for a break?" asked Rob.

"You're the boss," replied Yorkie.

Taking the weight from their tired legs, they sat amongst the dew and nettles.

"Your turn for a story, Rob," said Sam, giving him a playful punch.

"Suppose it is. Well, this is what happened next. There was so much propaganda, but in a way that's what gave me the idea. I mean the television channels had been restricted by then, satellite television had lost most of its channels, so I suppose the local paper was the next obvious step for them. In some ways it's worse. There's a local paper for nearly every town. Keeping track of all of them is a huge undertaking."

"The stories we had to run were ridiculous. 'Mrs Brentwood turns over her garden for vegetables.' I remember that one well - Loyal Mrs Brentwood, 62, has given her back garden up as part of the Food For All program. Her sixty foot garden is to be used for cultivating vegetables and will be worked on by a group from the Home Gardening Division of the local Job Ministry. This not only provides work, but will also produce much needed fruit and vegetables. As part of the program, Mrs Brentwood gets to keep a third of the produce grown. 'I'm ecstatic,' said Mrs Brentwood. 'I used to have nightmares about mowing my lawn with my bad back, but now I just sit back and watch the vegetables grow. I can't wait until the cabbages are ready.' If anyone has a large garden and would like to join the Food For All program, they should enquire at the local Ministry building."

"For ages I tried to be sarcastic when writing them, but it had to be subtle so I doubt anyone picked it up. Unfortunately, the reality was Mrs Brentwood was given an ultimatum. Chose to lose her house and move to Hastings or give up her big, flower filled garden. Knowing I'd spent hours hiding anagrams in the writing was one thing, but no one knew where to look. One other thing I did was use the letters to make words. First letter of each sentence made a hidden message. Failed though, I couldn't exactly print – there's a hidden message in this article."

Adjusting his position, his trousers now dew wet, he continued, "We had this old printer in the newspaper office. It was the original typeset printer the Basingstoke Bugle was printed on. Ancient antique thing it was, they just kept it as an advert for the paper in reception. But, it did actually work.

"I spent weeks fiddling with it at night when everyone had gone home. Eventually, I got it working. I printed a single sheet special edition of the Bugle. It didn't take too long to use the thing once I'd got the hang of it. I racked up a few hundred copies and stuck them through people's doors, carefully selected people. People I thought would be sympathetic."

"It didn't say a huge amount. Just pointed out the obvious: all news channels were the product of the state and people should fight it whenever and however. I suggested trying to set up something more formal. I don't mean something rivalling the French Resistance, just like a small collective. Obviously I couldn't suggest a meeting or give names in case it got in the wrong hands, but I said like-minded people should try and get together behind closed doors and from little acorns, trees would grow."

"I couldn't believe how stupid I'd been. I mean why print it on that old, antiquated thing. The office stank of ink for days afterwards. It was obvious it'd been used. But I didn't want to use the office PC as I was sure they'd hacked in and were looking at my files. I still gave it to them on a plate. The typescripts, you know the printing blocks, were so old the i's were missing their dots, and the h's were raised. Once they'd got hold of the special edition, two and two were quickly put together."

"I got the sack and a fortnight in a police cell, held under the anti-state laws. I was eventually let out on bail, my court case is due in a few months. But since then, for the last six months, I've been on a work program, helping to dig drainage channels, weeding Mrs Brentwood's garden and cleaning public toilets. I had to do it to get food. Mrs Brentwood isn't that nice either. 'I lost all my roses and geraniums so you plebs can grow your fucking carrots,' she used to say. As far as I know, an underground movement never got going in

Basingstoke. Sure, people used to moan in the streets and occasionally old friends would come round and gossip. But no one wanted to rock the boat. No one wanted to take the risk. Everyone was scared of losing food."

Again, they'd been following him intently. He'd only been talking ten minutes, but his mouth felt dry. The water needed to be saved, finding that cottage was a lucky break. Another one might not come along for days.

After waiting to see if Rob was going to add anymore, Quiety stood up. "Come on, let's go."

Sam re-joined him as he walked along the track. "I wish I'd lived in Basingstoke, I'd have helped."

Smiling, he replied, "Plenty of vacancies for gobby people in Basingstoke, you know."

Slotting her right arm through his left, they walked together, the wheezing Richard a few paces behind.

Chapter 9

Lunch came a few hours later. Yorkie looked like the sugar was wearing off and he was running on depleted reserves. Sam and Rob had barely spoken, but had stayed side by side. Richard had struck up a few small conversations, usually about his feet, and the two in front were equally as quiet.

The small clearing they sat in, still in the thick of the forest but a part that was just starting to wither, lay next to a stream. They'd so far crossed four streams, or the same one four times, but this stream was larger. A lunch break gave them the opportunity to work out whether they'd wade across or follow in the hope it got narrower.

Hacking open a can of stew, Quiety poured roughly a fifth into the three empty cans they'd kept. "You'll have to wait for a free can," he said to Rob.

Rob's bet was on Richard finishing his fifth first, but it was also the can he least wanted to share. Crunching into a sour apple, he waited.

"Your story next, Dave," said Sam.

Finishing his stew with a gag, he nodded. "Suppose it is. T'was a dark and windy night. No just kidding. It wasn't night at all, it was during the day. I was maintaining these choppers and cooking stuff for the crews. They had proper food too, no chicken stew there. They ate like kings. Proper meat, no mechanically recovered stuff, actual steaks and proper vegetables. I knew it was wrong, deep down we all did. I decided to do something, make some kind of stand. The wife was dead against it, can't blame her. Bastards better not have touched her."

Silence gripped as they thought of the loved ones left behind. Though Rob was single, he had family in Basingstoke. He found himself wondering what had happened to them after he was taken the other night. Not only that, now they'd escaped, would it make things worse? Would they assume the escape was planned? Would they interrogate them? Rob knew one thing. Sod the Highlands, he was heading back to Basingstoke to find out.

"I don't know if I can go on," said Quiety.

He'd depressed everyone in a heartbeat. As Yorkie munched on the lump of sugar, his thoughts looked miles away in Essex. Sam and

Richard similarly looked scared. Rob reckoned neither of them was married, definitely Richard, though they'd still have families like himself. Maybe Sam even had a boyfriend.

Probably another Estate Agent.

"I need to see my mum," she said.

Though they looked at her and smiled, sympathy was in short ration.

"Look," said Richard. "We have to keep talking. I'm enjoying these stories, but we all know what we've run from and I think we've realised what the result of that might be. Getting depressed ain't gonna change anything. Whatever it is we're in, we're in it together. We need to keep sharp and come out of this. Dave, you've got to tell us."

Rob knew he was right. If only to distract them from the truth, they needed to keep their minds active.

"Well, it's not as interesting as Rob's. I didn't steal no chicken stew either." He looked at Yorkie. "All I'm guilty of is sabotage. Both people and helicopters. With me being a cook you see, I could pretty much make anything I wanted. One day, as the rioting had got particularly bad, I did them a special curry. It wasn't mega-hot or even that spicy, it was just the combination of chilli powder and laxative that gave it a special effect."

"I grounded the whole squadron that day. The looters got away with loads, gave me a real chuckle. Anyway, we blamed it on food poisoning. Although we had good quality meat, it wasn't as fresh or as well refrigerated as before. Most of the chicken that arrived had E-coli written all over it."

"I couldn't get away with it regularly, so I started on the equipment, hiding essential bits, just delaying really. I also sneaked out some weapons. That was hard work. We were searched on the way in and out, but I had this holdall I kept my uniform in, so I made a false bottom. I got two pistols and a sub hidden in my back garden, plus plenty of ammo. Only I know it's there."

"Obviously, I got caught. It was bound to happen. It was a small, close knit place. While they were still friendly towards me, they were a bit wary of my sudden eyesight problems. So when things started to go wrong, and they suspected sabotage, they kept an eye on me. They eventually caught me trying to disable the starter on one of the choppers. I shouldn't have gone that far really, but each time I did something I had to better it. Became like a drug. I had to go further each time."

"They put me in a military prison first. That wasn't fun. In a cell alongside deserters, people who'd lost their minds and men who'd refused the recall, I was sort of at home. One by one though, they kept disappearing. Taken during the night. Then, after two months, it was my turn."

There was no reply to his story.

One by one they stood and continued by the side of the stream. Sam re-joined Dave at the lead, with Yorkie trailing between them and Rob. Richard, as usual was bringing up the rear.

"You doing okay?" Rob asked Yorkie.

"Yeah, course I am."

Though his eyes weren't as glazed he was still pale. Although perkier than yesterday, he looked weak. Rob wondered how long it would be before they had to carry him.

They continued through the forest, avoiding the more defined paths, and heading roughly North West. What little they knew of the New Forest's size, which wasn't helped by Sam's occasional insights, they knew within a day or two they'd emerge from it. That was when it would get tricky. Without the cover of trees, they'd be sitting ducks.

By four o'clock, their pace had slowed to a crawl and the forest was thinning. Rob and Quiety had broken from the others, scouting round a few plains, but still keeping within sight. Despite Sam's assurances that they were still in the middle of the Forest, Rob wasn't convinced.

Yorkie had grown tired and their current stop, an apple break, had the feeling of an all-nighter. The forest, still thick enough to give cover from the air, was becoming more heavily tracked. Posts lay occasionally as remainders of long forgotten walks and cycle paths. Rob was convinced a town was approaching, or at least some large ex-car park. Dave seemed of the same persuasion however much Sam said they were still in the middle of nowhere.

"Is it my turn?" asked Sam.

"I can't remember. I think so," Richard replied.

"Yeah go on, Sam," said Dave.

To the sound of Yorkie crunching sugar, Sam continued, "So I had everything. A house, a buy-to-let flat and one of those new Minis. I could barely make it from one month to the next without dipping more on the credit card but it didn't matter, did it?"

"The first thing we noticed in the Estate Agents was when the run started on that bank, you know the first one. It was the talk of the office. The problem was, that bank was about the only one people were getting mortgages from. Prices had risen so much the only chance new buyers had was getting one of their mortgages. I didn't click then what was about to happen."

"Overnight, new buyers couldn't get mortgages. As new mortgages were most of our work, it only took a month or so before sales dropped. House sales just weren't completing, they were failing halfway through. The funny thing was, there were still enough people trying to buy them, they just couldn't get mortgages. The ones that did sell had to knock thousands off."

"Pretty soon prices were falling big time, ten percent then fifteen. We had so little work it was embarrassing trying to look busy. Unsurprisingly, I got made redundant. I can't blame them, there was nothing to do. Getting made redundant was a problem. I had maxed out my credit cards, no job and was struggling to find new tenants for my flat."

"After a few months of nasty letters and no job, they took my car away. Next came the notice of repossession for the flat. I tried to fight it, but I was never going to win. Without repayments, the debt was just multiplying. Then, when the other two banks went under, that was when things really changed."

"Within a few more months, they took possession of my house. That annoyed me, as despite it being worthless, the bank still wanted it. They couldn't possibly sell it or even rent it out. They just didn't want me in it. I couldn't face moving back to my mum's, not after everything I'd said about me taking over the world, one buy-to-let at a time. I met up with an old friend who'd got into squatting with these guys. Pretty soon I was living in this squat. It was almost hidden in a half built block of flats, so it wasn't obvious we were there. With no job or anything, we just used to sit round all day moaning about what had gone wrong and blaming everyone but ourselves. And the consortium bailout, Christ, we must have gone over every aspect of that a million times."

"They were a bit radical really. I suppose deep down I've always been too, but the money and houses thing clouded my mind. Before long we were making a stand. Not in a big way, it started with just graffiti and attending the odd protest. But after protests were banned, we went for bigger things."

"Unlike you, Pat, we didn't have a name. We should have really. Southampton Squatters, I suppose."

"Southampton Subversive Front?" suggested Rob.

She shrugged her shoulders. It'd been a long time since he'd thought up a witty headline, the skill he once possessed seemed to have faltered.

"The graffiti got bigger and better. 'Make love not chicken stew' was my favourite. We also targeted attacks at the local ministry building and police station. Threw paint over cars and trucks, let down tyres, that sort of thing."

Yorkie was nodding his head. This was his domain. Rob's opinion of her, though pretty high since she'd used him as a crying post, was improving by the minute.

"Then one day it went to shit. We'd planned a big job, well not as big as yours, we didn't hijack stew or nothing, but this job was big to us. We graffiti'd loads of places saying, Day of action Saturday 13. It became a talking point round Southampton. A couple of anarchists that Greg, one of the squatters, knew were involved too. Well they called themselves anarchists, but they wouldn't know Anarchy if it bit them in the bollocks."

"It was a poor turnout. Only fifty or so hit the streets. The police out-numbered us four to one. They mopped us up and stuck us in this emergency centre they'd built. Just a bunch of portacabins in a secure part of the docks, but it did the trick. We were handcuffed, processed, fingerprinted, pictures taken then sent back to these cabins that were divided into little cells."

She paused. Rob thought she'd come to a hard part in the story.

"Slowly, they came back for us, one by one. They had this dossier on me. School, job history, even medical stuff, plus some images from CCTV of me paint bombing a police station. I had a balaclava on, but you could tell it was me. Also, they said my fingerprints were all over some robbery, but I've never robbed anywhere. They asked me some questions, who was in charge, who was leading this. They played hardball, even slapped me around, but

I didn't tell them anything. Then, they chucked me back in that portacabin cell and that's been it for the past two months."

"Then last night, they took me away."

Again, silence after Sam's story. Rob knew it was similar to all theirs but it didn't make it easier. How many others up and down the country were the same?

As they headed off, the sparser trees worried Rob. He thought of backtracking a few hours to more solid forestry, but that would give the advantage to anyone following. The edge of the forest grew near, miles of plains approached.

"We can't be through it already," said Sam. "It's bigger than this."

"Over there," said Quiety. "It looks like we're entering the world again."

In the distance they saw what looked like a village. An outlying large house lay across some fields about half a mile in front, with a main road leading from their left towards the distant cluster of houses.

"Where the fuck are we?" said Sam.

Considering this was her domain, Rob was disappointed she was lost. The village's benefits, clothes, food and maybe even medicine for Yorkie were outweighed by the knowledge that police, secret police and nosy neighbours wouldn't be welcoming.

"What do we do?" asked Richard.

None of them had a clue. Yorkie sat down. Rob noticed his face was pale again. He knew he'd struggle to go on further without help. It was only a matter of time before it came to a head.

"That large house. Is it a farmhouse?" asked Quiety.

"There's only one way to find out, and by then it's too late," said Rob. "Shit. We should have thought of a plan for this. Sorry lads, and Sam, I've let you down."

"Shut up you big twat," she said. "It's not your fault we're thick. Problem is, we can't walk all the way to Scotland, full stop. Even if we've got food and ini-cillen."

"I think you mean insulin," Richard butted in.

"Whatever. Problem is, we ain't got a plan. We're running. Do we carry on running, or sneak about here or something?"

She had a point and Rob knew it. They either carried on running and died of starvation or looked for help and got recaptured. Rob knew there had to be a medium point. Something that was risky, yet gave hope and a good chance of hiding.

Yorkie, who'd been quieter than Quiety and paler than Sam in the winter, took it on himself to decide. Collapse wasn't a strong enough word, he vertically slumped from sitting up to lying down in less than a second.

"Shit," most of them said. Scrabbling with the sugar, which Yorkie had put in his curtain-rucksack, Rob grabbed a lump and crushed it in his hands. "Open his mouth."

Quiety jumped on command while Richard and Sam stood mouths ajar, tongues hanging out. Quiety prised his mouth open and held it in place for Rob to dribble the crushed sugar in. The sweat from Yorkie's body soaked the straitjacket he was wearing. The smell, from both his unwashed teeth and body moved Rob close to gagging.

"How do you get him to swallow?" Asked Rob, the grains were just lying on his tongue.

"Slap him?" suggested Sam.

"Try some water," offered Richard.

Dribbling water down his throat, some of it was forced back through retching and coughing. Rob was no doctor but he thought those dribbles must have either hit his lungs or caught his gag reflex. Slowly, they dribbled more water and sugar onto his tongue. Within a few minutes, Yorkie's eyes were flickering and his body moving.

As Yorkie returned to something close to living, they sat round him. Rob noticed Sam had been crying. He knew he'd been close himself, but rushing around had staved it off. They all knew this moment had been coming, but they'd forced it back in their minds. So far back it had become a surprise.

"Told you to leave me," the very weak Yorkie said. His eyes searched out towards them, but he seemed to look through rather than at them.

"We decided not to. Democracy and all that," said Rob.

Democracy was later given another bash as the sugar bag was nearly empty. Most of their water had gone too, either in Yorkie's throat or splashed on the ground during the panic. The farmhouse and village would have to be looked at. If Yorkie were to be kept alive, they needed help.

Chapter 10

After a half hour break and the final can of stew, decisions had to be made. Yorkie was dozing against a tree, Sam kept checking he hadn't slipped into a coma, and the rest mingled round. By rights, Richard should have told the rest of his tale, but the atmosphere had changed. Rob knew they were thinking the same thing.

Yorkie: what to do with him?

The thought of leaving him in the middle of the night at the Farmhouse's doorstep like an abandoned baby, did occur to him. He presumed the others had thought of it too. It would be as much for his own good as theirs.

He needed medical help. But again, Rob's mind returned to the three musketeers' style of companionship they'd built. It was settled. Yorkie would get his help and either Rob would take him alone or the others could come, if they wanted. It would be their choice.

"I'm taking him to that farmhouse." Rob spoke with as much strength and stubbornness as he could muster. "The rest of you are going that way." He pointed across the small plain westwards towards another clump of trees. "I take the pistol, you take the sub. Once I'm sure he's okay and safe, I'll catch you up."

Rob had no idea how he was supposed to catch them up and find them. Once they'd disappeared into the forest that was it, he'd never see them again. Though half expecting them to go, he hoped they wouldn't.

"I'm coming with you," said Sam. The certainty in her voice was beyond reason, not that Rob would have tried to talk her out of it.

"We're all with you, Rob, but practically we should split up," said Quiety. "This would be my plan. You and Sam approach the house while me and Richard watch from here. If we see you get in trouble or you take too long, we'll help."

Richard nodded.

"Problem is," Rob continued, "Help's going to come in the form of a doctor or ambulance. What's the chance of finding a sympathetic doctor? Not much is it? No, me and Yorkie on our own."

Seeing their frowns, he realised he'd called him Yorkie. Though it was bound to happen, his reddening cheeks gave away his embarrassment. Sam's frown turned to a smile. "Anyway," she said, "Dave's plan needs more work."

Rob smiled through purple cheeks. "I don't see how. There's no point in us all getting captured."

"Going to that house is a bad move," said Richard. "Have you actually seen what we look like? They're going to ring the police straight away. What we need to do is wait until after dark and scout round. We'll see what's in the village then. There might be a surgery or chemist or something. If not, they'll be a shop and we'll get some sugar or glucose tablets or whatever."

"That's more like it," said Sam. She looked back at Yorkie. There was no doubt she was wondering if he'd last the night. "We might be able to get food and better clothes too."

"I'm sure we'll find loads to help ourselves to," said Rob. "But don't forget we're on the run. People are looking for us. If suddenly a few miles from where we were last seen five sets of clothes and food goes missing, it's a giveaway. There's only one way out of this, and it doesn't involve you three."

"Rob," said Sam. Hearing her say his name made him lose his train of thought. He turned and looked at her. Standing there, vulnerable and in a huge and smelly Rock Forever t-shirt, her tearful eyes burned into him. "Shut the fuck up and listen. We're not leaving you."

Breaking off his gaze from her eyes, he shrugged. "What's the plan then?"

The plan, long-winded endlessly-circling and in Sam's words, pants, was pretty much Richard's original plan: scout round after dark and hope for a miracle. Sam and Rob had been chosen for the task, though Rob would have to borrow Quiety's t-shirt, which far from ideal, was better than the alternative: Richard's. Quiety had suggested Sam and Rob together as they could pose as a couple if necessary. Rob thought this was a good plan, in more ways than one.

With daylight taking ages to fall behind the trees, and Yorkie drifting in and out of sleep, Richard gathered them together. It was his turn to finish his story.

"When house prices began to fall, it became clear that these packages of mortgages were more triple bypass than triple A. Problem was, the risk wasn't calculated correctly. The models we produced were fine, they worked, honest they did. You've got to believe that. It was the parameters we were using that were wrong. That was the problem."

"These packages of debt had been sold everywhere, not only by us. Everyone had done it. Banks and insurers were using them as Tier 1 Capital, which you can only do with a 'Triple A' investment, a safe investment. As confidence went, the value of these packages fell and everyone's capital was vaporising. With all this happening, my job was over. They disbanded the section but kept a few of us on and stuck us in the commodities trading arm. In order to try and protect themselves, they speculated on huge rises in precious metals and oil."

"It was self-fulfilling. Everyone gambled on the future price rising which pushed up the price. It was a joke. There were container ships full of oil at sea that no one wanted, yet the price was sky high. It rebuilt the bank's balance sheets, but all it really did was slow the inevitable. When the second round of runs started that was it, the end. I put every spare bit of money I had into gold in a Swiss vault. I hope it's still there, but I'm unlikely to ever be able to use it, am I?"

"The bank I worked for crashed through the floor. I do feel guilty. I mean I was only following orders but the consequences of my programming probably made it worse than it was. Sure, someone else would have done it, but that's not the point. I did do it."

"It all kicked off in Europe about the same time. Greece defaulted on their loans, which seemed to speed up the second credit crunch. It was like a set of dominos. Ireland, Portugal, Italy, Spain. Before we knew it, the value of everything had crashed. It was so fast. The German bailout just slowed things down. I always thought that ironic, you know. Given what happened in the Second World War, Germany effectively ended up owning or controlling most of Europe without a single shot being fired. Makes you wonder doesn't it."

"Of course Spain was the one that collapsed the bank. All the banks. It was just too big to rescue. Germany was broke itself by then, and America had their second round of collapses. It was just a matter of time before we went the same way."

69

"It was fear, wasn't it? That's what sped everything up. Fear of losing money made people panic and withdraw their money. It just laid open what the banking industry and money was: a fraud. The same money circulating round and round. As soon as you try and draw it all out, it fails."

"Obviously we got laid off. I owned my house so didn't need money for rent, not that money really existed anymore. I kind of spent my time on the internet writing blogs, and on this website forum about the crash. I spent hours looking round at other people's sites and that. Then the bailout came."

"There was huge speculation over who and what was being bailed what. But slowly it became clear. First the internet got slower, then access became restricted. Pretty soon you could guarantee that anything anti-Consortium written on a site would be removed within an hour. They must have had loads of people and computers searching for things to block. Me and a few old friends developed this coding system. It hid words inside strings of text. It looked harmless if you didn't have our key to decode it."

"We used to post coded recipes on the chicken stew recipe site. We passed on information about what was going on in various towns. After a while we got other people interested, I'd met other people from websites and the code was shared. I had this dream, silly you know but most dreams are. I thought we could build an army of supporters and take back the country, using the code we'd written. I suppose in that dream I'd have been a hero."

"As it happened, the code fell into the wrong hands. I don't know how. Suddenly, my internet connection and phone line went overnight. I knew what was coming. I just waited for them to smash the door in."

Looking up, Richard nervously smiled. The more Rob learnt about him, the more he liked him. Like all of them, he'd tried in his own way to make a stand. Rob only hoped there were others fighting too. There had to be. Though lethargy had become a national pastime, what was going on was wrong, anyone could see that. Everyone must be doing something, no matter how small.

Chapter 11

As darkness fell, so did the temperature. Due to lack of movement, the night-time chill hit hard. Dressed in Quiety's t-shirt, Rob went through the plan one last time before saying goodbye.

Armed with the pistol, which definitely had the safety on, Rob crouched and led Sam as they crossed the field, hidden from the farmhouse by a hedge. The low, crouching trot he'd perfected after fifty yards slowed as the edge approached. Turning to Sam, her eyes reflecting the moonlight, he whispered, "Any sign of life in the farm?"

She shrugged and looked towards the farm house.

Turning himself, Rob saw heavy curtains hung in the rear of the house. Upstairs, occasional light shone through, but a downstairs, curtainless window was in darkness.

"Can't see no one but you can't tell, can you?"

"Hmmm. Just keep sneaking round these hedges."

Leading the way, past the crops of growing cabbages and carrots, the pair stalked their way past the house, occasionally stopping to check the lights and farmhouse windows.

Like this field, most of the cattle grazing ground in the country had been converted back to vegetable crops. Britain's animal population had dropped ninety percent as a result. The reason was clear: no more expensive imported food. Britain had nothing to buy it with. The only chance of self-survival was to convert the country to vegetarianism. Of course, chicken stew now made up a large part of people's diets, but Rob considered eating the foul white liquid itself was vegetarianism. Maybe even cannibalism if the rumours were true.

Ten minutes of skirting round hedges, fields and trees bought them near the village. From their vantage point, in a hollowed hedge, the village appeared to be three streets long, criss-crossing regularly. It was the kind of place that'd been popular with holiday makers. No doubt a large number of the houses had been holiday cottages before the crash. It was safe to assume some of them were either squatted or bank owned but cared for by the ministry.

Rob guessed it was only a matter of time before the New Forest itself was chopped down for paper pulp, fire wood and vegetable growing land.

"Do you recognise it?" he asked.

"Not really. There's a few little villages dotted about that look the same. Quaint old pubs with horse brasses, little cottages and old style shops. There's usually a council estate shoved around the back where people can't see it."

Rob nodded. "I reckon we scout round the back first, see if we can find any deserted houses."

Sam nodded.

They moved a field nearer to the back gardens of the cottages. The small row of houses stood dark and silent. Their back gardens converted to allotments, they probably looked similar to their wartime days. The only difference being a wealth of unusable electronic gadgets inside them.

The fourth one stood out from the rest as, although the garden had been filled with growing vegetables, the cottage was empty. The lack of curtains, lights and furniture left them both beyond doubt no one lived there.

Turning to look at Sam, Rob said, "Do we try and get in?"

She shook her head. "Walls will be thin. If the neighbours hear us, they'll know we've broke in."

Rob nodded. He thought of saying, 'Well done, it was a trick question,' but knew she wouldn't believe it.

It took over fifteen minutes to scout the village. A few dogs barked as they approached some houses, but otherwise their creeping went unnoticed. The few dogs left in the country tended to be poorly fed and easily excitable anyway. Rob often wondered where all the dogs had ended up. His suspicion that a lot of them died of starvation, were eaten or turned into pig food before the pigs died out, was held by a lot of people.

Creeping into another bush, near the first row of cottages, he turned to Sam. "I'm a bit stumped."

She shook her head, indicating the same. "Didn't see a doctors or nothing."

"All that's left is to walk straight up the main street."

"Risky, but suppose we've got no choice?"

"I haven't seen any police or guards. Maybe they don't bother with small villages like this?" Rob scratched his chest. Quiety's t-shirt seemed to have come with something extra. Rob guessed it wasn't Quiety's fault. They'd been walking through forests, one of them was bound to pick up insects.

"I think they do, but if there's only one of them it's going to be low profile."

Rob nodded. "Come on then. We'll try and keep to the edge of the road. If we hear a noise, go into a garden and lie down."

"Anything else, boss?"

She bounced her head from side to side, her hair waving, almost floating round. It took a lot of effort to force his gaze from hers, but he did. "Just, if we get split up, head back to Yor...the others."

She nodded. "By the way, who's Yorkie? You've said it a few times now?"

"Just slipped out. Sorry. Don't tell him. It was a nickname for Pat before I knew his name." He felt his cheeks get hot.

"Have I got a nickname?"

Whether her pout was intentional or not, he wasn't sure. A million corny one-liners filled his head. Struggling through them, he searched for the least offensive.

"Gobby cow." He smiled.

Since he first heard her, while strung up in that van, he'd reckoned her left hook would be good. He wasn't disappointed. For what he hoped was a playful slap, more than necessary power was put into it. A small numbness throbbed in his cheek. He tried to say sorry, but it sounded like slurry.

She shook her head, the smile returned then faded. "Sorry, that was a bit hard, wasn't it? Did I break anything?"

"I'll live." His head now just inches from hers as she inspected the damage, he wanted to turn and take her in his arms. To finish what they'd started yesterday.

It wasn't going to happen. It wouldn't be fair on either of them. Yorkie was dying a few hundred yards away, they could get arrested any second and all he could think about was rutting in a bush with a gobby girl he'd just met. He felt slightly ashamed.

"Come on, let's go."

It must have been approaching midnight when they made their first sweep up the main road. Keeping to the left and crouching, the road was noiseless. Before, no matter how quiet the town, there would have been the odd car, drunken stumblers wandering home from the pub and the occasional dog walker. Now nothing. Just silence, streetlamps that weren't lit and roads that were no longer used.

The first few houses were set back from the road, big gardens and double garages boasted the upper end of town. Further along, the buildings got smaller as the centre approached. Long abandoned and converted shops were now used as coach houses, flats or stood empty.

Pausing, Rob noticed the road narrowed further as the main shops came into view. Spread on either side of the road, the houses were now gardenless, their doors directly opening on the pavements. Going on would mean no hiding place. Looking at Sam and nodding twice in the direction of the shops, she nodded back.

The centre of the village was just two shops: a supermarket he knew would only sell chicken stew and a newsagent that only sold propaganda. A deserted off-licence, fish and chip shop and hairdressers stood near. The supermarket might have headache tablets, but Rob knew it wouldn't hold syringes and insulin. The newsagent wouldn't be worth looking at anyway. Sugary sweets or sucrose tablets had long stopped being sold.

The shops would be alarmed anyway. Rioting had hit everywhere, even backwater newsagents. If they could get past the shutters, disable the alarm and not wake the owner up, its non-helpful bounty was theirs.

They crept on, past the shops hitting a four-way junction. An old road led towards the cottages, while a newer avenue led opposite towards the council estate. The road they were following continued past a church and pub, leading to houses.

Leading Sam into the graveyard, Rob paused behind a large headstone. Squatting, he looked at her. "What know?"

Her shrug said it all. Though the rest of the village remained unsearched, the chances of finding a doctor's surgery or insulin factory were nil. Sighing heavily, Rob was about to admit defeat when he heard a noise.

Though distant, the noise was definitely the low grunt of a diesel engine filled with poor quality bio-diesel. With no other noise around, the sound travelled for miles. Though fairly safe hidden behind the gravestone, he was aware the road was still nearby. Rob was unsure just who was coming and what they were looking for.

"Can you hear that?"

She nodded. Her gobbiness had evaporated the past half hour, being replaced by head signals.

"We need more cover."

Looking round, there was a choice of abandoned shops and a house. The pub across the street also looked inviting, but crossing the street would put them in the path of whatever was coming.

The final place was right beside them. A Norman built church, it stood at the centre of the town, reminding its residents that eternal salvation can be bought for the mere cost of a fifty pence weekly donation and the endurance of a two hour sermon. Its door, though closed, looked unlocked. It just seemed that sort of Church in that sort of area.

"Stay here a bit." Rob ran to the door and tried it.

Thee door squeaked open with enough noise to wake the village. Rob waved to Sam who ran after him. With the door closed, Rob looked round. Though not large in size, the church was full of pews. The moonlight flicked through the stained-glass windows, half lighting the altar. Standing there in the sanctity and calmness, they watched lights bounce round the room as the sound of the vehicle outside grew louder.

"We need to see what it is," whispered Rob, though the acoustics made it echo alarmingly.

"That window?"

"Yeah, come on."

Through a vestibule, the stained glass was light enough in places for them to see through. The chugging vehicle growing louder as it neared, Rob felt a warm, hand-like object grab his left hand. Turning slightly, Sam was looking out of the window, her face staring into the distance. Looking down, the smooth skin of her hand was loosely gripping his.

"We'll be alright," he said, with some conviction.

Letting go of her hand, he moved his arm around her shoulders, catching her goose-bump ridden arms on the way. The chill of night, though barely noticeable after their crab-like scrabbling, had left its mark. Turning, his eyes met hers. As the passing police car sped by, its blue light reflecting many colours through the stained-glass and onto their scummy-clothed bodies, they shared their first kiss.

His mouth numbed by Sam's, he pulled away. Lightheaded and out of breath he grinned. Looking down at her green, trusting eyes, he knew he could stay like that all night, but it didn't help their situation. Plus, Mother Mary was looking down from her statue very disapprovingly. If the wrath of the Consortium wasn't enough trouble to deal with, offending God's mum certainly wasn't going to help.

Rob never got the chance to carry the embrace further, a voice from behind them saying, "Excuse me, can I help?" broke them up.

Turning round, his heart dropped through the floor, Rob saw through the half-lit church a blackened figure walking towards them.

Unsure whether he should hide behind Sam or protect her, chivalry eventually came to his rescue. Taking a step forward, he tried to move in front of her, but she pushed him away and stood beside him.

As the figure entered the stained glass light, Rob was relieved to see it was a vicar. Dressed in a black smock with dog collar, he'd never been as pleased to see a vicar in his life.

"Can I help?" he repeated. Though confident, he seemed wary. Considering their clothes and possible smell, Rob wasn't surprised. They had robbers written all over them.

Sam stepped forward, pushing Rob out of the way. "Hi, we're a bit lost, so we, err, came in to warm up."

Leaning his head on his shoulder, he considered his reply. "You're very lost here, my child. Are you staying nearby?"

Sam nodded. "Camping trip. We're staying in the forest for a few nights."

It was a ridiculous thing to say. No one had been on holiday for over a year. Holiday's just didn't exist in the Consortium's Britain.

Though he knew he'd regret it, Rob made a decision to tell the truth. Or, a partial truth. They were in a church after all. "Thing is, one of our friends is unwell."

"Oh yes?" said the vicar. Although he still looked scared, he'd broken down a layer of fear and was climbing through to meet the next one.

"Yes," said Sam, "he's diabetic and his medicine got spoiled."

Again, the vicar pondered his reply. "Though the lord moves in mysterious ways, I've yet to see him conjure up insulin on demand."

Rob was mildly impressed with his wit. He'd never got on with the whole principle of god and churches, there just seemed too many contradictions. This vicar could possibly have been a stand-up comedian if a different calling had come. Beside him, Sam chuckled and had her best smile on. Hopefully another level of suspicion had been worn down. Instead of them being murderous robbers, they were now just lovable lead-sheet snatchers.

"Do you know where we might find some? Or perhaps a doctor?" asked the smiling Sam.

Rob did wonder if they were going too fast with this. Sure vicars are known to be helpful, it was somewhere in the job description, but here they were in the middle of the night, looking like shit dragged through a hedge and asking for the nearest chemist or doctor. They'd changed from friendly rogues to thieving druggies in a second.

The vicar forced a smile and shook his head.

"Doesn't matter," said Rob. "Perhaps we'll go to that phone box down the road and ring for help."

Sam hadn't appreciated the route he was taking. Her face dropped and her head shook involuntary. "Please, he really is unwell. Plus, we're not supposed to be on holiday. It's a long story, but we just fancied a few days away, like we used to before the..." She paused for effect. "Before all the troubles."

She was a good liar, maybe too good. Rob nodded agreement. The vicar's smile had grown as she talked. Maybe she'd broken through his last line of defence?

"There's no doctor here. Sorry. There is a nurse who lives just up the road, but she won't be able to help, I can't see her carrying insulin. I'm sure the police will understand if you tell them the truth."

"It's the curfew, you see," said Rob. "We're from Southampton and we didn't cross the checkpoints properly. I suppose we're scared of what might happen. You hear all these stories about people disappearing."

The vicar nodded. Rob knew he was no fool. This close to the Isle of Wight's holding centre, the vicar may have already sussed who they were. It would only make sense for the police or army to come round and warn them of escapees. Maybe the vicar had already rung for help and was stalling before they arrived.

"Come on Sam, we better go," said Rob, not hiding the panic in his voice.

Sam shrugged her shoulders at the vicar as Rob took her hand and pulled her towards the door.

"Wait," he said.

They froze and turned, breaking hand contact. Their wide eyes stared at him, knowing he held the power and almost pleaded with him to use it.

"I might know someone who can help." He looked more nervous than before. Either he knew what he was risking by offering help, or it was a last ditch attempt to keep them talking.

"If you could, we'd be grateful," said Sam.

"Follow me."

They followed him past the altar. As nervous as he was, Rob was starting to feel more comfortable. Maybe, just maybe, he would help.

Past the altar they entered what Rob could only describe as the vicar's dressing room. He tried to imagine him in here, warming up before his weekly show, but it wasn't a pretty image. The vicar offered them a seat on a cold pew as he sat behind a desk.

"One of my parishioners, the organ player actually, she's diabetic." Pulling a small black book from his drawer, he flicked to a page then picked up his phone.

Rob nervously fiddled with his t-shirt while the vicar waited for his call to be answered. Sitting down, he realised just how much the gun in his right pocket showed through the jeans. Nervously, he put his hand over it. The vicar must have noticed it, no wonder he looked so scared.

"Ah, Mrs Parkes," he said. "Sorry for ringing this late." He paused. "Yes I know, how is he?" Another pause. "Well, these things take time to heal, don't they? I'm ..."

Rob stopped listening and looked round the bare stone-lined room. Feeling Sam's body next to his shivering, he knew she was also feeling the cold. If this had a chance of working, they needed clothes as well as medicine. And food, obviously.

"...anyway to cut a long story short, I've got a friend who's lost his insulin. I mean I don't know how it works but is it the sort of thing than can be borrowed then replaced in the morning?" Pause. "Really, oh that's handy." Another pause. "Can I pop round and pick it up?" Last Pause. "Bless you. I'll be over in two shakes."

Smiles abounded as they looked at him sitting behind his small, ecclesiastical desk. "Any luck?" asked Rob.

He gently nodded. "She's got an emergency injection pen, whatever that is. I'm sure your friend will know what to do with it." Standing, he continued, "I'll go and fetch it. She just lives round the corner. I think you'll be safer waiting here."

Rob nodded. "Sorry."

"Don't be," he replied. "I'm only doing what I'm sure you'd do for someone in need."

"Be careful," said Sam. "A police car went by earlier."

"I know," he said, walking out. "I saw it."

Five minutes became ten then fifteen as they waited. The air grew cooler as the night got older. Rob tried his best to warm Sam by putting his arm around her. After their initial exchange, commenting on how nice the vicar was, they sat in silence looking at various pictures, candles and the other bare furnishings in the room.

Though Rob was worried any minute armed police would run in, he made no attempt to leave. Neither did Sam. Their fate and trust had been left with the seemingly kind vicar.

He returned after twenty minutes carrying a small holdall. "Still here then?" He smiled.

Rob shrugged his shoulders, unable to think of any reply.

"Did you get it?" asked Sam. She'd broken from Rob's hold when the vicar had returned. Rob guessed, and also thought himself, that showing bodily closeness in the heart of the church perhaps wasn't too sensible.

"Yes. Mrs Parkes really is quite kind. She insisted I bought you some jumpers and a flask of hot tea too." He gestured at the bag.

"Oh. She is a star," said Sam. "As are you," she added.

Rob stood up and offered his hand towards the vicar. "Thank you."

The vicar backed off slightly. Rob was sure he was still expecting them to hurt him. There was no easy way of convincing him that they were on the level, well nearly on the level.

Seeming to gain inner strength from somewhere, the vicar held his hand out which Rob limply shook. Handing the holdall to Sam with his other hand, the vicar said, "What happened to the other two?"

"Two?" Rob was confused so didn't need to act.

"Neither of us were born yesterday. Whatever your crimes may have been it is not for me to judge." He looked towards the roof before continuing. "But, whatever the crimes were, I know the punishment rendered nowadays is totally inappropriate. I hope they never find you."

"Yeah, there's five of us," said Sam. She'd cottoned on quicker that not only was he genuinely on their side, but it was widespread news they were on the run.

The vicar nodded and let go of Rob's hand. "You're not the first to come looking for help. I hope you're not the last either. But please can I ask that if the worst happens you keep my parishioners and church out of it?"

Rob nodded his head and heard Sam say, "Of course."

As Sam continued telling him how grateful they were, Rob could only think that he'd asked them to keep his parishioners and church out of it, not himself as most people would. Exiting through a rear door and heading for the back of the shops, they took an alley that was unlit and fairly safe. As they quietly walked along the alley, Rob again couldn't believe the selflessness they'd been shown.

Towards the end of the alley, the chugging diesel engine was heard again. Rob and Sam hid behind a few dustbins, well out of sight until the police car passed. Waiting another five minutes for luck, they re-crossed the main road, slid down the side of the farmhouse and back to roughly where they thought the others were.

Though they'd moved, Rob and Sam found them easily. Quiety explained the first time the police car went by, they'd panicked. Assuming Sam and Rob had been arrested, they starting packing and moved in case of sniffer dogs. They were going to wait three more hours before moving on.

"What's in the bag, Rob?" asked Richard.

Putting the bag down, and squatting next to it, Rob said, "Manna from heaven. Well from Mrs Parkes. We met this nice vicar, very helpful."

"So he knows about us then?" Richard looked worried.

"It's okay. He was helpful. I trust him." Rob turned to Sam, who agreed. "We didn't exactly go looking for him anyway. When we heard the car coming we went to hide in a church. The vicar just appeared and after a bit of persuading, he helped us."

Sam, who'd sat next to him, rummaged through the bag. "Bless her." She pulled out a few old and ragged jumpers, which were nonetheless clean, before she got to what she was looking for.

"So where are we, did he say?" asked Richard.

"Not really. It's just a small village. He did say others have been through before, others like us. He also said if we get caught, not to mention his help. He was a really nice bloke, you know."

"Here we are, looks like a pen though, is that right?" asked Sam.

"Yes," mumbled Yorkie. "Bring it here, duck."

Rob searched the bag as Sam helped Yorkie inject himself. He handed a jumper to Quiety and two to Sam for herself and Yorkie, Rob reckoned himself and Large Lad would have to go without. At the very least they could build a makeshift curtain-jumper.

At the bottom of the holdall lay a flask. It was an old flask, the sort that goes cold within a few hours, and Rob knew it needed drinking straight away. Next to it were a handful of teabags, a can of chicken stew, half a bag of sugar, a box of matches, and a hand drawn map. "She is so nice," said Rob. "An angel."

Hearing Yorkie mumbling to Sam about twisting the top of the pen, Rob looked at the map. It clearly showed they were still deep in the forest. An arrow pointed west, and though the map was rough it seemed to suggest another town was ten miles or so away.

"Stab it there then press that button for ten seconds," said Yorkie.

As Sam injected Yorkie, Rob collected some empty stew tins and poured the tea out. It was well sugared and lacking milk, but it tasted the best ever. Though a small flask didn't leave much to share, Rob knew if he'd drunk a gallon he'd still want more.

Half an hour of scant conversation passed as they waited for Yorkie to perk up. Rob half expected it to be like an adrenalin shot, instantly making the old man jump up and run a half marathon. The reality was much slower.

"I think we should move on," said Quiety.

"Agree," said Rob, "It's only a matter of time before that police car stops and looks around. Plus someone may have seen us."

Quiety nodded and Richard agreed.

"How's Pat?" Rob asked Sam.

"Fallen back asleep." Her vigil, tucked up under a curtain next to him, had been doting to the verge of extreme. After his jab, he'd drunk his tea and looked more lifelike, but he was still an ill man. They all knew it.

"How far can we carry him? None of us are exactly weightlifters, are we?"

"I'd be scared of dropping him," said Sam.

Quiety nodded. "She's got a point, but we're too near the village. It must be after two now, daylight will come soon. We've got to get out of here before daylight."

There was no denying it. "Come on," said Rob, "let's rig up a stretcher."

Chapter 12

The two largest curtains on top of each other gave roughly enough support, and Yorkie didn't wake when they rolled him onto it.

They headed for the road, Rob and Quiety at the rear, Sam and Richard in front. Though Yorkie was heavy they managed a fair speed. Stopping twenty metres from the road, they considered the next step.

"The police car's not been back yet," said Richard.

"I was thinking the same thing," said Rob.

"I suppose we just go for it. If the police turn up, we'll have to use the guns."

Richard's bloodlust surprised Rob. He'd gone from being feeble and lanky to Chuck Norris overnight. He was right though, they'd come this far and done so much to escape that a mere police car couldn't stand in their way.

"Just stop a minute and listen," said Sam. "Can we put Pat down too, my arm's killing."

"Course," said Rob, gently lowering him to the floor.

Listening to the rustle of trees and the odd bird flapping by, they were satisfied the police were nowhere near.

The silence was broken.

"What the fuck are you doing carrying me?"

Not really knowing what to say, Rob just looked at him.

"I ain't a fucking invalid, just diabetic."

He stood up, helped by Richard. "How long you been carrying me for."

"Couple of hours," lied Sam.

Quiety chuckled. "Don't listen to her, just a few minutes. Go on, get back down there, we don't mind."

"No. I ain't being carried like some slacker."

"Please," said Sam, in her best whiny voice.

"No."

That was final. Though wobbly on his feet, Yorkie had enough strength to stand unaided. Rob stood one side of him with Richard the other as they approached the road. His weak legs growing stronger with each step.

Crossing the road was uneventful, as was the next forty minutes of walking into the forest and away from the approaching sunlight. Sam took the lead with Yorkie and Quiety, while Richard helped Rob bring up the rear.

Rob found Richard chattier than normal; asking many questions about the village, the vicar and how long he thought they'd walk tonight.

Yorkie instigated the first stop. After so many hours rest, the others could have walked all night without breaks, but he wanted to top up his levels. The rest of the group stood round as Yorkie hid behind a tree and gave himself another shot.

They continued though the pace was slower. By the time the sun's rays hit their backs, they had slowed to a crawl.

Though Rob had been walking with Richard, occasionally Sam would drop back and join them, giving Rob a smile or playful slap on the arm. His stomach was becoming more knotted the closer they seemed to get. Trying to keep his reasonable head on was difficult. Sure they could be split up at any moment, even killed, but somewhere lurking in his mind was the perverse thought that he was glad this had happened. Glad it had bought them together.

"Time for a break?" said Rob.

"Aye. Reckon so," was the reply from up front.

Sitting down, with daylight now strong enough to see by, they sighed and flexed their legs. Richard opened up the holdall. "What's it to be, chicken stew or shall we try some tea?"

"Not got any water," said Quiety.

"We passed about three streams, we should have got some. How crap are we? I thought we weren't having fires because of the smoke?" said Sam.

"Next stream we get some. When I was in the RAF I did training, you know."

Rob sat back with a smirk, expecting a during the war style speech from Quiety.

"To leave no trace, we need to dig a hole first, make a little fire in it just using the driest of wood, and then bury the remains. Cover it with some brush and gorse after and we'll get away with it."

They nodded, it seemed plausible.

"Problem is smoke. If it rises above the trees we could be seen miles away by a chopper during the day. At night, if a chopper's got heat seeking cameras, they'll see us too."

"So it's cold tea in other words," interrupted Sam.

Quiety shrugged his shoulders.

"I say we save them; we might find another abandoned cottage," said Rob.

The murmurs of agreement became laughter then silence as the five shared a can of cold stew.

Though all of their stories had been told, Richard broke the silence. "You know, life working in the city seemed so exciting. There was all this money being generated. God knows how it was generated. Half the bankers themselves didn't know where it actually came from. It was just everywhere."

"We used to go to this wine bar after work every night, then onto a restaurant or Indian. I was spending over a thousand pounds a week, just on food and drink. After my mortgage there wasn't much left, even though they were paying me silly money. But there was this buzz everywhere. We were like the new industrialists. We were the ones who'd dragged the economy out of the eighties slump and were making it something again."

He paused and looked down at his poorly shod feet. "Seems shit now though, doesn't it. We created nothing. We just sent money in a big circle, each time round someone got richer while the poor got poorer. British companies that'd made things for years got stripped of assets or mountained with overseas debt while a few top knobs had all the benefits with none of the risk."

"But we didn't see it. Just couldn't see what we were doing. It was like a new world. The old rules didn't apply. Most of the people there I think wouldn't have given a shit if they had known what was happening. Some of us cared. I guess I got caught up in the moment, I believed the hype."

"You shouldn't believe hype," said Sam.

He nodded. "I just wish it'd been different."

"I know," said Sam. "We can't change what's happened. As you say, there were plenty of people who'd have done it intentionally just waiting to take your place. It's 'say la vie' ain't it."

"Whatever," said Richard, trying to imitate her accent.

"Come on children," said Yorkie. "Time to move."

Re-studying the map, they headed in a more north-westerly direction. The map appeared to be leading towards the edge of the forest and to what Sam thought was the Bournemouth road. They couldn't understand why it was sending them that way as opposed to north which would make more sense. They settled on either missing patrols or roadblocks and followed as best they could.

Lunch came and with it another stop and injection. Rob was certain they were nearing another main road. Most of the forest had been walked and they had the feet to prove it. Taking his flimsy shoes off, Rob inspected the calluses, broken skin and bruises on his aching feet. Like the others, he wasn't a natural walker. After the first day of walking, his legs had got in a routine of hurting but carrying on. Whatever was keeping them going, possibly the fear of dying, was strong enough to overcome sore feet.

Knowing their last proper sleep had been a day ago, exhaustion was setting in. Most of them had caught an hour or so while Yorkie was ill, but it wasn't proper sleep.

"Do we call it a day and get six hours sleep?" Richard asked.

Though Sam and Rob declared they weren't tired, it was obvious Pat and Quiety were.

"Maybe we ought to," agreed Rob.

Before long their curtain beds were set up on the ground, Rob next to Sam with the three men opposite. The shifts were split with Rob, Sam and Yorkie sleeping first, and Quiety and Richard second. Yorkie insisted he should be woken up with Rob and Sam. After some mutterings they agreed, if only to shut him up. Whether they actually woke him was a different story.

Tucked up in his curtain, with Sam in hers facing him, the nervous looks, smiling and giggling soon gave way to something more. It became clear to Rob that a diet of chicken stew and no toothpaste didn't make for a pleasant start to a relationship. On that thought, and with a warm Sam nicking most of his curtain, Rob drifted off to sleep.

Chapter 13

The gentle pushing of Sam's hand and the words, "Wake up you lazy shite," woke Rob. At six in the evening, it still felt like mid-afternoon, the current spell of good weather was fortunate if not a miracle during late summer. Slowly collecting his thoughts, he noticed Yorkie was up and pacing round the camp. The unlikely duo of Quiety and Large Lad were settling down in their curtains ready for an hour or two's sleep.

Re-trousering and standing, Rob yawned before taking a sip of stream water. Its foul taste added to his already upset stomach. He knew it needed to be boiled, but they couldn't risk a fire.

As Quiety and Richard fell asleep, Rob and Sam went for a brief look round their current position leaving Yorkie on watch.

"You sleep well?" asked Sam.

Rob knew it wasn't a question. "Think so. Can't think why I'm so tired." He smiled.

She smiled back. "My feet really ache this morning, I mean evening. I reckon we'd have been better off not stopping."

Rob agreed but there was no solution. They couldn't stop for two days to recover, they had to plod on.

Stopping by a tree, well out of sight of the others, he held her hand. Moving round to face her, he pulled gently on her right arm. Her initial flexing of muscles and reluctance to succumb dwindled. As her muscles relaxed, he pulled her closer. In her haste to get nearer, her kneecap caught the edge of his. A searing jag of pain raced up his leg.

"Jesus."

"Sorry. No I'm not sorry, that hurt me too," she replied.

Face to face, he moved nearer until their lips were almost touching. Gently, he placed both hands on her shoulders, slowly running his fingers round in small but increasing circles. Though Rob had a final destination in mind, the path they took resembled one of his old Spirograph pictures instead of any clear ambition or intent.

His muscles tensed as her hands grabbed either side of his waist. Cold fingers with jagged nails pressed into his sides, her right hand seemed intent on puncturing one of his kidneys. Flinching, he moved his face further into hers, moulding his nose into her cheek.

It was then that he heard a noise similar to cracking twigs coming from the south.

"Shhh," said Rob. His hands stopped all motion and clenched as he poked her in the armpit.

"What," she said loudly.

"Keep it down," he whispered. "There's a noise over there."

She turned, his hand bouncing off her shoulder as she spun. Gripping her waist tightly as she stood in front, Rob searched through the evening blackness. The crunching, snapping sound echoed as it grew louder.

"On the floor," he whispered.

"Yes sir." She giggled.

Lying stomach first, his arm over her shoulders, he searched for movement or non-forest colour.

As the twig snapping and rustling neared, Rob wondered what the hell to do. Yorkie, sitting a hundred yards or so away, had both guns. Not that Rob could have used it anyway. Whatever was out there was probably armed, had night-sights and wasn't friendly.

"Shall we go back?" he whispered.

"Dunno?"

As much as decision making sucked, Rob knew he had to get a grip. He'd come so close just then, his mind still full of Sam and Spirographs, but he needed to think, to snap out of this daydream and get back into the nightmare.

His mind was made up for him. Two human shapes drifted into view from the left, crunching and cracking their way over twigs and trunks. Triangulating their path in his mind, he estimated they were heading near, not exactly in their direction, but near enough. Near enough to see them.

"Shit," whispered Sam.

Unsure whether they had time to run or not, Rob eventually decided if he could hear them, they could hear him. What he hadn't thought was their speed and noisy movement may have given him the advantage.

Lying on the ground, heart racing and with Sam by his side, it became clear this may be how he left the world. Though destined to imprisonment while in the van, life had regained some purpose. He'd also met Sam, who, despite being a bit gobby and scratchy-nailed, he thought the world of.

So this was it. The end.

Chapter 14

The two people walked with purpose as they approached.

With night drawing in, their light clothing wasn't fully clear until they were twenty yards away. It was clothing Rob would never forget the look of: Consortium straitjackets.

The two figures, one male and one female had a spring in their step that had long since faded in Rob's group. As they neared, Rob and Sam pretended to be fallen tree trunks.

The man stopped. His companion narrowly avoided a collision with him as she stopped. "What?" she asked.

The man looked directly at Rob and Sam as he covered the woman with his arm. Pulling something from his pocket, which glistened in the moonlight, he forced the woman back with one hand while he pointed the knife at Sam and Rob.

Rob realised that though their clothing was dark on the dark floor of a forest at night, the whites of their eyes had betrayed them. Had they kept their eyes shut, they may never have been spotted.

"What is it?" said the woman.

"Shush," said the man.

Rob winced, though the man had a knife, he half expected the woman he was with to batter him for telling her to shush.

"Slowly back up," the man said to the woman.

Rob had a big decision to make, a decision he didn't want. These people were walking round with Consortium straitjackets on. Unless another new fashion hadn't hit Basingstoke, they were also escaped prisoners. However, it could be a trap. He couldn't think why the police or army would dress up like prisoners in order to get close to other prisoners, but it had to be considered. If they were like them, they needed help. They'd be safer together. However, two more mouths to feed and not much chicken stew could cause problems.

They shuffled a few more paces back. Rob could feel Sam breathing heavily. He could almost feel her heart beating through her shoulder. She was waiting for him to make the move. Again, the shit decision was his.

"Wait," called out Sam. She'd obviously got fed up waiting.

They edged back, the girl had her head turned looking for trees and brush to avoid while she dragged the man with her.

"Please wait." Sam shrugged off Rob and Sat up. "We've escaped too. We can help."

They stopped.

Mumbled words drifted towards Rob and Sam's ears. Their obvious debate over whether they could trust Rob and Sam was similar to Rob's internal debate, but without the chicken stew.

"Who are you?" the woman said.

"I'm Sam and this is Rob. We got captured a few nights back but the lorry crashed and we escaped."

"I'm Sally," she said. "We escaped from Beaulieu two days ago."

"Watch it," whispered Rob. It sounded similar to their own story. Too similar.

"Come and join us," said Sam. "Have you eaten?"

"John caught a rabbit yesterday," she replied, with something approaching pride. Rob wondered how on earth he'd managed it. Some type of snare or did he just find a rabbit hole and stick his arm in?

"Sounds nice," said Sam.

"We had to skin and gut it, that kind of took the edge off," the man named John replied.

"How did you catch it, John," asked Rob.

As Rob sat up and leant on Sam's arm, he noticed the two walking towards them, the knife now pointing down instead of towards them.

"We saw it run into this hole thing."

"Warren?" asked Rob.

"No, I'm John," he replied, a little confused.

"No I... carry on." Rob shook his head.

"Well I went up to the hole and stuck me hands in."

Now they were closer, Rob could see that Rabbit John was mid-forties. A quite heavy set and balding man, he looked far from the sharpest twig in the box. The woman, Sally, was mid-thirties, not much older than Rob. Her straitjacket fit her tightly, too tightly in a couple of places. However her face was almost oval shaped with very prominent top front teeth, not dissimilar to a rabbit. If Rob had been cruel, he'd have told her to watch out for John the rabbit catcher. She carried a small water bottle, while he had his knife and a big stick.

"Where've you been staying?" asked Sam.

"Here and there. We found this abandoned farmhouse, but..."

"The tunnel went back really far," said John, "so I started digging with me stick..."

"We didn't want to stay too long in case they came looking, but we stocked up on water and that..."

"Eventually, the little blighter comes running out. Nearly missed it I did, but I managed to grab its tail and back legs..."

"We've just been walking solidly for what seems like days, probably been going round in circles..."

"If that wasn't hard enough," John continued, "having to skin it then remove all the organs was horrible."

"Offal?" said Rob

"It was worse than awful pal, it was shocking. I was gagging, nearly threw up a few times. Poor Sally was actually sick."

By now, Elmar Fudd and Buggs Bunny had sat down, opposite but a respectful distance away. Rabbit Boy had placed the knife on the ground, still out of reach of Rob, but also quite far from himself. Rabbit girl, in such close proximity looked familiar to Rob, very familiar, yet he couldn't place her.

"It was horrible," she said. "I mean when you're starving it's amazing what you'll eat, but it was just all that blood and the smell."

Rabbit Boy nodded. "And if that wasn't bad enough, trying to cook the bastard was nearly impossible. I built this fire, you know like you learn in the scouts, but without matches I just had to rub two sticks together."

"He was at it for hours, weren't you? Swearing and cursing, blaming the sticks, saying he'd give his right leg for a box of matches."

Looking a bit embarrassed, Rabbit John shrugged his shoulders. "It went on for hours. Sal eventually fell asleep so I left her to it. You know what it's like when you start something but you ain't giving up? Well I was going to start that fire, I was determined, like."

"And then," she continued, "when I woke up, I was lovely and warm in front of the fire and the air smelt of burnt rabbit. Breakfast in bed we said, didn't we." She looked at him with a certain admiration.

Rabbit Boy shrugged his shoulders again, his cheeks filling with colour. "You know, just did my bit."

"You're off the telly aren't you?" interrupted Sam. "The weather girl from channel three."

She ran her fingers through her straw-like, un-conditioned hair. "Yes," she replied. "Though I'm not really a girl anymore, and I haven't worked since that day when..."

The jollity and introductions were interrupted by a diabetic ex-Yorkshire man wielding a sub-machine gun. "Don't move," Yorkie shouted.

Neanderthal rabbit man lost his bottle immediately. Curling into a ball, he moved towards Sally, looking for protection from the nasty man with the gun.

"Pat," shouted Sam. "It's fine, they've escaped like us."

Yorkie's eyes didn't leave the newcomers. "Get that knife, Rob."

Leaning over, with the nervous looking Sally holding onto the ball-shaped Rabbit Boy, Rob picked up the knife and moved it. Next to him, Sam stood and walked towards Yorkie, intentionally getting between the gun and the newcomers.

"Pat," she shouted. "Will you put that fucking gun down?"

He lowered the gun, but moved to his left so the Loony Tunes gang were still in sight. "Who are you?"

"It's okay, Pat. They're like us. Look they're even wearing straitjackets."

Nodding, Yorkie walked towards them, the gun now a limp piece of metal in his hand. "Where did you escape from?"

The weapon now pointing elsewhere, Rabbit Boy unfurled from his ball. "Beaulieu. Can you put that thing down, please? You're scaring Sally."

Trying not to laugh, Rob said, "Look let's just calm down and start from the beginning." He paused. "Pat, what's the time?"

Yorkie, looked at his forearm, twisting the gun as he did. Rabbit Boy ducked. "About two I think."

"Are the others sleeping?"

"Others?" said Sally.

"There's five of us," said Sam.

"Yeah," replied Yorkie. He took a few paces forward. Still four or five yards away, he added, "Dave got off straight away and Richard's snoring like an elephant."

"We don't want to wake them," said Rob. "Let's keep it down. Anyway, Pat this is John and Sally. John and Sally, this is Pat." Sam squeezed his arm. He half expected her to applaud him for getting their names right.

"Pleased to meet you," said Sally. John didn't say anything. Rob knew Yorkie had robbed him of his head stag position. They'd be rutting horns together before the night was out if this wasn't played right.

"John caught a rabbit, didn't you, John," said Sam, who had her diplomatic head on.

"Yeah," he replied. "Skinning and cooking it was the hardest part."

"Sounds nice, rabbit," replied Yorkie, "we've been living off cold stew."

"I hate that stew," said John. "What else is there to eat though?"

Yorkie took the remaining few steps forward and sat beside Rob. He placed the gun next to his leg. Rob forced a smile at Yorkie, before turning back to Rabbit Boy. "So, where does your story begin then?"

His confidence now returning, Rabbit Boy looked sideways at the lovely weather girl Sal before starting. "Well, as I say, I caught this rabbit and skinned it and Sal was nearly sick and..."

Despite it not being what Rob meant, he let it go. He wondered, and he knew Sam would too, whether the two rabbits had paired yet. Whether he'd been the perfect gentleman defending her honour or they'd been at it like, well, rabbits.

"...and then, after we'd eaten this rabbit, which although it was burnt tasted gorgeous. I mean I'm not saying I'm an ace cook or anything, but it was like Sally said, eating after so long without meat made it just heaven."

Sam's cold and bony fingers wormed their way into Rob's left hand, stealing the warmth he'd built up there.

"It also got a bit sickly. You know, after not eating much your stomach protests doesn't it? But after we'd eaten, we knew we needed to get going. We walked about half an hour, seriously that's all it was, then we came across this farmhouse. I wanted to avoid it but Sal, she says there might be someone who'll help. We staked it out for half hour, no one there, so we goes round the back and finds a loose window. I forced it open, using the knife like, and we goes inside."

"It was lovely," Sally butted in, "a real old farmhouse, cooking range, big wooden table and that, but the place was deserted. Everything had been taken, apart from the table and cooker."

"And the box of matches." John laughed. "After all that bloody effort getting that fire lit, within an hour we finds an old range cooker with logs ready and matches. Bloody typical ain't it?"

Sam squeezed Rob's hand. There were so many little things, observations he wanted to tell her. By the squeeze, he guessed she had a few too.

"That's bad luck, pal," said Yorkie.

"Aye, it was. But this farmhouse still had running water so we had a bath, coldish mind, the range thing took ages to heat the water. Then we got going again."

"Didn't you worry about the smoke?" asked Sam. "If anyone's following they'd have seen it?"

"Following?" said Sally. "I've got to admit, we never thought of that, they were so disorganised at Beaulieu they didn't know their arses from their elbows."

To hear the woman who'd always confidently talked about lows coming in from the west and occasional showers in the east swear like a navvy didn't feel right to Rob. Despite her dishevelled appearance, she still retained an outward glow of approachability and honesty. An authority figure from the old, good days.

"They probably haven't even realised we're missing yet." John smiled at weather girl Sal, she returned the smile. Sam squeezed Rob's hand tighter. "When we escaped we just walked out. I'd spent weeks secretly stealing the knife too, but when it came to the crunch, it was easy."

"What about the guards and army?" asked Sam.

"Their hearts aren't in it. Plus, they can be bought. The place we were at was a holding centre. They processed us, took name, date of birth, fingerprints, serial number and that, then they had to wait for the files to come from the regions that showed our crimes. Loads of people had to wait ages for the final bit, the boat to hell we called it."

"When I first got there I was terrified," said Sal, who'd somehow managed to grab hold of Rabbit Boy's hand without Rob noticing. "The first thing a guard did was offer me freedom, for, well the obvious thing."

Rob quickly realised it wasn't a personalised weather forecast.

"I turned it down, obviously. I'm not that kind of girl." She laughed to try and make light of it. "But I met John on my first day and he, well looked after me I suppose."

John's back straightened and his chest puffed out at her approval of his chivalry.

"They segregated us at night, but during the day we could mix together in part of the grounds and also in, like, a communal hall. I had a few bad words and got in some scuffles 'cos of who I was." She paused. "We had jobs as well. We both worked in the kitchen."

"That was how I got my knife," interrupted Rabbit Boy.

"We chose a day to leave. The guards changed over at one in the afternoon, but they always left the kitchen unattended for half an hour. So we just walked towards the fence, found a piece that wasn't watched and escaped. It really was easy."

A brief silence fell. Sam interrupted it, "All this time we've been eating cold stew and we could have heated it."

Rob shook his head. They could have had a proper bath as well. Though the cottage was a few days ago. They'd still be as festering as they were now even with it.

"When did you last sleep?" asked Yorkie.

"Over a day ago," said Rabbit Boy.

"Do you want to get a few hours before we move off?"

Rob knew it was an invitation of sorts to join them and they'd accept. They were safer together.

"Sounds good," said the weather girl.

"You can borrow mine and Rob's curtain-duvets," chipped in Sam.

"Best offer I've had in days," she replied with another nervous laugh.

Walking back to Quiety and Large Lad, Sam showed them to their bed for the next few hours. Regrouping back with Yorkie and

Rob, she shrugged her shoulders. "What do you reckon?" she whispered.

"Harmless," said Yorkie. "Even with that knife."

Rob nodded. "Shall we get some wood and make a fire? We can have a cup of tea when they wake up?"

"You're a genius, hun," said Sam.

"I think we deserve it after listening to that," said Yorkie.

Sam chuckled and turned to Rob, "Go on then, Mr Nickname, what have you got."

Seeing Yorkie's frown, he said, "Don't know what you mean?"

"Go on." She stuck her scratchiest finger in his forearm.

"Rabbit Boy and The Weather Girl?" he replied.

Sam shook her head. "You're losing it, Journo Boy."

Chapter 15

With the Rabbit Twins' arrival taking the passion from their
embrace, Rob and Sam collected wood while Yorkie watched the
camp. As morning broke through the trees, they shared a moment of
tranquillity watching a new day break. Another new day of freedom.

The most interesting news the new arrivals brought, was the
lack of any order amongst the Consortium's henchmen. They really
did rule on propaganda and fear. The actual ruling itself seemed a
second rate job.

Rob thought that unsurprising on reflection. Everything had
been so quick, things were made up as they went along. Given time,
the Consortium would tie up the loose ends, perfect the police state it
was making. But for now, things were chaotic. If only everyone
realised that. The whole thing could be smashed so easily.

As waking noises emerged from the camp, Yorkie and Rob dug
a small pit and built a fire while Sam filled three cans from the
stream. Spilling half of it on the way back, Rob topped up the cans
up from the water bottle.

Though Rabbit Boy's matches were wet, Yorkie soon got the
fire lit.

"What's the fire for?" asked Richard from his curtain lined pit.
"More to the point who are they? Who's that sleeping in your
curtain, Rob?"

"Well it's not fucking Goldilocks, is it?" said Yorkie.

"Ha ha. Too early for that," said Richard. "You feeling better
then, Pat?"

"Couple a waifs and strays we picked up last night. Sal and
John. Sal's famous. Used to do the weather on Channel 3," said Sam.

"Really?" Squinting, he had a better look. The mass of
unkempt hair covering her face made it hard to tell, but he eventually
nodded that yes, it was her.

"They can tell you their story later," said Rob. "Pass the time if
nothing else. One good thing, though. They got matches and it looks
like we're not being followed, so we're having a cup of tea to
celebrate."

"Sounds good to me. Don't suppose they've bought bacon and
eggs have they?"

Rob laughed. "You'd think you were dreaming if I said yes. They had roast rabbit the other day." He pointed at the new arrivals.

"Lucky bastards."

In time Quiety woke and was handed half a can of weak tea. He, like everyone, thought it heaven. The final two cans were saved for the newcomers and when they woke, the questions came.

"What I don't understand is," said Richard, who was not only on good form but also a bit drooly over the ex-weather girl. This hadn't gone unnoticed from either Sam, Rob or the rabbit catcher. "What could you have possibly done wrong to annoy them, Sally?"

Rob shuddered. Seeing Richard fawn over a woman was not a pretty sight.

"Periodic outbursts of rain in the northern parts of Scotland and Wales," she said.

To all of them it was like having a television on in front of them. It still didn't explain how she'd upset anyone.

"Code words. Quite simply. Relaying information from one party to another." She stopped and chewed her bottom lip. "Okay, by your faces, I need to start further back. Here's what I know."

Sam leant against Rob's left arm, making herself comfy.

"After the Consortium started to provide food, I was approached one night when I was waiting for my tube. It was all very clandestine, jolly exciting really. This young woman said to me, 'If you want to help your country, meet me on platform three in an hour.' Well, I kind of pondered it for a few seconds. I thought what can she mean?"

Though interested in her story, Rob was more interested in the expressions coming from Rabbit Boy's face. Daggers of hate were being thrown at Richard. He'd obviously heard this story before, they'd shared each other's company for a long time. Rob knew he was terrified of losing her.

"Well I sat down and thought about it. I mean sharing the news room, we were hearing all sorts of stories that weren't being told. I was always a bit of a rebel in my youth, I went on the Poll Tax march, so I thought I'd at least see what it was about."

"Standing on the station platform, I looked round but couldn't see her. I waited and waited. Just when I was close to giving up, the young woman appeared again. She looked at me, said, 'Hi Sal,' and ran over. She hugged me and though it felt obvious, I'm sure it looked just like a normal meeting between old friends. During the hug, she whispered, 'There's something in your pocket, read it when you get home.' Then she broke off the embrace, talked about her husband for ten seconds then apologised, said her train was due, and went."

"Well, I was stunned. Feeling in my pocket, I felt a piece of paper. I fiddled with it all the way home, wondering what on earth it would be and how she'd slipped it in there without me even feeling. When I got home, this scrap of paper said, 'If you're interested, be at The Crown in the Strand at 8.30 tomorrow. Destroy this piece of paper.' Well, it was all very exciting, like a spy book really. I half expected the paper to self destruct after I'd read it." She waited for laughter. It took a while to come.

"Well, to cut a long story short, they sent me round the houses. I was in the pub and someone bought me a drink and gave me a message to go to another pub. Then in that pub I was given a phone number and told to ring it from a call box. Finding a call box in central London that actually worked was the hardest part. Every one was vandalised."

Rob really wished she'd get to the point.

"Eventually I called this number and was told to go to a house in Mayfair the next evening. Well, I did and this very nice young man told me what was going on, the Consortium and how civil liberties were being eroded, we'd become no more than a police state. I could help by passing on information to various groups as part of my weather forecasts. I went back a few days later. Quite worryingly they said they were following me to make sure no one else was following me, but I learnt how to obtain and pass on these messages. Obviously, I eventually got caught."

Rob had many questions lurking in his head, he doubted he was alone. He also knew they had better get moving. "We better get going," he said. "But, who were they MI5, MI6?"

Standing up, she stretched, which in her ultra-tight straitjacket was probably illegal under some new law. "At first I didn't know, but eventually I found out. Now, please don't take this the wrong way, but if I tell you and we get captured, under torture you may give it away. I haven't been tortured, yet. I promised not to tell anyone. The or..." She paused. "Whoever they are, they're still trying to help. I'd hate to be responsible for spoiling that help."

Nodding, Rob stood up. Gathering their few bits together, and burying the fire's remains, they headed west.

An hour's walk breezed by. With Yorkie and Quiety up front, the two Bunnies and Richard took the middle with Sam and Rob bringing up the rear. The battle for domination and superiority was unravelling in front of Rob as the rabbit catcher and the computer geek vied for the weather girl's attention.

Slipping back, out of earshot, Sam whispered to Rob, "Something's definitely happened between them."

"I thought so last night. They were holding hands at one point."

"Richard needs telling. Don't want him to make a fool of himself."

He knew she was right. From their story, he knew they'd got close, but even then it didn't make the next step up guaranteed. She was definitely right about Richard though, he deserved better than to make a fool of himself.

Slipping his free arm round Sam's waist, his other full of curtain and empty cans, Rob planted a kiss on the top of her head. Two day old shower gel mixed in with head sweat made the process more a chore than it should have been.

Moving her own curtain to her other hand, she placed her hand round his waist. "What was that for?"

"Dunno. Just wanted to, I suppose."

"Good," she said.

Chapter 16

They walked for another hour until the trees cleared. In the distance stood a road, much larger than any they'd crossed before. Sam was certain the end of the New forest was marked by a dual carriageway, so this wasn't it. The map, for all its good, wasn't much help. Yorkie suggested a break while Sam tried to remember any other big roads in the forest.

Sitting again in their rough circle, the sighs and moans about aching limbs faded.

"Where do you come from, John?" asked Quiety.

"Ipswich," his reply.

After another short pause, Quiety said, "We've all told our stories, unfortunately you've missed them but I'm sure we can recap sometime. Not that you missed much with my story."

"Yo...Pat's was the best," said Rob.

"Yeah," agreed Sam, "he's a Basildon Bovver Boy." She dug her elbow into Rob's ribs, he supposed it was for his near name slip.

"It wasn't that interesting," said Yorkie. "Just a bunch of old men trying to make a difference."

"So what's yours, John?" said Rob.

"Me? Well, nothing really to it. Married at twenty, two kids by thirty, divorced by forty, be paying for them till I'm sixty. That's what I used to say. Won't now though, money's not important anymore, is it?" He paused. "My story ain't really that good to be honest. Not anywhere near as exciting as Sal's."

"Oh come now, John. You did your bit. Tell them about the lorries."

He shrugged his shoulders. "Mechanic, that's what I am. Got trained and apprenticed in the army fixing their fleets."

"When I left, I got a job with a bus company. Fixed them for years. Eventually became supervisor. Course, buses have been in decline a long time, eventually we got bought out and the repairing was contracted out. They took us all on, they had to, part of the agreement. One by one though, they made us redundant. I kept hold of my job, well, I had the wife and kids to support so I kept me head down. Until she left me of course, but I still kept working after that."

"When all that bank stuff happened I was well annoyed. I had two big mortgages on houses that were worth nothing, and well, things looked really bad. Just so as some bankers can get their bonuses."

"Then it got worse. The buses stopped running, but the boss says we're going to be fixing military vehicles and police cars instead. We were put up in digs at this stately home in the West Midlands. Given free food, beer and the like. Treated like kings, we were."

"But it weren't right. Deep down I knew it. Now, I'm a simple man..."

No shit, thought Rob.

"...but everyone else was suffering and we was living the life of Riley. We had a full size snooker table, you know. Well, to cut a long story short, I wanted out, but they wouldn't let me. So I started dipping me hand in. We were re-using parts, you know cos most of the parts had been coming from Japan and Poland and that all dried up. Some of the best parts I used to stash away and swap with this spiv type bloke who came round. I'd get food off him or fags or whatever and send it to the wife and kids, or ex-wife as she was them."

"I messed up though, used a few well dodgy brake pads and tracking rods that snapped or cracked. Lorries started crashing more often. They looked up the repair logs, saw it was me doing them, and put two and two together."

"Then, one night, they came for me."

Rob would only realise later that the lorry they'd been travelling in was possibly one that Rabbit Boy had fitted a dodgy part to. In all likelihood, they owed their escape to him.

When they set off again, Sam grabbed Richard by the arm and kept him lurking back, his eyes on the wonderful weather girl, while Rob joined the Bunnies and led them on. Rob was surprised how easily her plan worked.

Crossing the road was as before. No cars or vans had passed in the half hour they'd stopped.

Their trek continued for two hours. Beside the fawning Rabbit Killer and the lovely Sal, who kept trying in vain to straighten her hair, Rob chatted briefly about their travels.

Though Sal was only five years older than him, she had the air and maturity of a different generation. He'd be the first to admit she was a very charming and slightly mysterious lady. The fact she'd been dealing with spies just added to her appeal. No wonder these two dorks were smitten with her. Rabbit Boy himself was coming out from his shell and seemed to be showing a more intelligent side. His whole demeanour had changed since Yorkie gave him his knife back.

At their next stop under the mid-afternoon sun, the mood was lulled. With exhausted feet and no food in the kitty, they collectively realised they couldn't continue like this forever.

"Where are we going?" asked Rabbit Boy.

Silence.

"There's a camp in the Highlands apparently," said Sam, her heart didn't sound in it.

"You mean Scotland?"

She nodded. Rob leant against her, nearly knocking her over, to try and snap her out of the depression Rabbit Boy was intent on bringing. A poke in the ribs told him this wasn't the sort of time for leaning.

"Surely there's somewhere else? Our idea was to head for Bristol, find an empty flat and just mingle. In a large city you can get lost easily."

Rob knew he had a point. It was the same point they'd all been putting off. Deep down, they'd put off the inevitable, knowing they'd eventually be captured.

"I suppose that would work," said Yorkie. "Even a large town might work. You're right, it's to do with size."

Sam leant against Rob, her body limp on his. Apparently now had become a good time for leaning. "Bournemouth's nearby," she said.

"Hasn't that been overtaken by pensioners?" asked Richard.

"No more than usual I don't think." She placed her hand on Rob's knee digging it in to support her while she moved to get more comfortable. "Most of them went to Hastings and that."

"More police and Army by the sea," said Quiety. "You know, to stop people leaving."

Rob nodded. Though Europe offered no more security or wealth than Britain, hordes of youngsters had journeyed across the channel and travelled to Poland in search of a job and a stable wage. Rumours abounded of old Polish women saying, "All these British people, where are they coming from?"

The mood which had gone from hero to zero was rising back through the ranks. The thought of Bristol and the hope they could mingle undetected, while trying to do something to help was enough of an incentive to continue.

"Whatever and wherever," Quiety started, "we need food tonight or tomorrow. Bristol's a long way on an empty tum."

Rob noticed Rabbit Boy's eyes light up. The Elma Fudd within was stirring.

"Well," said Rob, "if this map's anything like correct then we should be near the dual carriageway by tonight. There must be another town soon."

"One thing we have to remember," said Yorkie. "Once we're out of the Forest, we lose cover. We'll have to sleep by day and walk at night."

That was going to make the journey harder. That wasn't their only problem. Rabbit Boy and Sal still had straitjackets on. They needed clothes, food, decent water and cover. Rob knew it was too much to ask. Yorkie's diabetic pen was getting low too. That was the most worrying thing.

"There really ain't much after the Forest," said Sam. "Army ground mainly. Not many towns or nothing. Ringwood's quite big, but god knows where that is."

"We'll find something," said Sal. "I know we will."

"At least the weather's good, eh Sal," said Quiety.

"Yeah. Don't ask me to forecast anything though, or don't believe me if I do. I'm usually wrong, as the papers constantly used to remind me."

Rob knew what she meant. Before the crashes, the papers had this dolly bird impression of her. The paparazzi would follow her everywhere, constantly trying to photograph her with a footballer or anyone they could get a story from. After meeting her, he knew the reality was different. She was friendlier in real life

Rob was pleased that Sam's little chat with Richard seemed to have worked. Though he looked a bit down, sitting on his own next to Quiety, Rob thought it had been for the best.

The break over, they packed and continued. This time, Richard joined the lead group of Yorkie and Quiety while Sam and Rob took the rear. Sneaking back a bit, Rob asked Sam about Richard. "How subtle were you?"

"Hey, I'm not gobby all the time you know. I just started talking about them and casually mentioned I thought they were together."

"What did he say?"

"His face dropped but he tried not to show it. I hate things like that."

Putting his arm round her shoulder, which with the rolled up curtain wasn't easy, Rob said, "To be honest. I don't think either of them are her type. I mean, Rabbit Boy's a bit, well, you know." He tried hard, but a polite word for thick wasn't appearing in his brain.

"I know what you mean. She's used to footballers and actors and that. She ain't his sort."

As the afternoon faded and tired feet slowed down, the edge of the Forest and a distant road approached. That was it, the end of the New Forest.

Chapter 17

Any break was welcome but this one was enforced by daylight. They'd decided to walk through the night or as far as possible until shelter was found or morning came.

Sitting in their group, Yorkie and Quiety were dozing while Richard, Sam and Sal lit a fire.

After much persuasion by Rabbit Boy, Rob had agreed to wander off in search of wildlife to stalk and kill. Rob went with him just to shut him up: he was pretty sure they had zero chance of finding anything. It just killed a few hours.

Walking slowly, with a curtain in one hand and a stout stick in the other, Rob saw the sheer concentration almost burnt onto Rabbit Boy's face. Trying to lighten the mood, he said, "Sal's nice, isn't she." He hadn't set out on a fishing trip, but if he did catch anything, Sam could only be grateful.

"Yep, fine woman she is." He rustled some undergrowth with his stick, looking for burrows.

"I suppose," Rob continued, "you must have got close, being on the run together." He dangled the line further out.

Nodding his head, Rabbit Boy said, "Well, yeah, you know there was just us, we talked a lot those few days. We got to know each other." The fish had seen the worm, but were looking for traps.

Rob was about to wiggle his line and throw a handful of maggots in to tempt the fish further when their path was blocked.

It happened so quickly, Rob wasn't convinced it had actually happened. A dreamlike feeling rose as two heavily set guards with full body armour jumped from a tree. With two others appearing from the undergrowth, all Rob could do was drop his stick and curtain. Two sets of wide eyes stared as guns were raised and pointed at his face. Only two words were spoken. "Get down."

Beside him, Rabbit Boy had dropped his knife and stick. Frozen to the spot, neither of them could get down as instructed. The surprise was so intense, so quick, that Rob later struggled to remember the exact sequence. The only certain thing was it ended with him lying face first in the floor, gagged and with cable tied hands.

One gun-wielding, special officer stood over them, his eyes unblinking as he stared, while the others headed towards the camp. There was no way he could warn them what was coming, no way he could tell Sam to run. No way of helping.

The noise of well-trained officers walking through the wood faded as they moved away. Listening hard, Rob eventually heard what he didn't want to hear.

A distant, "Freeze," was shouted. Visualising the scene, Rob knew the three remaining officers had surrounded the camp. Yorkie and Quiety, the two gun wielders of the group had been asleep when he left. If they were awake now, Rob knew gunfire would be the first signal. Though unsure of Quiety, Rob knew Yorkie would think nothing of shooting them. It was a bloodbath waiting to happen. Whether they'd all get lined up and shot later, Rob wasn't sure nor had even thought about, but at the moment he knew there was an outside possibility they'd be kept alive if no one shot the guards.

The distant screech of Sal was overpowered by some gobby girl shouting, "Get your facking hands off." Some mumbled words and orders were given, then a male voice screamed, "Don't move. Move a muscle and I'll blow your fucking head off." Unfortunately or fortunately, Rob didn't recognise the voice. It was one of the guards.

The next few minutes seemed to last forever as each shout, rustling, noise from the guards and Sam's swear words lingered. Rob finally realised it was over when some movement towards him, a guard running back suddenly became a voice.

"Five neutralised. These two, over there."

The gloved hand picking Rob up then pushing him bought back memories of two days ago and the lorry. At least no shots had been fired.

Yet.

Lying face down, next to the others, Rob wondered just how long they'd been followed. They'd obviously been waiting for the right moment. Maybe waiting for the group to separate. Perhaps waiting for the gun bearers to fall asleep? Though Quiety and Yorkie had long since stopped holding their guns at all times, they were within reach. That would have been obvious to anyone following.

The leader of the guards spoke into his radio. "Still in position and awaiting pick up. Over."

That sounded promising. Rob couldn't see how that could equate to death by firing squad. Though facing the ground, he could just catch Sam's eye from the corner of his own. Unable to do anything other than wink, he did. Twice. She closed her eyes slowly then opened them. Whatever that meant, he hoped he'd one day find out.

Chapter 18

Within half an hour, a military helicopter hugged the tree tops, eventually slowing and circling above. More police voices were heard, presumably the radio. A muffled reply told them to walk a hundred yards to a clearing.

Dragged one by one, and at gunpoint, they were pushed towards the waiting helicopter, which read Air-Sea Rescue. Chuckling somewhere deep inside at the irony, Rob plodded towards it.

He wondered briefly if he could run. Could he make it? There might be some confusion. The others might distract the police long enough for him to get away. Hell, they might even miss or the gun might jam. The chances were slim and he knew it. The only real temptation in running was death would be a quick end.

Approaching the helicopter Sal fell over. The downdraught from the blades was intense, and with his hands tied behind his back, Rob became unstable too. The police pushed them inside the chopper, forcing them to lie face down. Then, they went back for Sally and chucked her in. She landed awkwardly. Her mumbles through the gag were lost to the sound of the rotor blades.

The noisy, turbulent ride took ten minutes. More than enough time to ponder three wasted days of walking, sheer exhaustion and aching feet that would take months to heal. At least he was alive. Why would they call in a helicopter and fly them, presumably to the Isle of Wight, then kill them. That didn't make sense. Rob was more than confident they'd live. What sort of a life it would be, he wasn't sure. Just what did await on the Isle of Wight?

His stomach sank as the helicopter started its descent, the rotor blades slowing until it landed. The blades whined as their speed decreased, the noise now approaching unbearable. Though Quiety lay next to him, neither had made any attempt to look at each other: an armed guard nearby.

The rotors now nearly stopped, Rob sensed the others being picked up, one by one. Sure enough, Quiety was suddenly pulled upright. Twisting his head, Rob saw two black clad guards push him out of the helicopter. Rob's turn came next. One of them gripped him by the hands, the other his shoulder.

Pulled upwards, he struggled to find his feet on the floor. Carried to the edge, he was pushed out and into the arms of two waiting guards. The evening sun lit the sky in a red haze. Though unsure where he was, the landing pad appeared to be at the end of a runway. Around him, grassy fields ended in a high fence stretching to the horizon. A few old buildings lay scattered around; old Nissen huts were dwarfed by a concrete windowless tower. Radar equipment lay atop another smaller tower, whose window gave it away as a control tower.

Standing beside him were his six companions. Quiety had blood running across his gag, possibly a nose bleed. Sam's hair looked dishevelled. Her face pale with fear, a fear Rob didn't know she knew. The plucky, warm girl he'd only just met, looked lost in a sea of sharks. Richard breathed heavily through his nose. His hands tied behind his back left his stomach pushed out, accentuating his weight. Sal's straitjacket, which was still too tight and revealing, was covered in dust from her fall. All her weight was on her left foot, she'd obviously hurt her right one. Yorkie had a bring it on look in his face. His chest was puffed out, and eyes bored into the waiting guards. John the rabbit catcher looked lost, scared, a little boy without his knife. He stared at Sal, trying to catch her eye, but she was looking at the floor, avoiding everyone's eyes.

Looking back at Sam, Rob caught her eye. He could see her mouth trying to form a smile beneath the gag. He returned the gesture, and slightly shook his head. She shrugged her shoulders back, which looked painful with her hands tied.

The guards had doubled in number to eight. Balaclava wearing and with Special Forces uniforms on, their guns were trained on each of them.

An obvious leader, with more than one stripe on his lapel, spoke, "Welcome. You gave us quite the run about, didn't you? I don't know whether to congratulate you or not." Pausing, he added, "Right, move this way, towards the tower, single file. Now."

Yorkie took the lead, his chest still puffed out. Quiety and Sam took second and third place. Rob wanted to go last, just in case. In case of what he didn't know, but he knew he had to keep hope. However, Sal, John the Rabbit and Richard seemed to be fighting for last place. Rob left them to it and settled for the middle.

The tower loomed over them. Seagulls hovered above, their nesting site disturbed by the new arrivals. Entering a narrow doorway, strip lights flickered as the guard turned them on. The tower's ground floor, little bigger than a house, was divided into four small cells, an open area with table and chairs and an office behind that.

Yorkie was pushed into the first cell, barely six feet long by four wide. Containing a rough bed, toilet and sink it just rated as adequate. Slamming and locking the door behind the still handcuffed and gagged Yorkie, the guard herded the rest of them up a narrow flight of stairs, several guns trained on them as they walked.

The second floor had cells on either side, eight in all. Quiety was given the first, with Sam one at the other end. Catching her eyes as she was pushed into the cell, Rob winked. It was all he could do.

Rob was pushed into the nearest cell on the third floor. Once inside and with the door locked he looked round. A patch of damp hung in the corner. The flickering strip light outside only partially lit the cell. Despite the spiders and probably cockroaches, it was empty. Sitting on the bed, next to a folded blanket and sheet, he tried to sigh, but the gag meant he only got a warm nose and lips.

Hearing noises of movement, both from above and below, Rob waited. He wasn't sure how long he'd have to wait, but he hoped they'd remove the cable ties and gag. Maybe even a little food? Chances were it'd be the dregs of chicken stew.

He knew it would come to this. They were always going to get caught, it was just a matter of when. He was curious about the Isle of Wight. He'd imagined a Stasi style camp full of huts where intellectuals dug tunnels and radical activists vaulted over horses while dropping dirt onto the ground. Locked in his cell, he wondered where the baseball and glove was.

About a quarter hour gone, movement upstairs told Rob the guards were returning. A muffled voice, probably Rabbit Boy, was heard from above, giving Rob advance warning that they were de-gagging the group. When the guards got to his cell, their guns were still raised, aiming at him. Rob was ordered to turn round and walk backwards towards the cell bars.

Nervously waiting for a shot or a slap in the head, he felt gloved hands pat down his body starting at the feet and working up.

They were thorough. Incredibly thorough. Finally, the nosy hands cut the cable tie.

"If you move an inch, we'll shoot," said a guard.

Rob thought of nodding that he understood, but decided against it. The tie removed, his hands involuntarily flinched, free of their squashing grip. The gloved hand then moved up to the back of his neck, slowly unloosening the gag.

"Walk towards the far end then turn round."

Rob did as told. Each footstep taking a lifetime. He'd no idea what he was turning to, a volley of fire or a friendly face. Counting each footstep down until he reached the bars, he wondered again if this was it. Turning, he saw three rifles and their owners standing motionless. Trying to look one of them in the eye, Rob had no idea what was going to happen.

"Next cell," the leader said. One by one they peeled from their formation and headed towards Richard's cell. Rob sat on his bed, waiting, thinking and hoping to god Sam wasn't too mouthy when they took her gag off.

One by one, he counted the footsteps downstairs. Listening hard, he heard them go through the same procedure as his own. Sam had a few choice words to say, but no shots were fired. Eventually, after they'd reached the ground floor and relieved Yorkie of his handcuffs, the outside door slammed. He'd no idea if they were still in the building.

Lying down, he stared at the dark ceiling until food was delivered sometime later. It could have been a few hours, it could have been six. A plastic bowl of chicken stew was pushed through the bars by a guard, while another heavily armed one covered him.

"Thanks," said Rob. "The man on the bottom floor, he's..."

"I know," he replied, "he's diabetic. The girl below's already told us twice."

They walked on to Richard's cell and left him his food. "Thanks," Rob heard Richard say.

They delivered upstairs before leaving. Rob picked up the warmish bowl and sipped it. Watered down and with no spoon, he wondered what sort of weapon a spoon could possibly make. Shaking his head, he drank most of it before throwing the sheet over the bed and climbing under the blanket.

Sleep took a long time to come. As the night faded into the early hours and Richard's rhythmic snoring shook the cell's bars, Rob thought over and over their predicament. They might as well have not bothered running. It was inevitable. All those days of walking and only sore feet to show for it.

What a waste.

Chapter 19

Morning broke with shouting from downstairs. Rob thought it was morning, but without any windows he couldn't be sure. Though it'd taken him ages to drop off, he felt as if he'd slept well.

Walking to the bars, he looked at Richard's cell. There was no snoring so Rob presumed he was awake.

"What's going on," he whispered.

The reply took over ten seconds. "Don't know. Think it's Pat. They've been at it ten minutes or so. It was just talking first, but the voices are getting more and more raised."

Great, thought Rob. He knew if anyone, apart from Sam, could wind them up Yorkie could. Unsure what was happening he listened again, more intently. The person shouting was a guard or soldier, that was certain. What was going on wasn't clear.

A noise resembling a distant waterfall, accompanied by screaming was disturbing. The watery sound lasted a minute before stopping. The words, "You bastards," were definitely Yorkie's. More shouting came from a guard before footsteps climbed to Sam's floor.

Noticing the fire hose against the wall, and the small drain running through the centre of the corridor, Rob twigged what was happening: they were getting a shower. Their first in three or four days.

Quiety took his quietly. A whimper when the horizontal waterfall started told Rob the water was cold. Sam however could be heard shouting clearly. Rob wondered if they'd heard her back in Southampton.

"I ain't taking my fucking clothes off."

"Take them off now," the guard shouted.

"What you gonna do, shoot me?"

The sound of high pressure water hitting still-clothed gobby girl drowned out her swearing. Though a floor nearer, the water sounded more intense, like it was nearer its target and hitting limper flesh.

After ten seconds the water stopped. "Now," the guard shouted, "take off your clothes."

"Alright, alright." She coughed and spluttered. Rob struggled to guess where they'd been aiming. Maybe her face? What else would make her strip off?

A minute later the guard said, "There, not too difficult, was it?"

"Just get on with it," was her reply.

The splash of water hit again. Again, a screech at first, but then silence until it was turned off.

The clumping up the stairs continued, Rob could definitely distinguish two pairs of footsteps. The balaclava wearing, gun-toting guards stopped in front of his cell.

"Clothes off," the first one said.

"Why?" He knew why, but that wasn't the question.

"Just do it."

The second guard had a sack, which he'd dropped as he got the hosepipe from the wall. Reeling it out, he stood in front of the cell, his hand hovering over the nozzle.

Taking his baggy jeans, nearly week old pants and dirty jumper off, Rob clutched his hands in front of his tackle. Nervously, he looked at them trying to gauge what their eyes were looking at or for.

The blast of water pushed him back. Leaning into it, he involuntarily yelped. The coldness hadn't yet registered, it was the water's force that shocked and dragged away his breath.

The guard expertly sprayed his upper body before concentrating on each leg. Keeping his hands still to protect his bits, Rob tried to breathe deeper, air was struggling to reach his lungs. The guard made a turning gesture; Rob did as told and slowly rotated. His legs shaking and shivering, the water burned into his back as it moved up and down.

Then, as suddenly as it came on, it stopped. He stood facing the cell wall away from the guards as he heard them push some things through the bars then walk towards Richard's cell.

Richard screamed as the water hit him. Rob turned round, still shaking, to see that a towel, some soap, toothbrush, toothpaste and new clothes had been pushed through the bars. Turning on the cell's tap, he washed his face with soap before drying himself. Though he was cleaner than before, a power wash alone couldn't remove ground in dirt. He needed a soak in the tub.

Drying himself, he heard Richard's screams continue after the water had been turned off.

"Well get you some cream," one the guards said as they walked away.

Covering himself with the towel, Rob watched the guards go upstairs before talking to Richard. "What's wrong?"

"Just a bit sore, my clothes were rubbing me. The water took a layer of skin off."

Shivering again, Rob finished drying and grabbed the toothbrush. Scrubbing his teeth, Rob made his gums bleed trying to get rid of that four day old taste of unwashed mouth and stew. Two complete brushes later, he was happy they were clean and reached for his clothes. A pair of Y fronts, the like of which Rob hadn't seen for fifteen years, were loose, but he knew it was better than being too tight. The other clothes were a white t-shirt and a pair of dungarees. Putting them on, they were also loose. He thanked God there wasn't a mirror in the cell. He imagined he looked like a Dexys Midnight Runner cast off. Moving his damp sheet and blanket to the top of the bed, he sighed as he sat down.

The guards had finished hosing Rabbit Boy and Sal, and were making their way downstairs. Rob wanted to ask how long they were going to be there, what was going to happen next, but he didn't dare. He had a clear picture, growing every minute that death wasn't on the menu. Why would they hose them down before killing them? It didn't make sense. No, they were being prepared for something.

After another long patch of silence, broken by occasional words with Richard, Rob heard the downstairs door open. Again, there was hushed talking as the guards made their way through the building, visiting each cell.

Arriving at Rob's floor, they dropped off a bowl of chicken stew. Rob noticed in the guard's hand a tube of cream, obviously for Richard.

"Thanks," he heard Richard say.

As they left, he heard Sam shouting. Quiety was trying to talk to her, calm her down.

Finishing the stew, Rob sat on the wet bed. He remembered Sam had been locked up before, for weeks at Southampton docks. Sure, it sounded larger than their current cells, but he thought she'd be used to this. Was this something you got used to? His stomach ached as he heard her scream and swear. He'd give anything to free her. They'd never be together, but that wasn't the point. Maybe the freedom they'd all shared the past few days had made this worse? Feeling so close to being free had thrown away the waiting and acceptance they'd known was coming. It was evil. A form of torture. They'd tortured themselves by running.

The shouting, screaming and obvious tears must have lasted half an hour before finishing. Richard was very quiet, no doubt listening too. There was nothing they could do. Pure helplessness. Rob just cradled his head and thought of her; her smile, her jagged nails, the way she said whatever.

Eventually, it could have been after ten hours, six or two, more chicken stew was bought. He didn't realise he was hungry until he ate it.

Once the guards were gone, there was nothing but silence. Rob didn't feel like talking and Richard didn't seem to either. The occasional noise from upstairs or downstairs was rare. They all seemed resigned to this. Resigned to waiting for something to happen. Rob tried to battle the boredom by remembering their journey. Every detail he tried to put in the right order. Every one of their stories he tried to remember.

After another indeterminable length of time, the light went out, darkness invading every corner of the cell. His bed now almost dry, Rob lay down and pulled the blanket over himself. Sleep came quicker than the night before.

The same routine continued for three days, though there was only another shower blast on the second day. Rob assumed they were days from the lights-out sleep breaks. He'd marked a brick just above his bedstead with a fingernail each time he woke. Conversation with Richard was stilted, usually just an hour a day broken into small chunks. There was no lack of things to talk about: the mood wasn't right. They knew any moment something was going to happen.

Besides daydreaming, Rob started to do press ups, sit ups and even just walked round in circles in the four foot by one foot gap between bed and wall. Anything to occupy his mind or waste time. He imagined a few times how prisoners must feel. He knew this was different. Being in solitary was mind destroying. He had to keep his head in a better place to win. Any thought of how long he'd be trapped was banished. Happy thoughts, remembering old newspaper stories and even his diary kept him going. All the time, he was subconsciously waiting for it to happen.

Chapter 20

The day it happened, it surprised Rob by coming an hour after breakfast. He'd just been about to have his daily wash, he thought he'd acrobatically soak his aching feet in the sink, when the downstairs door opened. He heard many, heavy-booted footsteps on the hard concrete floor.

Listening hard, Rob couldn't tell what they were saying to Yorkie. Butterflies attacked his stomach. He knew this wasn't a shower. The change in routine was so marked. For the first time since they'd been recaptured, he was genuinely worried.

They seemed to hang around on the ground floor for minutes. The odd muffled shout and command wasn't distinguishable. Yorkie's cell door opening was. The vibrations carried through the whole building. They were taking him away. Was he ill? Had his insulin not been looked after by the guards? Maybe he was ill in some other way.

Rob listened again, he knew the others were. Another minute passed before the front door slammed. Then silence. A minute of no noise bought muffled voices from the floor below. Sam was obviously asking Quiety what had happened.

"Richard?" he said.

"What's happening?" said Richard.

"I don't know. Could you make out the voices?"

"No. I think they've taken him away." Richard's voice broke as he finished the sentence.

It was the words Rob didn't want to hear. From below he heard the unmistakeable voice of Sam shouting, "Pat, Pat, are you okay?"

They waited. No reply. A voice came from above. "What's going on?" Unmistakably Rabbit Boy, his concern clear.

"We think they've taken Pat," shouted Rob.

From below, Rob heard Sam shout Pat's name again and again. Since their separation, they'd barely spoke between the floors. Rob knew just like himself, all their moods had changed. They'd become resigned to this and had shut themselves off in their own world.

Rob wondered if they were being monitored. Hidden microphones and cameras could easily have been built into the building. What was the point though? They were hiding nothing. They were all guilty.

The shouting from below and above continued, seemingly for hours. Rob heard Richard be sick. His own stomach was in tatters too. What was going on?

A time later, the door opened. This time Sam was taken away. Her cries, questions about Yorkie and screams for help hurt, each like a punch to the kidneys. Silence as the front door slammed.

"It's the guards," shouted Quiety. "They took her away."

Rob thought Quiety was crying. Sal from above shouted what was going on, but Rob couldn't speak. The words wouldn't come out. Richard shouted what had happened, then added, "Sorry Rob," in a much quieter voice.

His eyes filled. He barely knew her, yet he did know her. He knew everything about her. Which side she slept on, how she ate, her wit, her gobby mouth. Everything. The tears came, unable to stop them he cradled his head in his hands for what seemed like hours.

They took Quiety with little fuss. Again, a long, deafeningly quiet wait afterwards. Rob's stomach started to grumble. It really had been hours since breakfast, it wasn't his mind playing tricks. Not knowing the time was torture enough without everything else. He tried not to think about what was coming. He was next, that was obvious.

They eventually came. As they climbed the floor, Richard said, "Thanks Rob, for everything." Rob guessed he'd been working on that line for hours. He'd probably spent ages trying to avoid the words sorry, good luck and see you. He wished he'd thought of a line, a little stand he could make, but it was too late. "You too, mate," he replied as three gun toting guards moved in front of his cell.

"Hands in the air and back up towards us."

Rob turned, facing the wall he knew every brick of. Every slight colour and blemish, every piece of cracked mortar. He backed up towards the cell gates.

"Slowly, move your hands behind your back. Do not make any sudden moves." The guard spoke quietly yet clearly.

He had no intention of doing anything rash or stupid. There was nothing he could do. The only possible weapons were a toothbrush and pillow. They had submachine guns. His hands were quickly cable tied then he was led downstairs, one guard in front the other two behind.

His legs ached instantly. Though the miles he'd walked were now a distant memory, his muscles felt seized. His exercises hadn't been enough.

As the front door opened, he squinted. Daylight hit his cowering eyes. Green grass, trees and the tarmac runway reminded him the world wasn't just a brick lined cell. The air was fresher, not stale, not stinking of his own sweat and waste. He took a deep breath and walked forward; the guard in front moved back to join the others.

"Walk straight ahead towards the building," the guard said.

The building in front, the concrete single-storey hut, looked so uninviting. Looking around as he paced towards it, Rob saw birds soaring above, a heat haze rising from the runway, and clouds drifting by. The free pleasures in life; nature, the sky, people, they really were things you only appreciated when they were removed.

With every step towards the hut, his heart beat faster. Where were the others? What had they done. Almost shaking, his pace slowed as he reached the door. Every step became a challenge. He felt like dropping to his knees, giving up, pleading with them not to kill him. That's what they were going to do. It was obvious.

"Halt."

As he stopped, one of the guards ran round, opened the door and stepped inside.

"Move inside."

A bare room, almost a corridor, it had three doors leading from it. Brick walls with nothing on them. He scanned the room, looking for help or any sign of the others. He felt tears again in his eyes and bit his bottom lip, almost slicing it through. He tasted blood before the tears stopped.

"Halt."

He stopped. The guard in front opened the middle door. A small windowless room inside. The walls looked thicker than the first, very thick. Covered with corrugated cardboard like egg boxes, Rob knew it was soundproof. A small desk in the middle of room had two chairs on one side and one the other. The floor concrete with patches of discolouration. He tried to convince himself it wasn't dried blood but filthy water from a leaking roof.

"In and sit down."

He took the single chair. Sitting while handcuffed behind his back was awkward, his centre of gravity wrong. Falling into the chair, he sighed as the door slammed. The table, though solid wasn't bolted down. He did consider moving it towards the door, trying to block it, but what was the point. Whatever was coming couldn't be stopped.

He sighed and stared at the walls. Another burst of time passed, maybe ten minutes or half an hour before the door opened.

A small, black-haired man walked in, followed by two guards. A folder and diary in his hand, he sat opposite, pushed his glasses up his nose then licked his fat lips. Taking his time to set down the folder and open his diary, he eventually asked, without looking up, "Name."

"Rob Birchwood."

"Address."

He reeled off his address. For some reason, he remembered the half eaten bowl of stew he'd left in the fridge the night before he was taken. He wondered who was living there now.

"Occupation."

"Journalist, well, ex junior reporter."

He still hadn't looked at Rob but wrote every reply in a flowing script.

"National Insurance number."

Again Rob reeled it off. The man's face was smoothly shaven and his suit clean and crisp, if too small for his stomach. Whoever he was, he didn't survive on stew.

"What was your crime, Rob?" His voice had changed, chattier, friendly. Still no eye contact. Rob suspected this was a well-rehearsed routine.

His stomach wrenched as he said, "I printed a paper." He then thought he should have said, 'I haven't yet been found guilty of any crime.'

He nodded. "Distribution of subversive material. An offence under article six of emergency law twelve."

Rob reckoned he'd been either a policeman or lawyer in the previous world.

"It hasn't gone to trial, yet," said Rob.

The man slowly looked up from his book. His eyes burned as they hit Rob's. He tried not to look away, not to flinch, but he couldn't help himself. He turned to the left, the guard was staring at his head, gun drawn and aimed towards his midriff. Looking down, at the marked table, he bit his lip then flicked his eyes back towards the man.

He shook his head then went back to his diary.

"Who were you working for, Rob?" The voice was the calmer one; the friend trying to help.

"No one."

"Did anyone approach you? Ask you to join any group?"

Rob shook his head. "No. I, err." He paused. It was obvious where this was going, even if he had been working for anyone he wouldn't give them away. This bloke was clever. The whole set up was clever. Thumbscrews and beatings were either a thing of the past or yet to come. For now, fast talking, calm voices and friendliness was the game.

"Well?" He looked up. Again, those eyes.

"I just thought it was wrong. I wanted to show the way I felt."

"Your country was in trouble, Rob. Everyone needed to pull together to help it out of the mess it was in. You thought you'd make that harder by distributing lies and propaganda. You've betrayed your country, Rob."

"No. I'd do anything for this country. This is all wrong. The secrets, the proclamations, the stew. It's all wrong."

"What if everyone acted the same as you? If everyone took to the streets and spread their lies, what then? Ever think about that? It'd be anarchy. The country needs to change, to adapt to a new way of life. What good would anarchy do? You let your country down, didn't you?"

"NO. No, I." He paused. Had he let them down? Shit. His words almost made sense. Collectively, did they have a responsibility to think larger? He leant back in his chair.

"Who made you do it, Rob? Who was it?"

"No. No one. I did it myself. It seemed wrong. No. It was wrong. Everything, it is wrong."

The man turned a page in his book. Rob's head was swimming, confused. The turmoil in his stomach had spread. Did he have the right, the moral right, to fall in line? What was best for society?

"How did we know?" Rob stopped, not really sure what he was trying to say. "At the end of all this, how do we know what they'll do? Will they let us be free?"

The guns no longer scared him. The man's mind did.

He looked up. "What right has one person got over the rest? What right did you have to assume you knew more than the Consortium? Where's your plans for production, Rob? Where's your solution to food? How are you going to pay off the creditors? Where's your new currency? What are your laws? What if people dissent from YOUR opinions? Is that allowed in Rob's New Country? Where do you draw the line? What crime isn't a crime? Have you got all that worked out, written down and have enough followers to police it? Can you keep the country safe from overseas attack? Can you? You can't even feed everyone? CAN YOU." His voice grew in strength. By the end as he shouted, Rob sank further into his chair.

"No, but it's..."

"It's what, Rob, it's different? It's not the same as it was? The world changed overnight. Deal with it. Everyone else has."

Rob looked at one of the guards. The face mask gave no clue to their owner's thoughts. Did he agree with this? Was he doing this job out of fear? He looked back at the man, the anger had left his face."

"I want to help you. The others you were travelling with, were they working for anyone, did they say anything?"

Rob immediately thought of Sal and her contact whoever it was. He felt himself blush as he shook his head. It must have been obvious he was lying. He was more than glad that Sal hadn't finished her story. She'd been right about that.

"You expect me to believe that? Which one was it? The old man, the young girl, the big one, eh? Which one?"

Rob was glad he hadn't singled out Sal. He didn't know what involuntary head shake or eye movement might have happened.

"We didn't really talk, just ran."

He wondered about Sam. If she was still okay. He wanted to ask about her, but couldn't. If they suspected closeness they'd use it.

125

He reckoned this same man had done all this to the others. It would make sense. The same person would pick up on things, the sort of things Rob was trying to hide.

"Yeah of course," he said. "A group of radicals meet for the first time and all they talk about is how nice the New Forest is now all the fucking tourists have gone. Who are they working for, Rob?"

"No one. None of us were. We just thought it was wrong and took a stand."

The man sighed and turned his page over. "Right, let's go back to the beginning."

It went on. He was hungry, tired, and almost brain dead but the questions still came. Each time a different angle, but the same ultimate question. Were they organised? Was there a resistance movement. Rob had a good idea there wasn't apart from Sal's brief revelation. He nearly gave her away at one point. The man had been through all of them in turn. Asking questions, wanting descriptions, needing to know their crimes.

He'd tried to lie, but it was obvious, even the previously silent guards sneered and shook their heads. A barrage of abuse from the once seemingly nice and helpful man failed to get the truth from him. Rob's last words were, she was here because of her previous political alliances and relationships. He stuck by it, eventually ignoring the question and just shaking his head.

The violence he'd been expecting hadn't come. He knew it would. So little information had been given, just what they'd all been arrested for. On reflection, Rob realised that the man must have known about Sal anyway. She'd been caught after all. She'd probably admitted then she had no clue who the message was from and what it actually was she was passing on.

As for Sam and Yorkie, who'd no doubt been interviewed before him, he knew neither of them would have sung. He half smiled as he thought of Sam giving as good as she got.

"What's funny, Rob?" He'd had a sip of water and was back for more.

Rob just shook his head. There was no way out of this. No more talking could cure this or even get a solution. They were going to have to beat it from him. He'd long since been scared of death.

126

Months of waiting and not sleeping had got him ready. He was a dead man walking. With knackered feet.

"Who are they?"

He shook his head again. "Why does there have to be a group?" Despite trying not to, he'd been goaded into it. Again.

"There always is. No amalgamation is smooth, Rob. The public can't always see what's good for them."

Rob could see in his eyes he actually believed it. Or was he trying to wind him up?

"Dissenters always group together. Whether it be the old unions or party factions. Even mates down the pub who've got a mate who knows someone. We need to know who they are. If this is going to work, if our country is to be saved, we need to know. Who are they, Rob?"

"I don't FUCKING know."

The man shot up from his chair and leaned over the table. Rob leant back as far as he could. The guards tensed their muscles, the guns now more closely aimed at his chest and head. The man's eyes almost bulged from his head as he slapped the table. "TELL ME."

"I don't know."

Rob looked down at his feet in the poorly shod shoes. This was it. No more answers. He'd just sit and stare at his shoes. They were going to shoot him anyway. He'd just let them get on with it. No more answers.

"Cat got your tongue, Rob?"

No move, nothing. Not even a head shake - that would be an answer. He'd just sit, staring at the far eastern made shoes. They weren't even shoes. Hard plastic, sweaty flip flops. Who had made these? Enforced labour no doubt, in some far off country. Maybe these were made at home? One of the labour camps. People worked hard for their bowl of stew a day. What was the point? What was the point of living anymore?

"You can go."

He wasn't sure if he was hearing things. Half looking up, his eyes stopped at the table and went back to his shoes. It was a trick. It had to be. Get him ready to leave, then hit him with another thousand unanswerable questions.

"I mean it. Stand up." He stood himself and walked towards the door.

Rob lifted his head, stared sideways at him as he opened the door, walked out then closed it. He looked back at the guards.

"Up, now."

Rob stood. With his hands tied, his balance wasn't great but he made it. One of the guards made for the door, the other moved behind him.

The first guard left the room then nodded for him to move out. Ushered into the rightmost room, Rob was surprised to see it was empty. He'd expected torture implements. He was sure they normally had dentists' chairs in this sort of room. Straps and machines, readouts, dials and implements of pain.

Nothing. No table, chair. Nothing.

"Stand in the middle and wait."

He walked the few paces then turned towards them. His eyes on theirs, he tried to gauge some idea of where this was going. There wasn't blood on the floor; that was good. The room wasn't soundproofed either. If they'd killed the others, the shots would have been heard in the tower.

"Turn around."

He sighed and turned round.

His legs turned to jelly as he faced the wall. Any second now, they were going to shoot him. His arms shaking, he waited.

Then the door opened. Steps on the concrete floor headed towards his left side. He moved his head to see the person. A woman in a white coat. If there was any doubts over her profession, the stethoscope round her neck made it clear. Behind him the guards moved. Steel touched the back of his neck.

"Move or try anything and we'll shoot."

The doctor, not seemingly bothered by the guards, looked carefully at his face then the rest of his clothed body. "Any illnesses, itching, sores, stomach upsets, problems breathing or chest pains?" Her voice was smooth and clear, but so matter of fact. No emotion.

Rob shook his head, the gun's barrel kissing his neck as he moved.

"You can talk."

"No. Just sore feet."

She seemed to half smile, like it was a bad joke she'd heard before. "You're a bit malnourished, but nothing unusual."

"Can you breathe through your nose alright? No cold or sinus problems?"

"No," Rob croaked. He didn't like where this was going.

"Okay, he's all yours." She turned and walked away. After the door slammed the cold steel weapon withdrew from his neck. He knew it was still right behind him. The guard hadn't moved, just pulled back his weapon.

The other guard moved in front. His gun hanging from his chest strap. In his hand, a roll of gaffer tape. Though the country couldn't produce food or power, it seemed to have a surplus of cable ties and gaffer tape. The guard pulled off a strip and slapped it over his mouth. The tacky exterior pulled at his lips. He tried to move his face, the left side pulled harder than the right.

Another large strip was placed around his head. His nose free to breathe, his mouth was now useless. Finally, a hood was placed over his head.

The blackness was immense. Truly dark. With his hands and mouth tied, he felt the most helpless ever, including in the lorry. A hand on his shoulder made him flinch.

"Turn round and walk."

He did as told. He heard the door open, he walked some more, turned right, walked again, turned right again and came to a stop. The hood was pulled from his head and he was pushed slightly forward, a brick wall immediately in front saved him from falling. A door closed behind him.

Chapter 21

The room was tiny, barely large enough to turn round in. He wondered where the hell the others were. The door in front was solid, soundproof even. He tried to retrace his steps in the mask. This was the far left room when he'd first come in. Maybe there were loads of little stand up cells in this room. Sam, Quiety or Yorkie could be just the other side of the wall. He thought of banging his head against it to get a response, but there was no point.

Looking at the floor, the harsh smell that'd caught in his throat became obvious. Human waste, long since dry, had yellowed the concrete underneath. Looking up, the roof was maybe three feet over his head. His arms ached. Really ached. They'd been tied behind him for hours. He'd been hoping for some end to this in the other room, but there wasn't. This was going on and on.

A noise outside was the front door opening. Several sets of footsteps clumped, obviously into the room next door. This would be Richard's turn. Rob wondered how long he'd last. He also wondered if the same tactics were used on each of them or did that bastard tailor his assault. After the door shut, Rob heard nothing except a distant hum, probably a generator or aircraft and an occasional nearby noise. A low, almost inaudible tap. Irregular, he was sure it was one of the others. Maybe he was kidding himself, but he tried to imagine who it was and what the message was. Slapping his cable tied hand against the wall sounded so quiet, but it made a noise. He half expected guards to rush in and slap him, but they didn't.

His slap was greeted by a procession of three different noises. Yorkie, Sam and Quiety. They were okay. Resting his head and back against the wall, he tried to slide down but there wasn't enough room. Twisting as he bent, he eventually managed to squat and, leaning back, he took some of the weight off his feet.

He closed his eyes.

The hours drifted by with few comings and goings. To kill time, he forced himself to remember the whole of the Back to the Future films, from the first to the last. He wasn't sure at one point if he'd drifted off to sleep or not. He'd got used to the pain in his legs, arms and mouth; it became normal like a week old toothache. He also lost count of the last one in. The person he thought was Sal, couldn't have been. He'd been convinced all of them had come through when another came in. He hadn't forgotten Rabbit Boy, he must just have dreamt or imagined the door opening.

He was expecting to face the man again. A second bout, now hungry tired and aching, would be the one that cracked them. He still couldn't see exactly what they hoped to get from this. They were a disparate group of loners and misfits. Hardly the head of some revolutionary group. Sal was the only one organised in any way, and he knew that she'd been only half fed information.

A door opened and some muffled mumbling was followed by footsteps leaving. The door shutting settled it: they were interviewing again. He shook his head and tried to stand, as he had every few hours. Leg muscles nearly seized, it took two minutes to get to his full height. Trying to move his arms and back bought surges of pain.

Ready for another hour or two wait, he tried to pick up his place in the second film.

The door opened again after only a few minutes. Another of the cells was opened and someone else taken away. This one resisted more than the last. Feisty. Rob smiled as much as the gaffer tape would allow him. His shoulders also dropped at the same time. What could be so quick? They hadn't bought Yorkie back. He tried to keep the thought of what might have happened to him from his mind, but it kept returning.

Outside or maybe in that room next door. Such a waste. None of them was stupid, they could have helped a more open government if it wasn't so insistent on removing people's rights. He shook his head. The end was coming. Worst thing of all, he was still only on the second Back to the Future film.

His turn came. The light from the bare bulb made him squint after hours of darkness. In front, two guards, submachine guns aimed at his chest. They nodded for him to walk. His legs crumbled as he tried to walk. So many hours of standing and leaning had seized every joint. He eventually shuffled out bow-legged, and walked to the door.

The middle door was open, which didn't surprise him, but they moved him past it and outside. The sunlight was harsh, as it had been when they took him in. A similar angle too. He'd been there the whole day and night. Maybe two nights?

He walked where they led him. Towards the tower. His legs almost jelly, he somehow kept walking to the door. The first guard stopped and raised his weapon.

"Halt."

Rob stopped.

"I'm going to remove your gag. Any sudden movement will make us attack. Understood?"

Rob nodded.

The guard behind walked round, then the first pointed his gun to the ground and approached.

"This will hurt, but it is less painful the faster it's ripped." He almost sounded human.

He could only imagine how much a slow rip would hurt.

"Fuck's sake." He twisted his mouth around, convinced his lips were still attached to the tape.

"Okay, inside."

One of the guards fell back behind and the door was opened. Inside Yorkie stood at the bars. "We're all okay, Rob. Pissed off, but okay."

The guards let Yorkie stay there as they led him upstairs. His eyes burned into the first guard as they went by. On the first floor, he caught a glimpse of Sam's arm, stuck out of the bars making a v-sign at the guards.

"Hi honey, I'm home," he said.

"About bloody time, your tea's ruined," she shouted back.

Plonked in his cell and the cable ties removed, Rob sat back on the bed. His arms were red and blue in places. They'd been behind him so long, they felt wrong in front of him, like strangers.

The door closed, a guard pushed a bowl of stew and a small bread roll under the bars before joining the other and heading downstairs.

Lying on the bed he sighed and closed his eyes. His mouth ached from the tape, he wanted to touch his lips with his hands, but couldn't move them. The dead useless things lay limp beside him.

"You okay, Rob?" Sam shouted from downstairs.

"Yeah, how about you?" he shouted back. His lips ached as each word rattled through them.

"We're fine." She said nothing else.

As much as he wanted to eat, being horizontal was heaven. He stayed for what seemed like hours before Richard walked by. He looked dishevelled, thinner and inwardly beaten.

"You okay?" Rob called as the guards left.

"Yeah." It wasn't convincing.

Rob tried to stand. His stomach muscles seemed to have disappeared overnight, leaving him to get up in an awkward set of shuffles. Leaning against the bars, he said, "Did they hurt you?"

"Not physically, no." He sighed heavily. "That bloke. What a bastard."

"I had him too. I think we all did."

"Clever too." His voice drifted off.

"Get some rest," said Rob. "Don't force yourself to eat too quickly."

"For once in my life, Rob, I don't feel hungry."

Rob sat on the bed and tried to work his hands so they could pick up the bread roll. It looked like a crusty cob. He hadn't seen one for ages, maybe six months. He'd no idea where it had come from. No doubt it was stale, maybe even inedible, but it looked so inviting. His hand shook violently as he grabbed it and bought it up to the bed. Lying back, he sighed, waiting for more life to return to his arms so he could eat it.

Chapter 22

The normal routine of stew with occasional showers continued. It took three days before Rob's arms felt anything like normal again. He'd made the bread roll last four meals, despite its staleness. Soaked in mystery stew, it tasted like heaven. A taste from the past.

The days rolled by. Every time the door went, he wondered if more questioning was coming. He knew he wasn't alone: all of them were waiting for it.

It came.

An hour before stew time on the afternoon of the tenth wall squiggle, the door opened. Silence filled the tower. Yorkie was shouting something but Rob didn't know what.

His heart sank. He couldn't take another bout of this. If this was what the Isle of Wight had to offer, they'd been right to be worried.

They guards took their time, maybe more than five minutes. However, they didn't leave. Booted feet clumped up the first staircase. He couldn't hear how many feet, it was just many.

Hearing the occasional voice, usually Sam's, he listened hard. Amongst shouting and screams, he clearly heard, "I ain't fucking wearing that," and, "You better not hurt me."

Eventually, some of the footsteps went downstairs while the others climbed to Rob's floor. Three guards emerged from the stairwell. Heavily armed, as before, one crouched opposite Rob's cell while the other two walked to the bars.

The guard pulled a balaclava and cable ties from his bag. "On your knees facing away. Arms behind your back."

Rob did as directed, though not in that order, and heard the guard unlock the cell door. This was different from last time, he'd realised that. Would the outcome be the same? Hands from behind tied him then the balaclava was forced over his head. Since it was missing eye holes but still had a mouth hole, Rob wondered if such a balaclava had its own name. Blindaclava maybe?

"Wait there." Some of the footsteps walked away. He knew they were headed towards Richard.

They went through a similar routine, though Richard didn't seem to be able to get his hands far enough round his back. His cries of pain told Rob they'd forced his arms together. Wincing, Rob waited until he heard them say stand up.

The footsteps returned, a voice barked behind his ear, "Stand up."

Standing, he allowed a guard to direct him by the shoulders to the stairs.

"Careful, one step at a time," said the guard before pushing Rob forward.

Reaching the bottom, Rob could just see through the poorly knitted Blindaclava. Three hazy images of Quiety, Yorkie and Sam kneeled down in front of the table. Reaching them he was also forced down. Two guards returned upstairs, leaving three watching over them.

The silence lasted minutes.

Eventually joined by the Rabbit Twins, a guard walked in front. "We're going for a little ride. Your co-operation is appreciated. Any attempt to escape will lead to a bloodbath. I'm sure that's understood. Right, stand up."

Standing while cable tied was starting to feel natural. In itself that was worrying. He wondered if he'd spend the rest of his short life not seeing his hands.

Outside, daylight hit his eyes even through the hat. His eyes had again become used to the soft strip lighting. Slowly walking, they occasionally bumped into each other. With Quiety to his left and Sam beside him, Rob so wanted to say something, anything, just to make contact, but he didn't dare.

They were helped into a lorry then lay face down. Crossing the bumpy field and poorly laid runway, they arrived on a much smoother surface. More than aware the guards were with them, none one of them even flinched.

Finally, slowing to a halt and turning in a circle, the chugging engine idled as something was moved or opened outside. A door slammed, followed by the lorry reversing for a few seconds.

The engine still running, the rear doors opened, letting some daylight back into Rob's eyes. One by one they were pulled from the lorry. As Rob was lifted by the arms and put back on the ground, he could just see the outline of a mesh fence. Their backs to the lorry, Rob wondered if this was it. Shot in the back from short range. He could see other guards nearby, to the left and right. Was this it? Their final journey.

"Keep very still, all of you," said the guard.

To Rob's surprise, no one spoke, not even Sam or Yorkie. This was it. He was going to end his days in some backend hole on the Isle of Wight. Shot dead with no doubt a pit already dug to dump their lifeless bodies in.

"We're about to free your hands. Any movement and you'll be shot."

Rob stiffened, wondering why they'd remove them. Perhaps they wanted them to try and escape to make the job of shooting them easier? It couldn't be easy for guards to live with killing people. Maybe thinking about it as self-defence made sleeping easier?

The ties removed, Rob kept his hands behind his back. The wood and metal fence in front moved away from them, opening in an arc. Either the mass graves were nearby or maybe it was the grounds of the chicken stew factory. Where they about to become the mysterious '24% Meat' ingredient?

"Walk forward fifteen steps."

The smell of grass filled Rob's nose as he counted each step. Savouring what could be his last smell, he reached the fifteenth and stopped, noticing he was roughly level with Quiety to his left and Rabbit Boy to the right.

The creaky fence or gate swung shut behind them, the sound of padlocks clasping around chain accompanying it.

"In five seconds you can take off your hoods but don't turn round. Five, four ..."

The countdown to death begun, Rob thought he'd probably prefer to die blind to the world, remember it in better days.

"One. Hats off."

Pulling his hat off, he squinted to avoid the midday sun. Turning his head slightly, he saw Sam, looking a combination of tearful, fresh faced and glowing. The sight of them all standing in their dungarees in the countryside reminded him of a Worzels tribute band he'd seen at the Crown one Sunday night. He smiled, eventually catching Sam's eyes. She half smiled back.

"You can turn round."

This was it. Heart in his mouth, Rob turned, catching Quiety's eyes on the way. He'd aged massively the past few days, he now looked like the old man he actually was.

Turned round, he looked at the gate. A heavily reinforced, barb-wire strewn thing attached to a high fence. The fence stretched in each direction to the horizon. Behind it stood another fence, fifteen or so metres back. Various towers, much higher than the fence, lined the length each of them filled with guns, guards and searchlights. The lorry that'd brought them, an old army truck, was driving out through the gates. The guard, now the other side of the fence was staring at them, gun in his hand.

"What you're in now is no man's land. The area covers fifty metres that way." He pointed behind them. "You've got a few minutes to get clear, but don't return. We shoot on sight. A mile or two behind you is a town, they'll tell you what to do there."

He turned and started walking towards the lorry.

"Oh," he added, "Welcome to the Isle of Wight."

Chapter 23

Squinting from the sun's rays, Rob moved towards Sam. Shading her own eyes, she moved to him. Holding her, he could feel her body tremble. He supposed he was trembling himself but couldn't feel it. Catching her eyes, he grinned. This was like a dream. For not the first time this week, he'd been convinced death was coming.

"Come on," said Yorkie. "You heard the man, let's go before they shoot us."

Taking his eyes from Sam, Rob saw the field they were standing in. Once pasture or grazing land, it was now knee high grass. Opposite the fence and a few hundred yards away was a small wood forming the field's boundary. The air was clean and fresh with the heavy aroma of grass. It felt friendly, despite the armed guards behind them.

Walking towards the wood, Rob realised just how sore his feet were. He was sure he wasn't alone. After all those days of walking, time off had started to heal them. That had been thrown on its head with a night or two standing up. Now, they'd just been healing again but had been interrupted.

His arm round Sam's dungareed waist, he walked towards the wood. As naturally as before, Yorkie and Quiety took the lead, with the Rabbit Twins and Richard in the middle.

"I thought we were dead," said Sam.

Rob squeezed her. "Me too. Were you okay? I heard you crying."

"I weren't crying." She smiled. "That was Dave. Blubbering like a girl, he was."

"I believe you..."

"I know, thousands wouldn't."

"Seriously though," said Rob, "What's going on here? This kind of feels almost safe now, doesn't it?"

"Don't tempt fate, hun."

"I know, but you know what I mean. We've been freed into something. God knows what." Thinking harder about it, Rob depressed himself further.

Walking into the wood gave a certain déjà vu. They continued through and out the other side, taking care to keep walking away from the now out of sight fence and guards. Yorkie's watch had been taken from him, so time was now an alien concept. After what could have been an hour, maybe more, Yorkie brought them to a halt.

"Rest here for a bit?" It wasn't a question.

Agreeing, they sat in their rough circle. Sam leaned against Rob, her bony shoulders digging into his chest.

"Is this definitely the Isle of Wight, Sam?" asked Sal.

"I think so. It's hard to tell from just countryside, but it's not a huge island so we should come across something soon."

"What do you reckon we're walking into?" asked Richard.

Rob shrugged his shoulders. He had his own opinion, but kept it to himself.

"I think," said Yorkie, "we should be careful. It don't make sense letting us loose like this. If there are others like us wandering round, there could be trouble."

"Reminds me of a drive-through safari park," said Sal. "Caged, yet free to roam. Pat's right, we need to be wary of other people. No doubt people have grouped together in gangs."

Sally looked so different in dungarees. Her hair looked clean, and even without make up she looked like she was on television. Confinement, though, had changed Rabbit Boy. A shadow of his former, in your face, self. He looked humbled. A humble little bunny.

The most remarkable thing was the beard growth. Unshaven now for nearly two weeks, Rob himself sported his biggest face-nest ever. Richard's was wiry, bare in places, he'd obviously never been able to grow a full one. Quiety and Yorkie had great monster beards. Like old sea dogs, they looked capable of hoarding a family of ospreys. Rabbit Boy's was blonde, much lighter than his hair. Larger sideburns than his moustache gave him a Victorian look.

"It can't be like that," said Richard, "there must be some sort of order and guards and that." Parts of Richard seemed to stick out of the dungarees in odd places. From the neck down Rob thought he resembled a crash-dieted Grandpa Walton.

"We can only hope," said Sam. "It could be, you know, a safety in numbers type of thing."

"Time will tell," said Yorkie.

Rob knew without food, water or shelter, they couldn't avoid other civilisation on the island. They needed help; whether they'd get any or not was a different question.

Another hour's walk through the grass filled countryside bought them to the top of a hill. Tired legs made hard work of it, especially Grandpa Walton's. Rob noticed Richard was also clutching his side by the brow of the hill. Maybe the dungarees were chaffing his sore patches?

From the top of the hill, the sea shone in the distance. Standing there, breathless, they all took in the summer afternoon's view. A more beautiful view hadn't been seen in a long time.

From east to west, the sea rolled into hills, making way for towns and villages before the hills carried on far to the west. Even from a distance, fences and watchtowers could be seen in front of the beaches. The biggest towns looked to be on their left, the east coast, but between the patch-work quilted fields, small towns and villages nestled.

"We're in the middle." Sam pointed. "That's Sandown, Ventnor and that's the needles right out there, but you can't see it. Cowes and Ryde are behind us, probably over the fence we came through. They've split the island in two."

"Them towns there." Yorkie pointed. "Are they big? Can't tell from here."

"Nah. They're villages. Half of them were Holiday cottages, the other half houses."

"What did people do for work round here, Sam," asked Sal.

"Out of the holiday season, not much."

Rob thought of the irony that only now did they have a burgeoning year round industry: the industry of imprisonment.

"Do we try that village then?" asked Quiety.

"We have to, I think," replied Yorkie. "Question is how do we go in? With big sticks or big hearts?"

"We have to give them the benefit of the doubt," said Quiety. "If you go in sticks blazing, you create an atmosphere. But, we need backup in case it goes wrong."

"Perhaps we should separate?" said Rob.

"Sal ought to hold back," said Rabbit Boy, his first words that weren't directed to Sal. "If anyone recognises her, they could do anything."

Rob suspected Rabbit Boy's next trick was to offer to look after the sticks. "Sam ought to hold back as well," he said.

"Fuck off," she said. "I'm going in first, with you."

"I can see your idea, John, but I'd like to go in first," said Sal. "If anyone should hold back, it should be the two strongest."

Rob nodded. "If we go in darkness it'll be easier to hide if it does go wrong."

They agreed. Not knowing the time and therefore when darkness would fall, they moved location to a tree. Sitting there for hours with little to talk of but speculation, they formed the plan for later.

Unfortunately for Rob and John the Rabbit, they were the chosen ones to bring up the rear. Rob certainly didn't want to and he guessed Rabbit Boy didn't for a similar reason, despite the fact he'd be in charge of the sticks. It had been decided though, and it made sense. They were the strongest and most agile. If force were needed, they were the best bets. However, Rob knew better. Yorkie, despite his fragile state had proved he had it in him to kill. That was still their secret though.

With daylight dipping over the horizon, they readied. Feet aching, they headed towards the town, which in the half-light was harder to find than it would have been two hours ago. Rob and Rabbit Boy initially kept fifty yards behind, but slowly, as the town approached, they dropped further back until the leading group was out of view.

Rabbit Boy picked up a large stick, more a tree trunk, as they neared town. From their direction, a road cut parallel then swept round to the start of the village. A few old houses lined the roads, expanding out as it grew into the centre.

As the others approached a fence, the pair hung back ensuring they were out of sight. After hopping the fence, the others made their way towards the first house. No streetlights or house lights, the village, even from their distance, resembled a ghost town. Rob's heart jumped as he watched them approach the house. Yorkie and

Quiety led with Richard and the two girls behind. Knocking on the door, Rob waited for who knew what to happen.

After a long pause, the door was opened by a dungareed man. The night made it too dark to see how old he was or judge his face, but Rob was sure that so far, so good.

After some talking, the dungareed man moved onto the street and pointed down the road. Rob turned and looked at Rabbit Boy, his expression fixed on his prey, ready to hunt it to the ground.

The prey didn't need hunting. Obvious thanks were given and the crew walked into the village. Sam and Sal turned round, waving at where they thought Rob and John were hiding, making come here gestures.

Rob shrugged his shoulders at John who seemed equally bemused. Walking towards them, the group continued, keeping the same distance apart. Rob noticed they occasionally turned, searching for them. He tried to wave, but they were trying to be incognito and it was apparently working.

Hitting the road and houses themselves, they bent and sneaked by a wilted hedge next to the gardens. Close up, they could see the houses were dark apart from the odd candle. The front gardens, once flower beds, had been dug with the first shoots of cabbages, carrots and runner beans appearing. Smoke rose from the chimney across the road. The fire, Rob guessed, wasn't for heating but for cooking or hot water. It felt like they'd travelled through a time warp, back to some pre-electric age.

Up ahead, they'd stopped at a junction. The group pointed in opposite directions, obvious confusion amongst them. Rob looked at Rabbit Boy who was shaking his head. Agreeing, Rob moved further forward, past another two cottages with candles and one with no light at all. The group carried on past the junction. A larger house with a bigger garden loomed in the distance. More hand pointing from the gang told Rob it was their destination.

They walked to the door and knocked. The house stood out being better lit. It also retained some of its garden. Sidling round a hedge to the front, Rob and John got nearer than before, getting a decent view of the front door. Seeing him grip his stick tighter, Rob knew Rabbit Boy was ready.

Listening hard, Rob could hear voices as someone came to the door. A man dressed in a guard uniform opened it, a heavy baton hanging from his belt. Rabbit Boy moved, as if to storm the door, but Rob put his hand on his shoulder. "Wait," he whispered.

He heard Yorkie tell the guard they'd been released but didn't know where to go or what to do.

"You're late tonight," he replied. "The office is shut. You'll have to come back tomorrow."

"What happens then?" asked Sal, who hadn't been recognised.

"I'll take your details and let you know where you can stay and what you have to do. You can't just roam around without any food, can you? They should have told you all this." The guard shrugged his shoulders. This wasn't the first time he'd explained this.

"Is there anywhere we can sleep tonight?" Sal continued.

"Number six's empty. Just up there."

"Is there a key?"

He laughed. "You don't need a key. Oh another thing. Don't bother trying to run or attack us, there really is nowhere to run to apart from an early grave. And, tell the two blokes in the bushes there's CCTV everywhere on the Island so I've already seen them creeping about."

"Thanks," said Sal. "I think," she quietly added.

Chapter 24

Number six was a deserted old cottage. Like the previous one they'd stayed in, anything of value had been removed. Downstairs, only the fireplace remained intact while the kitchen boasted a spacious nothingness. Trying the back door, Rob saw the overgrown garden; grass and weeds well over waist height. Most of the fence separating it from its neighbours had been torn down and the neighbours themselves had encroached a few feet into its garden, their own gardens full of sprouting vegetables.

Returning to the main room, Rob saw John go upstairs.

"Any fire wood out back?" asked Yorkie.

"Not unless you want to demolish the rest of the fence."

Sam emerged from a small cupboard under the stairs. In the moonlight, Rob could see a cobweb stuck to her hair. "Here," he said, "cobweb." Touching her flowing, slightly sticky hair he pulled most of it out, rubbing it on his dungarees. The stickiness remained, and it was much more than just cobweb.

"It's soap. I had to wash it in something."

Smiling, Rob put his arms round her and gently kissed her, rubbing his cobwebby hands on her back as he did. "Anything in there, Sam?"

Breaking away, she said, "Nah. Completely empty."

"Shall I go next door?" asked Sal. "See if I can borrow a cup of sugar and some matches?"

"Good idea," said Richard, "I'll come with you."

Flashing Rob a knowing look, Sam grabbed his hand. "Come on, let's see what John's up to."

The uncarpeted stairs were rickety underfoot. Reaching the top, he saw three small, door-less rooms filled the landing. The creeping eaves stole what little room there was from each of the bedrooms. The first room, a stripped out bathroom, contained only a seat-less toilet. Copper piping, along with the bathtub and sink had long since been removed.

Walking into the larger of the two bedrooms, Rabbit John was standing at the curtain-less window, looking along the street.

"You okay, John?" asked Sam.

He turned, his eyes tearful. "Yeah I'm fine, it's just final now."

Rob knew how he felt. To be almost free then get recaptured was cruel. This seemed to be the end of the line. Cottages with Victorian utilities.

"It's a bit shit isn't it, mate?" she replied. "We've got each other though, it's not all bad." She slipped her arm round Rob's waist.

"I just wish I could get a message to my kids. I miss them you know, really badly, and the ex too. Never thought I'd say that."

Sam removed her arm, walked towards John and placed it round him instead. He seemed more in need of it. Rob also approached and stood on his other side.

"Sorry," he said. "We're in the same boat, aren't we? Here's me acting like I'm something special."

"Course not," said Sam. "You're the only one of us with young kids, you're bound to feel it more."

As John started to cry, Rob considered tact wasn't her strongest point. She had a good shoulder to cry on though, and John made full use of it.

Feeling a spare part, Rob left the room and tried the other bedroom. It was also damp and curtain-less, but still carpeted. The window looked onto the overgrown rear and the fields beyond. Though darkness had fallen, Rob could see lights in the distance on a newly built building. About four stories high and long, it resembled an industrial unit, yet seemed to be in the middle of a field. Shaking his head, he looked further into the distance. A few other buildings and farms were scattered but nothing else was lit.

Sighing, he returned to the other room. John had finished sobbing and was explaining what his kids looked like. Sam was doing a great job of looking interested.

"I'll er, head back down," he said.

"Okay. Down in a minute, hun."

Clumping carefully downstairs, Rob re-entered the living room. Yorkie sat on the floor near the fireplace. "Dave's out back, getting some wood."

Rob nodded. "Does he need a hand?"

"Nah, he'll be rate. What's up there?" he pointed to the roof.

"Nothing. Literally nothing. Just a toilet with no water supply. They've even had the doors and curtains."

"Can't blame them, can you. Every man for himself."

Sitting near, Rob paused before looking at him. It was their first time alone since the cottage, when Yorkie ordered him to leave him to die. Much had happened since then, but they'd never really discussed it.

"I couldn't do it. Leave you, I mean. We all made the decision to help. I didn't force them. Richard was going to give you a piggyback if it came to it."

"Aye. Reckon I owe you some thanks I suppose. We came close to getting away, didn't we? Hope I didn't ruin all your chances."

"You didn't. I reckon you gave us an extra day's freedom. They'd have caught us anyway."

"That's enough soft talk, lad. Go and help Dave, he ain't as young as you."

Standing with a smile, Rob ventured outside into the jungle.

Quiety had pulled up the remaining fence panels and was trying to snap them, which without any tools was difficult. Helping him, Rob also picked some dried grass he thought would make good tinder.

Moving the wood inside, they built a fire in the grate. Although they were missing matches, Rob hoped Richard and Sal would return with them or some other method of lighting it.

"You reckon we should get them?"

"Nah," replied Yorkie, "I haven't heard owt? If they was trouble they'd be shouting."

"I had a peek through their back window," said Quiety. "Sal and Richard were sitting on the floor chatting to this bearded bloke and a woman, both wearing dungarees."

Rob thought it funny Dave had pointed out the man was bearded. They were all heavily bearded. Having no mirror hid it from yourself, but even Rob could see his grizzly bits from the bottom of his eyes.

"They'll be alright," said Yorkie.

Sam and John walked downstairs, John looked better to have got it from his system. Sitting next to Rob, Sam kissed him on the cheek then winked.

After a few minutes of silence, the front door opened and Sal and Richard bought in the man from next door.

146

"This is Jim," said Sal. As she introduced the assorted waifs and strays to him, Rob saw why Quiety had mentioned his beard: it was huge. Like two ferrets glued to his cheeks and a badger hanging off his chin.

"Nice to meet you," he said, most of his voice's power was lost, absorbed by the beard. "Shame it's not in better circumstances. Brenda's just heating some stew up. We haven't got a spare teapot and we've only got two cups, but you're welcome to borrow them and anything else too."

"Does anyone else live with you?" said Quiety.

"No, just us, we got moved here six months ago. We were a bit naughty I'm afraid, but I'm sure you were too. I'll get you a light for your fire, knew I'd forgotten something."

He left through the front door, returning with a box of matches. "Here, who wants the honours?"

Rabbit Boy, who'd regained not only his poise but also his caveman, fire-lighting ability jumped up and grabbed the matches. "I'll do it."

"So, what do you know then, Jim," asked Sam.

"Not much really." He stroked his hairy cheeks. "Did you come via Beaulieu?"

"No, we escaped from a lorry crash just before. Apart from Sal and John, they were at Beaulieu but did a runner."

He stroked his beard again, it seemed to please him, like a child's pacifier. "I take it you got caught. Quite a few escape but they always get em."

"Yeah," replied Rob. "Just on the edge of the forest, we'd walked for miles too. Typical ain't it?"

"What did you do," asked Sal, "If you don't mind me asking, that is."

Rob wondered how anyone could mind the Nation's Favourite asking any question at all.

"Well, it's a long story, but I guess time is all we've got now. I was a telephone engineer, worked for thirty years, straight from school. I survived the layoffs in the early nineties. It all went digital you see, two thirds of the engineers weren't needed anymore, but they still kept some of us. Most of the older ones wanted redundancy, big payoff, see?"

"I kind of grew up with digital technology. Okay so the work we did wasn't exactly rocket science, we we're just electricians with fancy gadgets, but you have to know how it works to be able to fix it. Anyway, about four years ago I was leading a team of engineers, I didn't do so much fixing and fitting then, just used to visit new customers, try to win back old ones and advise people on how they could improve their equipment."

"Then it all went wrong. I had a good house, big mortgage because me and the wife was always moving. Had a buy-to-let too, in Manchester, my eldest went to University there you see. We bought a flat and rented it to him and his student mates. After he left, we carried on renting it out. When house prices fell, we started to worry. I mean knocking past the door of fifty and still borrowing a quarter of a million pounds. Things didn't look good."

"Half this equity we supposedly had vanished in a year, the price of the flat went through the floor, fell by sixty percent. We were on the verge of losing everything we'd put by for our retirement, which I was determined wasn't going to happen. Then one day, around the time of the food riots, I met this man."

As Rabbit Boy got the fire crackling, Rob watched Jim speak, dazzled by the flickering firelight catching his mound of facial hair. Brenda interrupted Rob's beard-gazing as she walked through the door with a big pan of stew and six empty cans. As Richard got up to help her, the bearded wonder also stood.

"This is Brenda, my partner in crime and chicken stew."

"Hello." She gave a cursory glance round the room.

Brenda also appeared to be in her fifties. Her long brown hair, which needed a decent cut and styling, partially covered her face. Her dungarees gave her a trim appearance, quite muscular even. Rob wondered what the hell a lady of that age could have done to end up here. She certainly wasn't a weather girl like Sal.

Yorkie completed the introductions and, as Brenda poured the stew she realised she was an empty can missing. "Oh, sorry I thought there were six, I'll get another can."

"No it's fine," said Sam, "me and Rob'll share."

"It's really no bother, I..."

"It's okay. So where are you from Brenda?"

"Oh, I'm just from Dorking, nothing interesting."

As she finished pouring the sixth can and started handing them over, Richard said, "You must have done something interesting to be here."

"No, I just did the same as everyone else."

"Brenda's very humble. She did more than me certainly, she became a local hero."

"Oh no, it wasn't like that. I just helped out that's all."

"What did you do?" asked Sal.

"Well." Her face blushed as she spoke. "I'm just a normal housewife. My husband worked for an oil company, used to work away a lot visiting sites and brokering deals." She sighed. "My children left home years ago, Sherry's married and lives in the States and Hubert was at college in Bognor Regis. Anyway, being on my own so much, well things got boring, for want of a better word, so I started going to the local Woman's Institute for company."

Rob could see her along with the rest of them, swapping scone recipes and drinking tea.

"We had great fun, Jumble sales to raise money for the church roof, tea dances, cake making competitions and occasionally we'd have talks by various people. We had a famous author once, well, Joany said he was famous, I'd never heard of him. We had such a good time, great companionship."

She gazed at the floor, her mind far away. "We didn't fully understand what was happening when the bank runs started. Some of us had lots of money there, all our savings. We weren't rich, okay we were well off compared to some, but it was money we couldn't afford to lose. It was going to help in our retirements or something to give the grandchildren. Well, we all started queuing to get our money back. I helped to give people lifts to the bank and took down flasks of tea, we had this sort of rota going."

"Well, as you know, our money was safe then, the first time, but then house prices started falling. It sounds ridiculous, but house prices were our life. We'd spend half of each meeting talking about who's bought what and how much a new extension would add to the value. It wasn't our fault, it was everywhere, the television, newspapers. All those people getting rich from selling houses. It was the new thing."

Rob felt himself cringe. It wasn't her fault? No, she was just a pawn in the biggest Ponzi scheme ever. House price inflation was a miracle: everyone got rich the higher prices went. Only problem was it relied on some mug coming in at the bottom mortgaging their life away to give people thirty years older more money than they could ever spend. It wasn't their fault though. No one could have imagined the damage they were causing.

"We couldn't believe it. Our houses we'd boasted so much about were suddenly worth less. Some people had used the equity to buy flats, or go on holiday. Some had helped out their children. All that money just disappeared in months, it was terrible. Then the other banks crashed. That was when it got really bad. I still can't believe they never bailed them out the way they did those first banks. I suppose the problem was too big by then, they couldn't bail it out."

"Our meetings carried on, but we'd all changed. Those glorious years of tea, cake and gossip melted as one by one we lost our savings and houses."

She sighed again. Forgotten memories had returned. "We lost our lovely house that was the worst day of my life. Then, to top it all, my husband announced he was staying in the Ukraine where he'd been working on an oil pipeline. Seems he found a younger model that had somewhere to live. I moved in with Maude from the Institute, she owned her house outright. I was angry, we were angry. That was when I started my rebellion phase."

Rob wondered what counted as a rebellion for the chattering classes. Sponge cake without jam? A picnic without olives? He did feel sorry for her, her husband disappearing like that. He wasn't the only one. The old Soviet Union, with its natural resources of coal, oil and minerals had proved a magnet to Western engineers wanting out of the mess Britain was in. Many intelligent people joined the brain drain abroad, getting well paid jobs in a country that had both food and something to offer the world.

"What did you do?" asked Sam.

Teary eyed, she continued. "First of all, we carried on our charity work, except we were helping British people rather than starving Africans. They do say charity begins at home, don't they? Before long it became more than just charity and helping. We were angry, especially when all these Consortium foreigners started to run the country. So we started protests. Just small ones: banks, council, local government. Small targets, but our message was clear, we didn't like what was happening. We wanted a say in the changes."

Rob thought what a great slogan that would make for a bunch of marching sixty-year olds. 'We're not very happy with all this,' he imagined them politely saying.

"Of course, the protests got larger. When the curfews started, we thought about stopping, I mean we we're respectable people. But you've got to stand up and fight, haven't you? So we did. Before long we were marching everywhere, chanting things, telling people what was happening and asking, politely of course, for a say ourselves in how things were run. The problem was, as far as we could see, the people who'd made the mistakes that'd ruined this country, it was those who thought they had the answers. But they didn't, did they?"

She sighed. "The protests got too popular. They rounded a few of us up, made examples out of us." She paused. "Sent us here."

Her story ended abruptly. Sipping the quarter can of stew that Sam had left him, Rob looked again at Brenda and Jim. An unlikely couple in the old world, but in this new, not very brave one, anything went. Looking again at Jim, his gaze turned to the ferrety beard he wore. Facial hair had never ranked high in his list of worries during a worldwide economic collapse and the resulting failure of governments and countries, but Rob had no doubt things were going to get a lot hairier from now on.

"So what do we do then?" asked Quiety. "I mean I've gathered we have to work, but doing what?"

"Don't know whether I ought to spoil the fun or not?" Jim looked at Brenda. Noticing her eyes were full of tears, he held her hand. "Okay, you work six days a week eight till six. Get one day off but that varies. We don't all get Sunday off or whatever. You get a can of soup a day and a bar of soap a month plus other little bits. That's it. It's not a great life to be honest, there's no pension scheme, sick pay, nothing like that." He laughed. An attempt to make light of a hopeless situation.

"What do we actually have to do?" asked Sam. Her leaning and bony elbow once more digging into Rob.

"Well, there are two different jobs, you rotate them. Electricity generation and general work, we call that municipal work."

"Electricity?" Sam's face scrunched into a ball.

"Yeah, unbelievable isn't it. It's like a big gym, exercise bikes everywhere. You pedal and pedal and pedal, but you don't go anywhere. Apparently they're everywhere, in all the camps. You know, the gypsies, tramps and thieves one, even the old folks have to do a few hours a day."

"So what, is it like connected to a motor or something?" Rabbit Boy looked confused.

"Yeah, you remember those old bicycle lights we used to have that had dynamos? The ones that stop working when you stop peddling? It's like that, only a much larger scale."

"Surely that can't generate enough to help anything," said Rob. He'd endured and learnt a lot about power cuts and electricity rationing. With most of the fuel for power stations coming from imported coal or oil, Britain had no easy replacement. Sure, the nuclear stations that were on the verge of meltdown were bought back into use and some coal mines had re-opened, but that still left a large electrical hole that was unexplained. Rob couldn't imagine how a bunch of peddling dissidents could provide enough to replace oil and coal.

"There's about two thousand bikes working at a time here. The noise is incredible, but you get used to it. There's another seven buildings on the other island too. According to Ron, one of the guys there, each bike produces eighty watts an hour. That's well over a thousand kilowatts. That's like a thousand kettles boiling at once, or ten thousand televisions. And that's just our building. Most electricity used through the day is just for radio, television and what's left of our industry. So, yeah it does help. The other camps are even bigger from what I've heard. There's over a million drop outs and people on sick leave pedalling every day in Wales."

"That's incredible," said Sal. "No wonder there's so many power cuts."

"They're building three more sites here too. Once they round up more dissidents they'll build more I'm sure. Still a lot of empty houses here."

"It sounds like one of those hamster wheels," said Sam. "This is crazy. I bet it's hard work pedalling all day."

"Secret is," said Brenda, "to take it steady. There's a red mark that you have to keep above. If your pace drops too low you don't get any stew. You get a quarter hour break every hour, so it's not too bad." She almost sounded like she enjoyed it.

"I suppose you can't refuse?" asked Yorkie.

"Not if you want food, no. You occasionally get a minor rebellion or people choosing not to work and steal from others, but they don't last long. They just get sent to prison where they're forced to pedal."

"What happens every other day, you said Mu-cipinal?" asked Sam.

"Municipal," corrected Richard.

"Yeah alright Dad, whatever." She poked Rob in the ribs for Richard's insolence. Rob thought it mildly unfair.

"It's like a day off job, if that makes sense. Some of us do bits around the Island, whether it's in the water filtration plant, digging fields or repairing houses that have been ransacked. Others make things, like the old folks do in Eastbourne."

"What do they do?" asked Richard.

"Make small items of tat that get sold to the Chinese. Cheap labour you see. Kind of opposite of the imports we used to get. Well, we're now making them for a bowl of rice, well stew, a day while the Chinese live the easy life."

Rob wondered if he really was dreaming. He also wondered how this had gone on without it leaking to the public. He supposed regular food had made things easier to stomach or forget about, not that chicken stew was easy to stomach. "What do you mean, tat?"

"Phew, um, toys, you know all those little fighting toys the Chinese love, streamers and bunting for their New Year. They have these Yuan shops over there, you know, Yuan World, Yuan Land? They're a bit like our old pound shops were everything breaks within days but people still buy it anyway. My job's to seal a deck of playing cards. I pick up 52 different cards, each has got a celebrated Chinese worker on them, put them in order then wrap it. Can of stew a day for ten hours of that."

"I sew little sequins onto tiny purses, they give them to each other for their New Year, like a luck thing. Feel like I'm cross-eyed by the time I get home." Rob thought she looked cross-eyed too.

"Wonder what job we'll get?" said Sam.

"You two are young and fit, they'll probably get you renovating and rebuilding houses, maybe even the fields," said Beardy Jim.

Sam nodded. Her face had dropped in the last half hour from the smiling, approachable friend to a depressed mid twenty-something who's just seen forty years hard labour approach. The rest were silent too. Rabbit Boy played with his fire, stoking, rebuilding and generally looking lost in the flames. Yorkie mused quietly, nursing an empty stew can. Richard, sitting next to Sal, looked at Jim and then Brenda for more conversation, while Sal plucked at a broken finger nail with another one, probably making it more jagged. Quiety, sat on his own at the back, fiddled with his dungaree strap, picking at a loose piece of cotton. Rob sighed then squeezed Sam tighter, trying to remind her she wasn't alone.

"We should think about sleep," said Jim.

Brenda nodded. "We've got a spare room, no bed I'm afraid, but if anyone wants it you're more than welcome. We've also got a spare blanket. The downstairs is free too if anyone else wants that?"

"Yo..." Rob stopped and restarted, "Pat should have the room and blanket."

"I told you afore, I'm not an invalid. I'm staying here with the fire."

"Sal should have the room." Sam gazed into the fire.

"Oh no," she started, "I couldn't possibly..."

One by one, they agreed that Sal should have the room. She eventually and gracefully accepted. Richard asked if he could have Jim and Brenda's downstairs, which prompted a big dig in Rob's ribs from Sam.

As the four left, the remaining five sat in silence, taking in the heat of Rabbit Boy's fire. Though the late summer evening was warm, the house devoid of life and heat for so long had a chill. As Quiety, Yorkie and Rabbity lay on the floor, settling in for the night, Sam turned to Rob, whispering, "Want to go for a walk?"

Nodding, he stood up. "We're just gonna, you know," was all he said as they left through the back door.

Walking towards an open field, which appeared to have been half ploughed, Sam stopped and turned to Rob.

"Are you okay?" he asked.

"Yeah." She sighed. "As well as you can be. I don't..." She stopped and looked at the half dug ground.

Following her eyes down, Rob guessed the field had been ploughed by hand, it being too rough for a plough, whether horse or tractor drawn. Municipal or Mu-cipinal, Rob thought and smiled. Looking at her, she was miles away, hurting in some internal struggle. "What's wrong, Sam?"

"Them. Bloody Beardy Weirdy and the Golden Girl. They've..." She paused again. "Aww," she shouted. "I can't say the right words sometimes."

"Calm down and start at the beginning. We've got all night. Get it worked out in your head first." Kissing the top of her forehead, Rob expected a punch or dig, but it never came. She wrapped her arms round his back and pulled him down to her level. They shared a gentle kiss.

Pulling away, Sam looked at her feet again while leaning her head on his chest.

"Whenever you're ready," he said, his mouth full of her soapy, red hair.

"It don't matter," she mumbled.

"It does. Whatever it is, share it. It'll eat away otherwise."

"Come here then, going to need to sit down."

Rob was more than apprehensive as he followed her and sat on the dewy grass that hadn't been cut. Many things whirred through his mind. The obvious, she doesn't like me, had been pushed to the back by their embrace. But what could she be so worried about? What could possibly be so bad?

"I'm going to take my time, so no interrupting." She poked her boniest elbow into his already sore ribs.

"I wish you wouldn't do that."

"I said no interrupting." She poked again. Taking a deep breath she started. "You're a journalist, well, sort of journalist."

Thanks, he thought.

"I can't explain things as well as you, but looking at them two. It made me angry, mad even." She paused, Rob didn't speak. "They had a bit about them once. They wanted to change things, however small or whatever they were. But look at what they've become. It's like they've changed, lost their spirit. They're just accepting what's happened and they're getting on with work, whether it's making electric or purses. Also, making electric, what the fuck's that all about? Do they seriously expect us to just do that and be happy?"

Two questions in a row, but Rob wasn't answering either.

"They've given up, haven't they?"

The third.

"That's it, life's over, we've been caught, let's become Consortium monkeys for a can of stew a day."

She paused. Rob tried hard to think of something; nothing came.

"I don't want to be like that. No offense, but I don't want to be here in ten years warming up stew and trimming your beard."

Rob took little offense. As much as he'd fallen for her, it wasn't the kind of fairy tale existence he'd dreamed of. Plus he wouldn't trust her anyway near a pair of scissors.

"I know we fucked up getting caught, but I'm not sure I can handle this. When we was running, it was great, a laugh, felt like we had some purpose, some reason. Fuck, we could have ended up anywhere, maybe done something to help."

She pulled a piece of grass and fiddled with it. "I can't do this, just give up and get old with Beardy Weirdy and the Women's Institute of Stew."

"You don't have to." Rob figured she'd said enough, got her point over. "We'll keep fighting. We've done it before haven't we? I did my sort of journalism thing and you started riots. Together, just think of the havoc we could cause."

She started crying. Real big, bawling and snuffling crying. Thinking back, he could have worded that better. He put his arm round her, but she was not only cold from the night time air, she was also cold to his touch. That gobby thing that'd leaned into and moulded round him earlier was stiff as a board. Lost in a world there was no escape from.

"What I'm trying to say," he continued, "is you don't ever have to stop fighting. There could be people here already doing it, planning stuff, digging tunnels."

"Vaulting over horses?"

"Yeah, that too. Thing is, Sam, we don't know yet. For all we know Beardy McBeard could be the head of the Island's underground escape force. He's hardly going to tell us the first night we meet is he? All these people fought before, not all of them will give up so easily. I feel the same. I don't want spend the rest of my life here either on this Island, making electricity and eating your stew."

"What's wrong with my stew?"

"Nothing. But that's not the point." He felt himself getting flustered. "You started that anyway. I'd pedal to Land's End and back every day to sleep with you, I mean to live with you, erm, I mean to eat your stew."

Shit.

That was it. It'd been said. He'd not only let the cat out of the bag but it was coughing up fur balls on the carpet.

Sam turned round, dropping her grass. "Did you just say what I think you did?"

"No." He smiled. "I meant you warm up stew very well."

One bony hand went for his waist, while the other headed for the back of his neck. There was no messing around, Spirographing or disturbances. Within seconds a writhing mass of dungarees flattened the grass.

Sometime later, when the stars lit the sky, they returned to the house.

"Good names, by the way," said Rob. "Beardy Weirdy and the Women's Institute of Stew."

"I had a good teacher," She winked.

"Shall we go upstairs?" asked Rob.

"What, again?"

"No, I just meant a bit of privacy, you know."

The fire now a mass of embers, Sam agreed to move to the master bedroom. Some warmth had climbed the stairs and entered the rooms, but the floor was cold. Rob wondered how the three downstairs had got to sleep without anything to lie on or any covers. Yet they had.

Lying beside her, her soapy hair scratching and suffocating him with her every move, Rob wouldn't have swapped it for the world.

Not for all the stew in China.

Chapter 25

"Morning."

As Rob woke, the freshly washed face of Sam smiled as she handed him half a can of weak tea. "Ayuh." His mouth wasn't yet in gear.

"Beardy and Weirdy let me use their bathroom. The water was warm too, can you believe that, a shower that isn't cold?"

Smiling and yawning, Rob tried to move his arm. Frozen cold and stiff, it felt like someone had used it all night as a pillow. "What time is it?"

"Seven. Jimboy says we should get to the guard's house early, show willing. Twat."

Rob shook his head. "Hey, remember, he might be Secret Squirrel?"

"His beard might be a secret squirrel." She turned, and faced the empty doorway. "Thanks," her voice had become weaker, vulnerable, "for saying the right things."

"Don't say it like that. The time will come, just don't forget it."

"Yeah, see you in a bit."

She left the bedroom, turning her head and winking as she made for the stairs. Taking another sip of his tea, he yawned and shook his head. He needed to wake up, today was important.

Downstairs, Rabbit Boy had relit and was stoking the fire while the remainder of the gang drank heavily watered down tea. Sam sat next to Richard, while Sal was telling Quiety and Yorkie how well she'd slept and how she'd also had a hot shower.

Saying good morning, Rob sat between Sam and Richard. Richard looked like he'd slept well. He also looked ten times trimmer than when they'd first met. Sure, he'd seen him a lot recently, but it wasn't until he'd stepped back that he realised just how much weight he'd lost.

Sam was listening to Sal recount her shower with something close to admiration. Even Rob would admit it was weird having a celebrity so close. Last night seemed to have relaxed everything, removed the panic from their hearts. Everything looked different this morning.

Beardy and Weirdy walked in; they looked exactly the same. No change there.

"All ready?" asked Beardy.

"As ready as we'll ever be," replied Yorkie.

"You'll be okay," said Weirdy. "Don't forget to let us know where you end up."

"Aye, we will. Thanks again for the stew and tea. We'll repay you as soon as we can."

"Oh don't worry about that, we've got cans of the stuff. Jim's cabbages are nearly ready so we'll be living off cabbage stew soon. Make a change from that chicken stuff."

Rob thought if ever there was a good time to avoid a dinner party at the Beard Twins, it was during cabbage stew season. He had visions of Jim with bits of watery cabbage hanging from his beard.

"We get to keep half the veggies we grow," Jim said with some pride. "Don't tell anyone, but I made rhubarb wine last year."

Brenda looked annoyed and slightly worried about this revelation. Rob thought he'd definitely avoid cabbage stew and rhubarb wine. That had messy written all over it. He gently nudged Sam, to prove his Beardy Secret Squirrel point. Her gaze back showed she needed a lot more convincing.

"I haven't had a drink in months," said Yorkie. "We had a few moonshiners round our way, but they soon gave up, it was too obvious where it came from."

"Ever made your own hooch?" said Richard. "I did once, you stick some bread in a bottle of lemonade and it ferments. Tasted horrible, but did the job."

"Yeah, we did that," said Sam.

"Can't beat homebrew," said Beardy, "especially wine. My rhubarb's not doing too well this year, so I'm thinking of trying cabbage wine."

Rob shivered. Determined to change the subject, he said, "Who gets the other half of the veggies?"

"Guards take them. Whether they declare them or not I don't know. You're always going to get corruption, aren't you? It could be worse, believe me, it has been worse."

Rob was about to ask what he meant, but the others were standing, ready to find out what the Island was really about and how they fitted in. Though Beardy and Weirdy had already told them, nerves were still rattled.

Standing, he winked at Sam as they left. Beardy and Weirdy took back their empty cans and saucepan before leaving for work. Gathering outside, Yorkie led them to the guard's house.

Rob guessed he wasn't the only one with a knotted stomach as they opened the gate and walked into the almost pristine garden. Rustling up the path, Yorkie led with Quiety at his side. Sam and Rob stood behind, just in front of Sal sandwiched by Rabbit Boy and Richard.

Knocking on the door made Rob's butterflies flutter faster. As Yorkie's heavy hand bashed the solid wood, they waited.

Within a minute, the door opened. The guard from last night looked half-asleep and half dressed. "You're early, wasn't expecting you for another hour. Come in."

He led them into the front room. The only door leaving the room was obviously recently installed and very sturdy. Just a desk, chair and an old filing cabinet stood in the carpeted and curtained room. Sitting behind his desk, he looked up. A friendly faced, middle-aged man, his demeanour hid his power and standing. In a previous life he may have been a tax inspector or accountant. Now he was arguably one of the most important men on the Island. His brown eyes and well shaven face beckoned the stares of the seven waifs before him.

"Right who's first? I need name, old address and occupation."

Yorkie stepped forward and reeled off his details. The man nodded as he wrote in a red ledger book, capturing everything Yorkie said. His details given, the man pondered them. "Not many mines here, I'm afraid. Did you do any building work when you laboured?"

"Aye."

"Good, that's easy then." He pulled a piece of paper from the filing cabinet. A pre-printed form, he filled it in, almost exactly matching the scrawl in his ledger. Taking his time, and devouring each written word, he left the last two boxes blank.

"Who's next?"

Quiety stepped forward and went through the same slow process. The job allocated to Quiety was something in the factory.

Afterwards, Sam gave her details, the guard becoming interested in her ex-estate agency skills, particularly the lettings side. "Know anything about repairs and maintenance?"

"It was outsourced, but I decorated both my houses myself."

"I'll put you on decoration then." He flashed her a smile that Rob wasn't alone in disliking.

Rob and Richard's turns produced jobs in the fields. He shared a worrying look with Sam at the thought of being split up. Yorkie appeared to sense that and moved, standing next to Sam, reminding her that he'd be there.

Sal was recognised before even giving her name. "Is your real name Sally Dentwood," he asked, with a smile that more than half the group now disliked.

She twiddled her hair with her fingers. "Yes, it is."

"I just need your address. I can guess your occupation."

After writing out her form, he said, "I think we need something more fitting than the factory." He scratched his smooth chin. "The village shop always needs help. It's not rocket science, or weather science for that matter." He waited until he got his laugh. "Just stacking shelves and serving your fellow Islanders."

That left John, who gave his occupation as fitter, which he clarified, under questioning, to car mechanic. "Presumably you can fix anything mechanical or electrical?" he asked.

He nodded.

"The power plant always needs mechanics, that's you all sorted then. Right, now sleeping arrangements." He looked at Sal then Sam, before looking casually at the rest of them. Rob felt his arm muscles tighten.

Standing, he walked to the filing cabinet and pulled a different file. Slipping its three sheets of paper out, each a pre-printed form, he looked hard at them.

"You'd be better at this than me," he said to Sam. "Right, we have a lovely period cottage on the main road. Running water, stove and back boiler for hot water. Two bedrooms. Also, there's a fantastic two bedroom new build apartment on the edge of the town. An old holiday apartment, it affords generous views of the bay and countryside. Again, running cold water, but no heating or hot water I'm afraid. Lastly we have my favourite, a sixties townhouse on the new estate. Three bedrooms, fireplace has been reconverted, running water, hot and cold. How did I do?"

Rob could see Sam's face and body fuming. Steam appeared to be flowing from her nose. She was more than ready to slap this twat down. Remarkably, she just shrugged her shoulders. Someone would pay for this later. Rob reckoned it might be himself.

"Looks like two of you get the cold flat, sorry apartment. Do you want to draw straws between yourselves or something?"

Though he appeared moderately kind, Rob could tell he was well aware of his power and importance. He was loving every minute. He'd probably chosen a flat without a fire on purpose.

"I'm sure we can squeeze into the two houses," said Sal.

"No difference to me, Sal." He savoured her name. Shaking his head afterwards as if he couldn't believe it was actually her. "I just need to write your addresses down."

"Me Rob and Sal will have the cottage, everyone else can share the house," said Sam. Rob didn't disagree, though both Rabbity and Richard didn't look pleased.

"Okay." He filled in another box on each of the forms, taking his time, enjoying every pen stroke. "Okay, I'll need you all to sign here, he pointed to the last empty box on a form, and then I'll give you your number."

As they signed, he gave them numbers. Rob's was 5136982. Sam's 3169944. Males and females seemed to be on a different pattern.

"Now," he said. "Ration books."

Proceeding again to his filing cabinet, he drew out seven small printed booklets. Printing seemed to have become a growth industry under the Consortium's regime. Filling in each of their names in turn wasted another quarter hour. He was nothing if not methodical.

"Here you are. Take it to work with you and at the end of each day they'll stamp it. No stamp no stew. There's also weekly items at the back of the booklet. One slice of bread a week, three tea bags and a weekly supply of vitamins. Monthly goods are also on the back, one bar of soap, one small tube of toothpaste, and one bottle of shampoo. Other things can be purchased or swapped in the shop, but Sal will find out about them. I'm sure she'll explain it later."

Handing out the ration books, he sighed. Whether he enjoyed his job was debatable, but he certainly made the most of it.

A slow knocking noise came from behind the sturdy door. Rob quickly realised stairs were behind it and someone was walking down them. The handle turned, but the door was obviously locked from this side. Turning round, the guard walked to the door, pulled out a chain of keys and unlocked it.

A woman walked through, Rob guessed mid-twenties. Her dungarees seemed cleaner, and of better quality than the others. Her face reddened as she saw them, staring at her, wondering what the hell she was doing.

"My cleaner." He smiled his false smile again that Rob knew Sam would want to wipe from his face.

Walking past, she tried not to catch their eyes. Rob again wondered what she was up to. Or what he was up to.

As she left, he continued, "Today, you can move into your houses and get your shopping. Tomorrow, you'll start at the power plant. If you haven't yet seen it, it's the huge building to the West. You need to be there by eight, they'll explain what you have to do, if you don't already know. Make sure you take your ration book so it can be stamped. The day after tomorrow, your other jobs start. Meet outside here and find your correct job team. Again don't forget your ration book."

He turned to Rabbit Boy, "Except you, of course. Introduce yourself to the gaffer at the power plant tomorrow morning, he'll decide what to do with you." Looking at the filing cabinet, he shook his head before retrieving two more pieces of paper. "Nearly forgot that, didn't I?"

Slowly, he filled in the sheets, which Rob read upside down as being acquisition forms for new houses. Again he took his time before handing one to Sam and the other to Yorkie.

"That's about it," he said. "I take it there aren't any questions, are there?"

"He's diabetic," said Sal, pointing at Yorkie. "His insulin pen got left back at that concrete prison. Is there a hospital or doctors?" Yorkie shook his head, not wanting any fuss.

"The infirmary's a few towns away, on the coast. There's a Nurse who lives in the village. She kind of doubles as emergency help. She lives two doors from the village shop. She'll have some, if not she can radio the hospital and get something sorted."

Yorkie nodded.

"Any other questions?"

There weren't. Rob presumed everyone else was as creeped out as he was. They just wanted out.

"Okay. Enjoy yourselves."

Leaving the building, Rob put his arm round Sam's shoulders. "Well done. I thought at one point you were going to slap him."

"Don't. I just want to forget." She breathed deeply. "What an absolute fu..."

"Shh. He'll hear. Come on, I'll take you shopping."

Chapter 26

The shop had once been a proper village shop but was now just a chicken stew warehouse. An old post office grilled-counter separated the back from front. The back, rammed full of stew cans was only broken by some luxury items, if luxury was the correct word for soap. The shopkeeper, a balding middle-aged man sat on a small stool, a mass of paperwork in front of him.

Sal stepped forward, seemingly wanting to get off on the right foot. "Hello."

The man didn't look up from his pile. "Just a minute."

They waited. It really was a minute before he put the papers down, sighed, and stood. "What can I do you for?"

"Hello, I'm Sal. The guard up the road sent us."

"Oh right, newcomers are you? Got your ration books?"

"Yes we have, thanks. He also said I was to help you, a job here starting in two days?"

His eyes lit up. "Oh, about time I got some help, I've had no help since the last one." He disconcertingly left the sentence hanging. "I'm Bill, nice to meet you." He shoved his hand through the gap designed for stamps and pension books.

Gently shaking it, Sal said, "And you. We've also got another sheet of paper, for the houses?"

"Ah yes. Form 134b if I'm not mistaken. Right, this is going to take a few minutes, a lot of paperwork I'm afraid. Reaching below the counter, he picked up a ledger book, similar to the guard's and some blank forms, each slightly different. "Now, where is it?" Rifling through the papers, he pulled out two blank ones. "Right, the form for the first house?"

Rob noticed the form Sal handed over was for their house.

"Three occupants, so you want three bowls, and spoons." He wandered out back, returning with enamel bowls and cutlery, the like Rob hadn't seen since a camping trip. "One saucepan, one kettle." He again returned with two thin looking and not very large vessels. "You'll have to use old cans for cups I'm afraid, they've stopped making them."

Sal nodded, putting on her best, 'Sunny skies will continue for the rest of the week,' smile.

"I'll come to it in a bit, but you need to return your empty cans when you pick up your rations. I can let you off a few though. Anyway, two boxes of matches, three sleeping bags and three jumpers, what sizes. Small, medium or large."

"Well, I was always a size ten, but I don't really know?" Sal pushed the side of her hair, straightening it.

He looked her up and down. "Medium. Who else is in this house?"

"Me and Rob." Sam pointed at Rob.

"You're small, he's large. Right, I'll just finish off this form."

Methodically and slowly, he ticked a few boxes, wrote various sizes in other boxes then signed the form. Rob wondered what poor sod had the job of receiving all these forms and doing something with them. The civil service must have more than trebled the past two years.

"I think that's it," he said, without looking up. Opening the small door to the right of the counter, he handed their gear through.

Their turn over, the three waited while the bachelor pad received its furnishings. The jumper sizes sorted, four large, again he took a lifetime filling out his relevant paperwork.

"Now that's sorted, you'll be wanting your stew then?" He motioned for their ration books.

Half an hour later, and with armfuls of sleeping bags, stew, soap and tea bags, they left. Sal had maybe overdone saying how much she was looking forward to working there. Outside the shop, they paused: their paths about to split.

"Shall we meet up later?" asked Yorkie.

"Yeah," said Sal. "Come round ours after you've settled in and eaten."

"Will do. Good luck."

"Don't forget to go and see the nurse," said Sam.

"I will. Just get this stuff back first."

"I'll check up later," she said.

Both Rabbit Boy and Richard left longing looks in the weather girl's direction, but she turned and nodded towards the street their cottage was in. Rob offered to carry both their sleeping bags, but they wouldn't let him. A few minutes later, they arrived at the front door.

Unlocked, the cottage was chilled through lack of heating. A spacious downstairs living room, with staircase running up the side, the cottage was well tended. A few of the stairs looked recently fixed. The floor carpeted, though not particularly clean, was the only regular item of furnishing. The old wood or coal burning fire had a back boiler, water inside just waiting to be heated.

"Need some chairs," said Sam.

"Mmmm," said Sal. "What are we supposed to sit on? How do we heat these pots up?"

Inspecting the fire place, Rob found a metal tripod hidden behind the grate. It appeared to fit in three holes in the brick work surrounding the fireplace. "This?"

"Mmmm." She didn't look impressed.

Opening the kitchen door, Rob saw another bare room. An old gas cooker stood its ground next to empty and doorless cupboards. Whether the cooker worked or not was irrelevant. Gas wasn't piped to Britain anymore. The remaining gas in the North Sea fields was sold, or more specifically swapped, to the Russians, Norwegians and Danes in return for food and luxuries. Unfortunately, the likes of Rob never saw the proceeds. The guards, army and politicians were the only benefactors. Their need of Danish bacon and bread from Russian wheat exceeded the needs of ordinary people.

The basin was fairly new, with a cold tap and a hole where the hot had once been. Turning the water on Rob expected mud to drip out, but it didn't. Fairly fresh and cold water chugged through at a good pressure. Nodding his head, Rob walked to the large larder that backed onto the stairwell's rear. A small selection of dried branches and rotting wood lay at the far end, out of sight of most casual viewers.

"Heh heh." He gathered up the wood.

Returning to the kitchen, Sam had the tap running full. "Aren't you the proper caveman?" She pointed to his wood pile.

"Ugh." Putting the dried wood on the sideboard, he moved behind her, placing his hands on her shoulders. "You okay?"

"Suppose. Bit odd isn't it?"

"Yeah. Where's Sal?"

"Upstairs, checking out the bedrooms. Thought I'd get the kettle on."

"Probably a day or two's wood here. God knows what happens when we run out." The more he thought about it, the more it puzzled him. There couldn't possibly be enough wood on the island to keep everyone warm and heat up stew. And this was summer, what would happen in winter?

The pan now full, she turned the tap off and placed it down. Turning round, she put her hands on his waist, moved her face nearer and kissed him.

Breaking away before it became something more, she said, "Come on, fire needs lighting."

Picking up his wood, and leaving shavings, splinters and leaves all over the work surface, Rob went into the front room and assembled the fire. As Sam went upstairs to find Sal, Rob pondered this new life.

Certain things were bugging him. What was the point of producing such a small amount of electricity? Why wasn't there a spare set of underwear? How were they going to keep warm this winter? How was this going to end? How could they wash their clothes without any spare ones to wear while they dried?

Shaking his head, he carried on making the fire. He hadn't done as good a job as Rabbit Boy would have, but it would suffice.

Upstairs, he could hear Sal and Sam laughing. Feeling left out, he joined them. The stairs themselves, though bare wood, were in good order. Even the repaired ones didn't wobble when stepped on.

The upstairs consisted of a small, carpet-less corridor with three doors leading off. Sal and Sam were in the last room. Walking towards it, he sneaked in the first room; a box bedroom. Flimsy, almost see through curtains hung on the walls while an old wardrobe was missing one of its two doors. The bed itself was a single mattress lying on the floor. Devoid of any bed sheet or quilt, and with a few stains, it wasn't appealing.

Next, the bathroom. Half the floor was carpeted, but a large chunk was missing where the bath used to be. In its place stood a thin plastic shower cubicle, hastily plumbed into hot and cold taps. The toilet was clean yet dusty and the sink though clean, housed a few dead spiders.

A few more questions hit Rob. What about toilet paper? Towels? This was crazy. They couldn't be expected to live like this and work six days a week.

Shaking his head, he knocked on the last door in the corridor.

"Come in," said Sal.

Sam laughed as he entered. "You don't have to knock."

He shrugged his shoulders. "You know."

The room, again uncarpeted and flimsy curtained, had two single mattresses on the floor, one slightly larger than the other. Separated by another wardrobe, this one no doors at all, Rob wondered if some point was being made by the bed's distance from each other.

Sam smiled. "Separate beds."

Rob nodded. A smile grew on his face in expectation of being asked to move them closer. "Mattresses have seen better days, haven't they?"

Sal nodded. "Could be worse. I'm not sure how, but it could be."

"Come on," said Rob, "let's put that kettle on."

The fire lit and the dampness slowly eaten away, the water boiled. Not having empty cans, they decided on making a saucepan of tea and sharing it. The saucepan, though small, didn't make an ideal drinking vessel being both unwieldy and quick to cool down. They each supped a few mouthfuls of very weak poor quality tea.

"What's next?" asked Sal.

"Suppose we check out the garden," said Rob. He'd already taken a peek outside. Grassed over, and not cut this year, it was a fair size. Next door's gardens on both sides seemed to be thriving with growing vegetables. Though they'd probably missed this year's season for planting, Rob reckoned a few potatoes and cabbages would half grow. Where did you get seeds from? That was the question.

"I might have a shower. Do you reckon the water's hot yet?" asked Sal.

"It's only been burning a few minutes. The pipe upstairs should get hot as the water does, maybe check that?"

"I'll give it a few more minutes."

169

"Come on, let's see the garden," said Sam, putting down the tea.

Through the unlocked back door, Rob surveyed the garden. The fence long gone and burned, the garden backed onto a field, separated by a thorn and blackberry bush. The field behind was roughly ploughed with small shoots growing, Rob had no idea what they were, but it was some kind of grain.

The most notable thing was a six by four patch of paving slabs, possibly the ex-home of a shed or greenhouse. The house three doors down had a shed that looked the right shape. "I used to write a lot of stories of thefts from sheds. Never written a theft of a shed story."

"We ought to kick their arses later," said Sam.

"Shall we see who's living there first?" said Sal.

Sam shrugged her shoulders. The view from the garden, over the fields and hills, was of the metallic power station. Its peddlers inside no doubt suffering from aching legs as their day neared the half-way point. Rob knew he'd find out tomorrow just how hard it was. Whether they'd earn their stew or not was debatable. It seemed a bitter spiral: you needed energy to work, if you don't work hard enough you don't get any stew, so you have less energy the next day. Surely there'd be a breaking point somewhere. How many didn't make it?

"It'll look nice with a bit of decking and a Jacuzzi" said Sam.

They laughed before returning inside.

Rob was chosen to test the shower and hot water. Gingerly, he ran the tap before getting in. The water was warm, not overly hot or cold, but was also dark yellow in colour. In the minute it took running before the colour improved, it became much colder.

Grabbing his soap, he washed. Despite being poor quality soap, it helped wipe away the grime, chicken stew and wood smoke. Washing as quickly as he could, and timing himself by counting, he reckoned three minutes had passed and the water was still just bearable. Finally, Rob washed his t-shirt and pants in the bottom of the shower cubicle. Though he felt sorry for Sam and Sal's feet, there was no other way he could think of cleaning them.

Shaking himself dry and wringing out his t-shirt, he waited a few minutes for the drips of water to slide down him. Satisfied he was as dry as possible, he put his dirty dungarees back on. Realising he looked like a Worzel stripper-gram, he shrugged his shoulders before heading back downstairs, his wet pants and t-shirt in hand.

"Any good," asked Sal.

"Not bad. Lost most of the hot water while it purged the gunk out, but it's clear now."

"We need a washing line outside." Sam pointed at his t-shirt and the pants wrapped inside. "Suppose you could hang it on the windowsill for now."

Rob nodded and went outside to do as told.

"Nice muscles by the way," she added. He didn't know if she was being sarcastic or not.

The quietness of the mid-afternoon struck him. With everyone, absolutely everyone, at work the village had a ghost town feel. Rob supposed some people wouldn't be working, they'd have their weekly day off. He imagined them at home, exhausted in their tatty dungarees maybe enjoying a can of stew or tea. What a life. What a crap life.

Back inside, Sal was getting ready to go upstairs. The fire didn't have much life left and with wood at a premium, Sam was getting anxious she'd be having a cold water shower.

When Sal went upstairs, Rob moved next to Sam. Sitting beside her, with his arm looped through the back of her dungarees, he said, "What's the plan then?"

"Dunno. What plan?"

He shrugged his shoulders. "The escape plan. Tunnel our way to the mainland with soup cans or make a boat from dungarees, soap and shower cubicles?"

The smile he'd seen the previous night returned. "What about building a big horse, like the Horse of Troy thing? Except make it out of stew cans. It'd only take a few weeks' worth?"

A scream came from upstairs, not a scared scream, but a definite this water's too cold scream.

"Stick another bit of wood on, hun. Sounds like the water's getting chilly."

Doing as he was told, again, he then sat next to her.

"Fancy a walk when you and Sal's done showering?"

"Yeah. I was going to nip to the nurse anyway, but I could pop in on the way."

"Why? Is something wrong? You're not ill are you?"

"No, nothing like that. I want to ask about, you know, pills."

It took Rob a few minutes and several misinterpreted questions to realise she meant the pill rather than other, more specific pills. It hadn't occurred to him last night, the moment had just go to them. He presumed it had occurred to her, it must have. Like toilet rolls and towels, birth control must have a place in this new world. After all, who'd want to bring a child into this?

"There must be something here. I mean Beardy and Weirdy must be at it like rabbits," she said. "If she's not past her prime, so to speak."

"Thanks, that's an image that'll take some shifting."

"Wonder what his wife would make of that. And his beard come to think of it, what would she think of that?" Pausing for a second, she turned, which twisted his hand the wrong way inside her dungarees. "Have you got a girlfriend or wife?"

He instantly went on the defensive, not that he'd anything to hide. "No, seriously, no. I'm not married. Haven't had a girlfriend for years. Honest. I haven't."

Smiling, she said, "I know, you already said. I don't think it matters anyway, does it? I haven't seen anyone since I lost my house. Those crusty anarchists were a good laugh, but not really my type."

"I will cut my beard. I'll find a way."

Pulling him closer, she got entangled in his beard for five minutes while Sal finished her coldish shower.

With Sal downstairs and Sam singing in the shower, Rob realised that not only were there no towels or toilet paper, they didn't have a can opener either. What kind of fucked up regime gives you mountains of canned chicken stew and no can opener? The nail and pair of pliers they'd previously used back in the forest were long gone and nothing he'd found in the house would come close to making a dent in it.

"The shop must have one," said Sal.

"Yeah. Suppose it's not that far away, is it?"

Taking the can and rinsed out saucepan, he left the cottage. The afternoon sun still bright and warm. His hair and beard fluff now dry, he took in the afternoon street. Still deathly quiet, no sign of anyone.

172

The shop was open and warm. Being in a suntrap, Rob wondered what good the heat was doing the canned stew. The shop keeper explained that because of the metal shortage, can openers were no longer available. He suggested borrowing one from a neighbour or getting hold of a screwdriver and brick. However, as he was new, he let Rob borrow his own, an act akin to lending someone a hundred quid in the old days. Rob couldn't thank him enough and left with some small part of his faith restored.

Walking back to the cottage, Rob saw curtains flicker three doors down. Unsure whether to wave or ignore, he carried on, but kept an eye out. With no net curtains up, it was obvious the silhouette inside was either very small, on their knees or a child.

Entering the cottage, Rob couldn't shift this from his mind.

"Did you get one?" asked Sal.

"Yeah, but it's only a loan. He suggests we get hold of a screwdriver."

The noise of water hitting plastic from above had stopped. Rob presumed Sam must be drip drying.

"I'll nip down B&Q shall I?" Sal was not really one for sarcasm, but this was a new world and new worlds deserved new thoughts.

"Think there's someone three doors down. Could be a child, not sure though."

"Children, here? God that's awful. Do you think we ought to go and say something?"

"No. I think we'd scare them to death. It could just be a short person." Rob tipped the stew into the saucepan. Glooping out, the familiar smell hit his nose, reminding him how hungry he was. "Shall I water it down?"

"We should build a stock of stew in case we don't earn any." Sal flicked her still wet hair, hiding part of it behind her ear.

"I was thinking the same." Rob went to the kitchen and half-filled the can with water. Returning, he swirled it round, catching the remaining few dregs of chicken-like meat stuck to the sides.

Placing the saucepan on the nearly depleted fire, Rob sat on the floor.

As the stew warmed, the freshened Sam came downstairs. Her hair wet and complexion clearer, Rob couldn't help but smile as he saw her. She returned the smile.

Sharing the nearly warm stew in their bowls, Rob poured slightly less for himself and made sure Sam got the biggest lump of suspicious chicken. Eating in silence, they finished it quickly. Sal offered to wash up, and neither Rob nor Sam counter offered.

Chapter 27

Stepping into the late afternoon sun, they tried to look in the house three doors down. Its curtains still drawn, but no longer rustling, they gave up and walked towards the village centre.

"I'm going to nip to the Nurse's," said Sam to Sal.

"Okay," she said.

Sal never asked why, which given her caring nature, suggested to Rob she already knew why. Chances are it had been discussed while he was showering, they'd maybe planned the whole walk charade they were now performing.

At the Nurse's house, which was obvious thanks to the carefully painted 'Village Hospital' on the door, Rob and Sal waited a respectful distance as Sam knocked.

"Just a minute," a voice called from inside.

Sometime later, more than a minute, the door opened revealing a mid-thirties, short woman. Her black hair long, she had what Rob considered to be a kind smile. The perfect nursing smile.

"Come in."

Sam followed her inside.

Waiting outside, there are only so many times you can comment on the weather, especially with an ex-weathergirl, or look up and down the street. Five minutes felt like an hour.

Eventually, Sam emerged smiling. A knowing look and nod was flashed between herself and Sal that Rob pretended not to notice, then they were off.

Walking through the village, heading a roundabout route to the bachelor pad, the once pretty holiday village had become nothing less than a big allotment with houses in between.

"Should have asked the shop keeper about seeds," said Rob.

"I can do that when I start work," said Sal.

"You might be able to sneak us some extra soap or stew," said Sam, though her heart didn't seem in it.

Depression was an obvious problem, one that Rob hoped he'd spot coming. He felt it was his job to keep spirits up, being the man of the house. Though he'd never put it that way to Sam. That was asking for more bruised ribs. Thinking of a joke, any joke or funny comment was difficult for him at the best of times. Making up debatably funny nicknames was as far as he went. Keeping morale up was going to be hard.

"Best not on the first few days," Sal replied. She maybe hadn't realised it was a joke.

Reaching the lads' house, its front garden had been recently dug over with a third of it already yielding some potatoes and cabbages.

"They've been busy digging for victory," said Rob. Their smiles returned, if only for a brief period. Knocking on the door, he added, "Avon calling."

Sal giggled in a way Rob hadn't heard for years. He remembered that famous clip of her collapsing with laughter live on the television after the anchor man had fluffed a line and accidently implied she was a man in drag. The lines on her face creased the same way. Maybe laughter was the cure?

Yorkie opened the door, looking genuinely happy to see them. "Hello. Come in, come in, we're just having a cuppa."

Walking inside, the first thing to strike Rob was the smell. A musty pong hung in the air. Immediately he felt both sorry for them and also relived they'd chosen the other house.

The hall gave way to stairs and two doors, one the front room the other the kitchen. The front room was large, maybe too large to keep warm with a small fire, but it gave enough room for all of them.

"Sorry about the smell," Quiety said. "There were three dead rats in here when we arrived. Stinks, doesn't it?"

"It's fine," Sal lied. "Where are the boys?"

"Off hunting for wood."

Rob's image of Rabbit Boy hunting for wood bought back the smile the smell had wiped away.

"Not a bad size, is it?" said Sam. Not only was the size good, but it also had a sofa. Though faded, worn and full of holes, and possibly rats, it was a sofa. "What's the kitchen like?"

"I'll do you the proper tour," said Quiety. "We just had enough wood for a small fire, but tea's taking ages to warm."

Rob wasn't surprised. The fire place was huge, not compact like their own. They'd definitely picked the best house.

The kitchen was a good size, with a wobbly table but no chairs. An old fridge stood in the corner, useless without electricity. The sink and taps were similar to their own, the hot one missing, the cold one dirty. Looking out at the back garden, it had been dug over and partially planted. Smaller than their own garden, they'd still be hard pressed to grow much with the lack of time this year.

"Neighbours have been busy," said Quiety. "We'll pop round later. Hopefully if we get off on the right foot, they'll give us some of that veg."

"We're going to need seeds or whatever," said Rob. "Have to find out where they come from."

Quiety nodded. "Didn't see none in that shop. I suppose you could ask." He nodded at Sal. "Right, upstairs."

Leading them up the carpeted stairs, Quiety opened the first room, the box room. "Richard picked the short straw. Actually maybe me and Pat picked the short one. We're sharing."

Richard's sleeping bag rolled up on the mattress was the only furnishing. The room was clean though and the walls recently whitewashed.

"Next bedroom's John's, he definitely got the long straw." The room, similar in furnishing to Richard's was nearly twice the size. A cursory glance was all they needed to inspect it.

Moving on, they saw the main bedroom. A small chest of drawers stood in the corner, dwarfed by the lack of anything but the bed in the room. The double bed looked hardly used.

"Fancy a swap. We've got two singles?" said Sam.

"Please." He smiled. "It could get awkward otherwise."

"Rob, go and swap it, hun."

"Bit heavy for just me," he said. "Shall we wait for the wood hunters to come back first?"

She nodded before walking out of the room and into the bathroom.

The bathroom was an actual bathroom: it had a bath. Though old, it was intact but the hot water had been rerouted to a shower attachment screwed to the wall. The basin and toilet were similar to their own, reclaimed.

"And that concludes the tour."

Downstairs, Yorkie had poured four bowls of tea. He passed them round, leaving nothing for himself.

"Me and Rob'll share," said Sam.

It took some persuading, but the stubborn Yorkie eventually agreed and supped his tea noisily. Little conversation came as they struggled to either make light of the situation or find something to talk about. Rob knew it would come, it just needed time. As Sam had pointed out yesterday, this new life couldn't be permanent. Something had to happen, something had to change.

With the saucepan re-boiling the same tea bag, the two wood hunters returned, armed with a meagre handful of sticks.

"We found a wood," said Richard, "but it's fenced off and guarded. These sticks were from a hedgerow, last year's growth mainly."

"We reckon they're keeping the trees for the winter," said Rabbit Boy, swigging his weak tea.

"There's some recently planted trees, too, fast growing pine. It'll still take five years or so to get to a decent size. That little wood ain't going to last this village five years."

The conversation ended. Sam poked Rob in the ribs, reminding him to swap the mattresses. Gesturing at the two woodsmen, Rob said maybe they should get their breath back first. She kind of agreed.

"You should go with them, see the nurse," she said to Yorkie.

"Aye, maybe." His heart didn't sound in it.

"We should probably make the most of this hot water," said Quiety. "That wood won't last all night."

"You go now, Dave," said Yorkie. "I'll have one when I get back from the quack's, then the two lads can have the rest."

"We better get moving now then," said Sam, who obviously really wanted the bed immediately.

Chapter 28

Getting the mattress downstairs proved less of a Laurel and Hardy routine than Rob had imagined. Outside, in the late afternoon sun, Rob, Richard and John suspended the mattress on their right arms with Sam, Yorkie and Sal supervising.

At the cottage, getting the mattress up the thin, curvy stairs wasn't easy, but was managed in a true ordered-chaos. Bringing the other mattresses down one at a time, Sam and Rob helped take them back to the lad's house, while Sal stayed behind.

On their fourteenth stop with the awkward mattress, Rob noticed the village was coming to life. People were returning from their jobs. Several of them nodded and said hello. No one stopped to chat, though as they were struggling with the mattresses, it wasn't surprising.

Dropping the mattresses off, Rob and Sam returned to their cottage. Their silence broken as it came into view. "What did the nurse say?" asked Rob.

"Oh, sorry forgot, didn't I?"

Rob shrugged. His felt his cheeks burning and it wasn't from the heat.

"She gave some tablets, a week's worth. I'll have to go to the main hospital on my day off for a proper prescription."

Rob was lost for words, nothing intelligent leaping forward. He could think of a lot of corny things, plus many things that'd have him going to the lads' house to swap the mattresses back. Devoid of anything, he took her hand and kissed her soapy head.

Near the house, Rob noticed Sal outside talking to someone. As they approached, Rob could see the man, early forties and wearing dungarees. They were getting on well. Very well.

"Sal," said Sam.

"Hi." Her face was full of colour. "You won't believe this, but this is Ralf, my old producer. He lives three doors away."

"Which side?" asked Rob, his mind being only on the shed thief.

Ralf pointed to his house. It was him. Extending his hand to Rob, he said, "Nice to meet you."

Rob shook his hand back, making it as firm as he could. He tried hard to contain his anger and hoped it didn't show. "I'm Rob," he said. That was my shed, he didn't say.

"And this is Sam," said Sal.

"Hi Sam, nice to meet you."

Rob could see Sam has gone star struck again. A real life television-producing, shed-stealing star was living three doors away.

"Hello. Small world isn't it?"

"Yes," he said.

Though he also possessed a beard, it'd been recently trimmed. Other than that, he was the same as them: a dungaree wearing ex-something who'd annoyed someone. Rob wondered if Ralf and Sal had been in it together in more ways than one.

"We'll, er, make a drink," said Sam, pushing Rob towards the door.

As Sam drowned the already lifeless teabag in water and put it back on the fire, Rob glanced out of the window. "Do you reckon? Those two?"

"Maybe. They look very familiar."

"I thought she went for footballers and rock stars?"

"A lot of that's just made up though, ain't it?" She prodded the fire remains with a stick. "You know what those journalists are like."

"Hmmm," he murmured.

The afternoon slipped into evening. The lads popped round after tea. Anxiousness about tomorrow was rife. After they'd left, Sam and Sal were chatting about the old days, while Rob prodded the fire and washed up the bowls.

"Bit weird meeting Ralf again," said Sal.

Sam pounced like a waiting cat. "Did you know each other well?"

Sal played with a piece of her hair. "We worked together for years. I mean you get close, don't you."

"What did he do? To get here, I mean, did he do the same as you?"

"Do you know, I'm not sure. He wasn't involved in the weather forecasts, unless they never told me, but I can't see how we wouldn't have sussed each other out."

180

Sal's face dropped, fell a mile. Her hands reaching for her head, she said, "Oh no. It's my fault, isn't it?"

Rob stole a glance at Sam, she half shrugged then moved to Sal, placing her arms round her shoulders. The two became a merging mess of soapy hair and dungaree as they hugged each other.

"I bet they thought we were working together. It's my fault, isn't it?"

"You don't know that. He might have done something else." She didn't look as if she could think what. Looking to Rob for inspiration, he too shrugged his shoulders. Chances are it was because of Sal, but that didn't make it her fault.

Her tears came. The first since they'd met. Sam joined in, and Rob, though he'd enough to cry about, couldn't. Feeling helpless, he prodded the fire.

Something needed to happen. They had to do something. This wasn't how it ended.

Chapter 29

An early night became restless for all of them, worry about the next day the cause. Waking the next morning, Rob's instincts told him they were late. Not having a clock was playing havoc with his mind. How could they be on time for work when they didn't know the time?

Leaving Sam in the bathroom, Rob went downstairs. Putting on the t-shirt he'd left outside all night, he saw Sal in the kitchen struggling to open a can.

"I didn't sleep very well," she said. "I was scared of oversleeping."

"Me too," said Rob. "What is the time?"

"I'll go and see Ralf, he'll know," she said.

Rob nodded and put some sticks on the fire, but didn't light them.

Sam soon came down, looking fresh and ready for work.

"Sal's just finding out the time."

Nodding, she kissed him and slapped him on the rear. "Go and get ready then."

He did. Halfway through his cold water wash, he heard Sal return and the pair of them talking. There was no sign of rushing, so he assumed they weren't late. On his return downstairs, the fire was crackling in the grate with a pot of stew on. "What's the time?"

"Ten to six. I woke him up. He said you're not on breakfast telly anymore, Sal." She laughed. Someone needed too.

"We need a clock or watch," said Sam.

"There's a watch repairer apparently in the big town, can't remember its name. He swaps watches for cans of stew and fresh veg.

"Have to go cabbage rustling, won't we?" said Rob.

"I was thinking more of asking for an advance, from the shop," said Sal.

Rob nodded and smiled. Her working there could be very useful.

"He's going to drop in at seven thirty, Ralf that is, show us the way."

"What about the others?" Rob remembered they'd arranged to meet at their house, as it was nearer the power plant.

"Run over and tell them we'll pick them up," said Sam.

Knowing he couldn't refuse, he left the cottage. "Save us some stew," he said.

Yorkie and Quiety were up and trying to warm up stew with very little wood. Rob said he couldn't stay long and explained the change of plan. Yorkie looked much better, more alert, having had a good dose of insulin from the nurse. Like Sam, he too had to visit the hospital on his day off for a long term supply. The plan was for a gang trip there on their day off. A day in the big town, sampling what sort of society dissidents had made for themselves.

Walking back, Rob wondered at this new society. He'd had visions of being in a prison, under lock and key, armed guards everywhere. The level of freedom had surprised him. Though expected to work, they at least had some freedom.

The problems with any sort of society, crimes both against the person and theft of property had not so far been seen. At the end of the day, there was nothing to steal, besides food and sheds, but surely like any society, greed would show itself in some way? He found it hard to believe the perfect communal society had been created.

Reaching the cottage, his legs already tired, though more in anticipation of the huge cycle ride coming, he sat down.

"They alright?"

"Yeah. The two oldies were up, no sign of the hunters."

Sal laughed. "Hunters?"

Remembering she didn't know his name game, he clarified, "The wood hunters, you know, what Yor... Pat said yesterday. The name just kind of stuck."

Shaking her head, she stirred the stew round. "This isn't warming very well. Cold alright for everyone?"

"Yeah," said Sam. "Put that teabag back on too. See if we can get a few more cups out of it."

They finished their tepid water with a hint of tea just before Ralf came round. By Ralf's side was another man and woman. At a guess, Rob would have them in their forties.

"This is Jane and Freddy," said Ralf.

Rob covered his mouth. If only Ralf had been called Rod. Was that too much to ask? He noticed Sam also nearly laughing.

"This is Sam and Rob, we met yesterday," said Sal.

"Hello," said the overenthusiastic Jane. "Nice to meet you, really, really nice."

Handshakes all round led to them leaving.

Rob's stomach sloshed with the biggest bout of butterflies he'd had since playing King Herod in a nativity play when he was eight. Sam took his hand, her bony fingers shaking and digging in tight. This was it. Crunch time. Their new life really had begun.

Sal took the lead with Ralf and Jane while Freddy hung back, nearer to Rob and Sam.

"How long you been here?" asked Sam.

"About three months. Jane and I arrived together. I used to mark off every day, but I stopped after six weeks."

A manic depressive Freddy was not needed at this time.

"What did you do before, your job I mean?"

"Nothing too interesting. I worked for the council, used to produce reports for their Recycling stats."

Rob had to agree that really didn't sound interesting.

"What about yourselves?"

"Rob was a reporter for the Basingstoke Bugle. I worked in an Estate Agency."

He nodded. "This your first day?"

They nodded back.

"You get used to it. I won't lie and say it's easy. The first few days kills your legs. You'll feel like you've walked up a mountain. After a few weeks though, once your muscles have grown and got used to it, it's nothing."

"Thanks," said Rob.

The rest of the gang collected, they walked through the field toward the power station. Hundreds of people were walking from all directions. It reminded Rob of a computer game he played years ago: Lemmings.

Sam's fingernails dug deeper into Rob's hand the closer they got. As they neared the plant, it towered over them. From a distance it was big. Close up, massive. Rob could only guess what it would look like inside.

Sam's stomach growled. Rob himself wondered if the stew would repeat on them. Maybe eating hadn't been a good idea.

Approaching the large door at the front, Ralf turned to them. "When you get inside, there's an office on the left. New starters go there. There's quite a crowd when you get that near, so if we get separated, I'll see you later."

Joining the throng of people walking through the doors, Rob held tightly to Sam, who was doing the same to him. Inside the doors, it resembled what Rob could only describe as the foyer of a football ground or concert hall. Huge corridors peeled off in either direction, skirting the middle brick-lined portion. Signs overhead read directions for the workers using colour-coded directional arrows. Another sign for new starters pointed to the left, as Ralf had said.

Moving to the left, against the ever forward scrum of people, Rob and Sam reached the small New Starter corridor and stopped just inside, waiting for the others. A white faced Yorkie was soon joined by an out of breath Richard and a quiet Quiety. Sal and John were the last two in. Sal had her left hand on his shoulder, being led. Rob wondered again just what the deal was with them. Or what the deal had once been.

Regrouping, Yorkie said, "Guess this is it. If we get separated, meet outside to the left of the building at home time?"

Agreeing, Rob wondered just how long it would be before their group disintegrated. After all, Sal had met her old boss, the day jobs started tomorrow which would lead to more friends, before long, the New Forest runners that had so nearly escaped would in a month probably just be a memory.

The corridor ended at a door, the word 'knock' helpfully written on it.

Knocking received the reply, "Come in." Inside a fifty foot square room, people mingled behind tables and chairs. Yorkie stepped forward to the first table where a stern woman was sitting. Dressed in dungarees, as were most of the others, it was obvious she was one of them but her job didn't involve peddling.

"New starters?" she asked.

"Aye."

Pulling seven forms from the top of her tray, she clicked on her pen. "Who's first?"

Name, address and new serial number were given over one by one and written neatly on the paper. John the rabbit waited until last then said, "I'm an engineer. They said you might be able to use me?"

Sighing, she replaced the form in her pile and pulled a different one from her top drawer. Again, name and number were given then John was given directions to store room ten, about half way round the circular corridor.

Leaving he tried to smile and mumbled, "See you."

"Good luck." Sal placed a hand on his shoulder.

The stern woman took her time checking the forms before taking them to a uniformed guard in the centre of the room. Looking at them, he studied each in turn before writing something, Rob presumed a signature, on each form. She then went to another desk and gave the paperwork to another dungareed worker.

Returning after a few anxious minutes, she sat down. "Haven't got six spots together I'm afraid. The best we can do is split you in half. Now, who goes with who?"

"Me, Rob and Sal," said Sam very quickly.

The paperwork finalised, a bearded dungaree wearer led them towards the hall. In the circular corridor, the combined sound of pedalling was already starting to vibrate the brickwork and metal walls. A low pitched, bee-like hum battered their ears. At first, Rob tried to block it, but it soon became obvious, as it got louder, that it was futile.

"Okay," said the beard, "entrance four, that's Sam, Sal and Rob."

Opening the door, the sound buffeted out louder than before. Rob scrunched up his face.

Inside was a sight Rob never thought he'd see. A thousand dungareed dissidents, in various states of beard growth, sat at exercise bikes peddling. Though in a circle, each quadrant contained raised walkways between them. The roof had been lowered compared to the corridor and each peddle bike had a lead rising up to meet and go through it. Rob suspected the electricity was combined, monitored and fed into the grid upstairs.

The exercise bikes themselves were not all the same. Some were from gyms and health clubs with an extra box added to the side or rear. Others looked more in-house, made from a cycle frame, heavy rear wheel and again, a metal enclosed box obviously containing the dynamo. Each bike had both a revolution counter and what appeared to be a chart, similar to a lorry's Tachograph. Guards stood round the sides of the room, behind chicken wire fence. They were heavily armed. The first guns Rob had seen inside the Island's camp. He'd no doubt they had a barracks inside the plant and were separated at all times.

The noise, though still colossal, was becoming bearable. The beard guiding them, gestured to Sam Rob and Sal to move over to the fourth row back and the other three to wait by the door. A row of three empty bikes, proper exercise bikes were waiting.

"You'll get the hang of it pretty easily," he shouted above the noise. "Just peddle and keep the revs above the red line. Try and find a rhythm and don't waste too much energy." He motioned for Rob to get on first.

Sitting on the seat, which wasn't very comfortable, Rob started peddling. Stuck in the lowest gear possible, it took all his effort to get it moving.

"I know it seems hard at first, but the secret is to keep moving slowly."

Building up speed, his legs already ached after only seconds. How was he going to last ten hours?

Sal and Sam took their seats, either side of him. A few people nearby nodded and smiled, some of them recognising Sal the weather girl. Sam had a few choice words to say about the peddling, but once up to speed, she settled into a rhythm.

"This quadrant's break is half past until quarter to." He pointed to the big clock up on the wall next to a blank television screen and a huge ammeter. Circular, it obviously registered the total output. With everyone peddling it was reading well over the red line drawn on it. All four quadrants were peddling, whereas most of the time only three would be.

"You passed the toilets on the way in. If you really do need to leave your station when it's not your break, attract someone's attention first." He pointed to the dungaree wearers, pacing the gaps between each quadrant. "Any questions?"

"Yeah," said Sam. "How do we get your job?"

He smiled. "Luck of the draw and a bad knee, I'm afraid. You'll get used to it, honestly. Sorry." His smile faded. Rob thought it important to remember that he was like them, a dissident. He'd just been in the right place at the right time with the wrong knees.

Their peddling underway, Rob watched the second hand of the clock ticking round. The rhythm was roughly two revolutions per second. Over the coming hours he could do little more than count those revolutions and work out how many rotations were left before home time.

Chapter 30

The first break, after less than half an hour, went too quickly. Rob's legs were already hurting. Sam and Sal were complaining too. The people around them sympathised. After the first few days, they kept saying, it gets easier. That was little comfort for now. Rob went to the toilet during his break. He didn't need to, he just knew he'd be desperate in ten minutes if he didn't go.

The men's room was just a big sheet of aluminium lining the wall with recessed bricks to drain the waste away. The smell was unbelievably ripe. His eyes stung with pain as he left and returned to the bikes.

The next half hour seemed to go faster. Rob could see the three lads in the opposite quadrant, they seemed to be on the hour to quarter past break. This seemed unfair, they had to peddle a full hour before their first break. Perhaps they got to go quarter of an hour earlier?

Upon the hour, the television came to life. Previously just a blackened screen, it now showed two pictures, the first a larger image of the ammeter, which was just ticking over the red line, and the second the state run news channel. Unseen speakers burst into life overhead. The ever smiling news reader talked of how cabbage production was up in the home-counties and also how patriotic school children in Britain were to help out by manufacturing shoes for two hours a day. These shoes, the news reader said, would be sold to China and India and the proceeds used to buy more food and medicine.

Mutterings rose round the hall; they were dissidents after all. A couple of them shouted shame, but none of them stopped peddling. Not one.

At quarter past the hour, during the changeover of breaks, the ammeter dipped well below the red line. The news report went off the television, replaced by a flashing red message, 'Power too low.' Rob noticed the people in front pedalling faster, to compensate for the loss. Within a minute, the message had gone, replaced by the news report which was just ending with the weather.

"She doesn't know a warm front from her arse," said Sal.

Rob smiled. He suppressed a laugh as it would waste too much energy.

The news and weather finished, an anchor man appeared. "You're watching Power Station TV," he said. "Bringing News and Entertainment to you as you bring power to the nation."

The peddlers avidly watched the screen. "Coming up next, the first part of today's film, Honey I shrunk the kids."

Moans filled the hall. The man peddling in front of Rob turned and said, "They said it was Ben Hur today." He shook his head.

The dinner break came. Some munched apples and berries, while others ate what looked like flat, home-made bread. Having no food themselves, the three went hungry. Rob could still feel his legs moving despite being sitting next to the bike. The bread looked interesting. Rob wondered how they'd got hold of flour. It wasn't for sale in the shop.

"I kept dipping below the red line," said Sal. "I'm not sure I can last all day."

"It doesn't matter," said Rob. "We've still got a can left from yesterday, and we're not going to eat three cans between us, are we?"

She shrugged her shoulders. "I want to do my bit."

"I'm sure you will," said Sam. "You're in the shop tomorrow remember?" She winked at Sal.

Half smiling, Sal said, "Yeah I suppose."

The break was over too quickly. The film was still showing, interrupted every quarter hour by a news break, repeating the same thing over and over. Not being too interested in the film, Rob spent the afternoon looking round, remembering faces amongst the peddlers and trying to give them nicknames. He soon realised there's only a few ways you can alter the nickname beardy, and most of those just weren't funny.

The mid-afternoon stint was the hardest. Every vein below Rob's waist felt like it was exploding. Legs became numb, lifeless. Cramp gripped his calves twice in an hour, forcing him to stop at one point. Beside him, Sam was continuing. Though pale and exhausted, her legs were trundling round, completing the revolutions needed for a can of stew. The other side, Sal had all but given up. Longer breaks of a minute in every six or seven were needed for her to get some energy back. When she was peddling she was way under the red line. In a perfect world, Rob supposed she may as well give up now, go home and get some rest. She wasn't going to earn any stew now, however hard she peddled.

Rob himself slowed during the late afternoon stint. Convinced the clock was broken or going backwards, time had become his enemy. The film had finished its broken stint and was replaced by re-runs of EastEnders. According to the man beside Sal, who'd become chattier as the day moved on, they were showing EastEnders in full from the start. The Eighties haircuts and long gone characters bought back memories of Rob's youth. Happier times. Shame it was EastEnders though. He thought The Bill would have gone down better.

The last half hour was the worst. A group of ten people walked round the first quadrant, Yorkie and the two lads' area, looking at their tachograph charts. They seemed to be stamping almost everyone's ration books, which Rob was quite relieved about. They then moved onto the fourth quarter, the ones due their break at quarter to the hour. Rob thought they would just leave at quarter to: there was no point having a break then going home after.

Finally, at quarter to, when Rob's legs seared with pain, a quarter of the hall disappeared. Rob saw Richard wave in their direction and indicate, through some form of semaphore, they'd wait as agreed.

Rob waved back. He hoped it would be interpreted as okay.

Slowly, fifteen minutes ticked by. The tachograph checker looked at Sal's and shook his head. "Sorry, I know it's your first day, and we are lenient but I can't stamp this. Sorry." Instead of the stamp, he drew a large X through the box.

Both Rob and Sam got their stamps, but Sal was mortified at failing.

Outside, the three lads were sitting down. Richard was beyond pale and not very fresh smelling. He now seemed almost thin. Yorkie too was pale and exhausted, yet still with it. Quiety looked in the best condition of all. Rob presumed the RAF had left him fitter than most.

John was conspicuous by his absence. "Anyone seen John?" asked Sal.

"No. Not all day," said Yorkie. "Don't know if he's gone or not."

"Suppose we give him a few minutes then head off?" said Quiety.

The others mumbled agreement. Sitting down, Rob sighed as his heavy legs finally got some rest.

A few minutes of silence led to them standing and leaving. They were all sure John would understand their exhaustion just made them want to go home and rest.

As Rob stood, Sam nudged him and pointed to someone walking from the power station. The girl from the guard's house. The one who looked embarrassed to be emerging from his upstairs. The one the guard called his cleaner.

On her own, Rob wondered who or what she was. She was in dungarees and certainly looked like she'd peddled to Mongolia and back, yet she was on her own.

"Weird," said Sam.

"Hmmm," he agreed.

Rabbit Boy was back at the lads' house with a fire burning and tea and stew cooking. Beside him a pile of wood, enough for a few days, and also a few extra cans of stew.

"I'm so sorry," he said. "You must be knackered. I feel terrible, you know that don't you? Tea's on me tonight, for all of us."

"Don't be soft, lad," said Yorkie. "It's not your fault. What you been doing then?"

"Not a lot I'm afraid." His cheeks reddened as he returned to his fire. "Rewired a few coils, you know the dynamos? Mainly we just sat round drinking tea. Sorry, compared to what you've been through I feel a fraud."

"Where'd the wood come from?" asked Richard.

"They had a pile of it, told me to take some. I said we were struggling to get any. I liberated a few pairs of wire cutters too, you can open cans with them."

"Can we have one?" asked Sam.

"Yeah, that's why I got two. I thought to myself, better get one for Sal and the two others as well as us."

Sam gave Rob a knowing look.

"Thanks," said Sal. "I didn't feel comfortable borrowing that can opener."

Richard went for a shower before dinner while the others lay round on the floor, exhausted and close to sleep. After dinner, the three returned to the cottage, lit a fire, had a shower each and went to bed. The sun still not close to setting, Rob knew it was only about eight o'clock, but he didn't care, he could have slept for days, even weeks.

Waking from a dream, with a warm and starfish shaped Sam beside him, Rob could hear repetitive drumming. Waking more, he realised it was knocking on the door. Waking even more, he realised he didn't know the time and from the sound of the knocking, they were late.

Hastily pulling on his dungarees, he flew downstairs. Halfway down his legs locked, the pain of cycling returning. Bowlegged, he finished the last few steps.

Freddy, minus Ralf the Rod and Jane, was the knocker. "It's about ten past seven, Sal said to wake you?"

"Thanks mate. Don't want to be late."

"I do the fields too. I'll pop round again if you like. Just before eight, we meet just over the road."

"Thanks, pal." He slowly dragged his legs back upstairs and woke Sam and Sal despite their moaning. Rob washed first before lighting the fire and putting some stew and tea on. The first teabag was finally spent. Rob was still amazed just how much tea tasting water you could get from one bag.

Slowly Sam then Sal emerged, walking stiffly and looking tired despite their long sleeps. Supping fairly strong tea, still half asleep, they muttered how tired they were and how much their legs hurt.

Freddy returned and the three departed. Rob realised none of them had woken the others. His legs weren't up to running so he kept quiet, hoping somehow they'd woken up themselves.

Outside the shop, which Sal went into, were three queues of people.

"Ours is the last one," said Freddy. "Yours is the first," he pointed Sam towards the first queue. The others hadn't arrived, though Rob thought there was still time.

They did arrive late, but were still earlier than the coaches.

Stepping off the first coach, a guard said, "House renovation."

As the dissidents boarded the coach, Rob watched Sam all the way. As she climbed the stairs, she turned and tried to smile. Rob tried to smile back, but knew it wasn't convincing.

Half the people on the next coach got off along with two guards. One of the guards removed four spades from the luggage compartment. "Factory work," the other guard said as the second queue, including Quiety, got on. The guard joined them as the coach drove off.

The newcomers to the last group, the field workers including Rob and Richard were ordered to pick a spade and join the others walking towards the field behind the back of Rob's house. Two spades were left over; possibly indicating two hadn't made it in.

Digging over a dry, barren field by hand would be back breaking without having cycled fifty miles the day before. Exhausted within an hour, Rob went through the motions, every bone, joint and muscle aching. Richard was suffering worse. The hot midday sun made him sweat through every pore and his arms, not used to ever doing physical work, had turned to jelly by lunchtime.

As they sat in a small group during their lunch break, the guard came round and beckoned for a quiet word with Rob and Richard

"Your first day, isn't it?"

Rob nodded.

"I do understand. I don't expect too much the first week, just try your best and build your muscles up. No slacking though, I know the difference between being dog tired and slacking."

Richard thanked him, though it didn't come out too sincerely. The guard suggested thanks were not needed and sat under a tree on his own to eat his lunch.

The afternoon slipped away with each spade full of soil becoming smaller and smaller. By the end of the afternoon you could almost count the grains of dust on each spade.

Returning the short distance home, Rob and Richard were filthy with dusty soil. Being the first home, Rob made the fire and put the kettle and pot of stew on. Richard was initially going to stay for a cuppa, but found himself nodding off so made his excuses and left.

Sam came home within ten minutes, her hair a mess of white paint and plaster.

"How did it go?" he asked.

"Not too bad. Poor old Pat's been bricklaying all day. There's these half-finished flats a few miles away. I've been re-plastering walls then painting them. You look whacked, hun, was it hard work?"

"Digging a field by hand. The one behind the house funnily enough." He didn't think it was funny, just a turn of phrase. "At least I get to keep the spade."

She insisted Rob had the first shower. He guessed he must have smelt worse than he realised. The tepid water hitting his aching back, arms and legs did little to relax or soothe him. His dungarees were trashed, but he'd no chance of getting them dry by the morning. Plus, what else would he wear in the evening? Sam probably wouldn't mind him strutting round in his trollies, but Sal lived there too. He decided in the end to wash his pants and t-shirt. He'd have to go top and bottomless again this evening.

Downstairs, Sal had returned and was telling Sam about her day's work. Stacking shelves, drinking tea and talking to customers seemed to be as hard as it got in the world of retail. She did however manage to get some cabbage seeds from the shopkeeper.

"If you could dig over the garden, Rob," she said, "we could get them planted before it's too late."

Rob had taken a lot so far. Been on the run for days, trying his hardest to help everyone and keep spirits up. He'd also worked himself to the bone for two cans of stew. But this was the final straw. Feeling his eyes nearly pop out he took a deep breath in advance of the tirade he knew was coming from his mouth.

Sam had sensed this and interrupted him after the words, "For fuck's sake..." She explained to Sal that Rob had been digging all day and a busman's holiday was not needed.

Sal withdrew slightly, apologising profusely. She hadn't been thinking properly, she really hadn't. Throughout and after tea, an uncomfortable air between the three was only ended when Sal went for a shower.

"I know she's a thoughtless cow," said Sam, "but apologise anyway. It's hard enough here without fighting amongst ourselves."

"I know you're right," he said. "She just doesn't think sometimes, does she?"

Sam leaned against him, her bony elbow hitting his tender muscles. "Just apologise, hun. It's too small to fall out."

He agreed and after Sal came back down, he apologised. Sal was determined to apologise more, which in itself nearly caused another argument until Sam told both of them to, "Fucking shut it, I'm knackered."

"I will dig it," said Rob. "Just give me a day or two."

"I'll help," said Sal. "I can do a little bit in the evenings after the shop. Not tonight though, I think I need all my strength for tomorrow."

"We all do," said Sam, "my legs still ache from yesterday."

Rob took longer to fall asleep. Though tired, his annoyance at falling out with Sal weighed heavy. Don't let the bastards win by driving you apart, he kept telling himself.

Don't let them win.

Chapter 31

Four days flew by, each the same as before. Wake up, work, dinner, sleep. By the fifth day, both the peddling and ploughing had become easier for Rob. Keeping his head in a strong and much better place was the hard part.

Richard continued digging and peddling and was now officially thin and also starving all the time. He looked healthier in the face, almost a new person.

Yorkie continued plodding on in his own way, as did Quiety. Rabbit John brought back more and more booty from the Power station, a lost watch, a handful of fresh carrots and even an old transistor radio. The carrots were kept for their day off dinner but unfortunately as the radio had no battery, it was almost useless.

Sal continued meeting people and enjoying it. Over four days she managed to turn over a square yard of earth in the garden after her shifts. Sam said it was like watching Margo digging in the Good Life.

Sam, despite being on the verge of exhaustion all the time, continued to keep her spirits up which also kept the others going. She'd also befriended the mystery cleaner from the guard's house. It wasn't that Sam needed or even wanted other friends, it was just that the girl looked both lost and embarrassed by her day off job. The nosy cow in Sam needed to know more.

Waking after a long sleep, Rob was more than ready for the day off. Sam was already up: he could hear her and Sal downstairs. Joining them, Sam gave him a warm smile, reminding him of what they'd shared last night. After being dog tired the past four days, they'd somehow managed more than just a goodnight kiss.

"Ready for a day at the seaside, Rob?" asked Sal. She actually looked excited at the prospect.

"It's the day off I'm looking forward too."

Sam handed him a can of weak tea and sat beside him. "There's some stew on, when you're ready."

"Any sign of the lads?"

"John's out the back, digging the garden," said Sal.

"But it's his day off?"

"He says every day's a day off for him. He wanted to help."

Rob nodded. Though they'd made up over the digging incident, it was still a raw nerve. "Sorry," he said for the thirtieth time.

"We've done this before, Rob. I'm the one that's sorry."

"Whatever," said Sam. "Come on drink up, we've got sandcastles to build."

Picking up the other lads, they hit the road in search of Shanklin. Their tired legs protested after the first hour and two miles. According to the road signs, there were another four miles to go. Stopping for a break, they found shade from a tree.

"Like being in the New Forest isn't it?" said Quiety.

Yorkie nodded. "Aye. We must have walked miles you know."

"Most of it in circles, probably," said Rob.

Finishing their break, they continued. Occasionally, they met others walking the other way, or got overtaken by people from their own village. In the main though, the road was deserted.

By the time they arrived on the outskirts of the town at one o'clock, their legs didn't feel like they'd been given a day off.

The town, once a bustling resort, now had two large power plants dominating the skyline; one in each corner. More houses were empty than their own village. Rob guessed it was pot luck which way you came in. Apparently there were three ways into the island. Their entrance was not the usual route. Some of the houses had work parties preparing them for other, poor sods, while some looked beyond repair.

At a crossroads, with a view of the sea, the sign pointed inland for the hospital. Taking a moment, they looked at the beach. A shingle bay with the shoreline surrounded by shops that should have been rammed this time of year. Yet it was deserted. A row of empty, dirty squares marked where beach huts once stood. In front of them, two lines of twelve foot high razor wire reached to the sky. The beach deserted and cordoned off, only the armed guards parading between the two sets of wire could now enjoy it. Two high and hastily constructed watch towers stood at each end of the beach. Huge searchlights on top of the towers were for night time use.

"I guess we're not going for a paddle, then," said Richard.

"Suppose we should have guessed. Still, at least there are shops," said Sal.

They'd come armed with spare cans of stew and two pairs of wire cutters that John had lifted from work. They needed another watch. An alarm clock would be better, much better, but a watch would do. If any was left over, they fancied something to go with the carrots. Potatoes would be heaven. They'd bake them over the fire and have their chicken stew with real carrots. Chances were, they'd end up with nothing.

"We better get going," said Pat.

"Yeah, said Sam. "Should we meet you later or what?"

"We'll come with you," said Rob.

The others agreed. They were in this together. Plus, with the beach closed, there wasn't much else to do. Stew swapping and shopping wouldn't take all day.

Rob thought the hospital had once been a Victorian asylum or care home. Obviously a cottage hospital until recently, it seemed well equipped and still had that hospital smell. It wouldn't have been the only one on the island, but it was certainly the only one this side of the fence. Few people were waiting to be seen, but there were fewer doctors and nurses. Rob supposed they'd prioritised the best for the guards and soldiers on the other side of the fence. Dissidents' health came low down the pecking order. He wondered if the doctors and nurses were like them, here against their will. If so, who had they annoyed?

Yorkie was seen first after waiting an hour. Emerging with an old paper bag containing his prescription, he sat beside them. Now just after two in the afternoon, most of them were worried they'd be back late. It seemed only fair to wait for Sam to be seen: she'd have done the same for them.

Though Rob and Sal knew what Sam was seeing the doctor for, the other men didn't either seem bothered or have the balls to ask. Sam was eventually seen and came out by half two.

Sal found the shops, the shopkeeper's directions being fairly good. Most of the old parades and shopping centres were now just either stew shops or converted into flats. However, a row back from the seafront, a tiny row of old shops were the island's attempt at a bartering economy. Four shops: a grocers, a watch and clock repairer, a clothes shop, and a knick-knack shop.

The watch shop was locked, as they all were, but inside two men sat by candlelight, fiddling with complex springs, coils and tiny pieces of shaped metal. Sam knocked on the window, one of the men waved without looking up from the watch he seemed to be repairing.

As waves go, Rob was unsure if it was a go away or a hang on wave. They were hanging on anyway: they hadn't come this far for anything but a watch and food. The wave did mean wait; after a few minutes he stood up and unlocked the door.

"What have you got?" he asked.

"We're after an alarm clock and a watch," said Sam. "We've got a pair of wire-cutters and three cans of stew." Rob thought she was maybe pitching too high for her first attempt at bartering.

Shaking his head, he said, "You'll not get much for that. One or the other, not both."

Sam turned to the others, "Clock?"

They agreed, they didn't dare disagree.

"We'll have the clock then."

Yorkie handed over the pliers and Richard pulled out three stew cans from the front pocket of his dungarees. They'd been taking it in turns to carry them while walking, but he'd somehow ended up with them for longer than his turn.

The clock had once been a carriage clock. Not gold or anything expensive, like something from a seaside tat shop. During its overhaul, a different front had been secured: it looked suspiciously like a flattened stew can. The battery compartment had been replaced with a winding mechanism also of stew can origin.

"Can you make a whole clock from a stew can?" asked Quiety with real interest.

"Probably," he replied. "The springs are difficult. We reuse old ones."

All of them impressed, they thanked him and went to the grocers. Again, entrance was obtained by knocking and waiting.

The shop, musty from lack of cleaning fluids had mainly bare shelves. Cans, mainly stew, were stacked near the entrance, though they did sell other tins: corned beef, peach halves and a can of Scotch Broth. On each can was a label, expressing the cost in terms of stew cans. The corned beef was forty cans, peaches one hundred and the Scotch Broth thirty.

Yorkie pulled the other wire cutter from his pocket. "What do we get for this?"

Screwing up his face, he said, "Five cans of stew."

Looking round the rest of the store, a small basket with tiny new potatoes had 'five cans a pot' written on it. Mini carrots were also five cans each, as were apples. Runner beans, mini pea pods and tomatoes were two cans each. Rob knew it was still too early for most vegetables. They'd become used to year round imported fruit and veg. Returning to pre-globalisation seasons was hard to get used to.

After much deliberation, they decided to leave it. What good was one potato between five?

"That corned beef, eh?" said Yorkie as they walked to the other shops. "What I'd give for corned beef hash."

"With baked beans and gravy," said Quiety.

"Oh stop it you two," said Sal. "You're making me hungry."

"Steak and chips," said Richard. "Button mushrooms, onion rings, peas."

"Stop it."

The clothes shop resembled a charity shop, the only difference the cost. Nothing under fifty cans of stew was available. God only knew what the shopkeepers were doing with all the stew, it didn't bear thinking about. The cheapest items were dungarees and t-shirts, whatever had happened to the old owners, they were no longer in need of clothes. They'd been given a new lease of life and a quick rinse in water. Underwear appeared to be both scarce and the most expensive items.

Moving to the knick-knack shop, it sold literally everything you couldn't eat, wear or tell the time by. Richard gazed longingly at an old laptop in a corner. The shopkeeper told him it did work, obviously there was no electricity to test it, but the price of five hundred cans of stew was the sticking point.

Returning home, Sal promised she'd cook for them all and no one disagreed. By the time they arrived and warmed up the stew it was getting on for half seven.

Calling John in, who'd been outside digging again, Sal served the stew with the carrots John had obtained during the week.

The carrots were the highlight. By the time they were cut, each ended up with a tiny piece. Some ate it first, savouring the taste, while others kept it for last, like the treat it was. Rob ate his first. Sal had cooked it well. Still full of flavour and a real crunch when you bit through. It was nothing at all like the mushy red blobs that came in the mystery stew.

Finishing, they sat round, legs tired after the walk. As Sal started to speak, Rob could tell she'd been building up to this for a few days. They were hardly together anymore, but today, despite the waiting and disappointment over the prices, they'd rekindled the friendship they'd had while walking.

"I hope I'm not speaking out of turn here, I know Sam agrees with me and I think the rest of you do, but. Is there anything we can do? I mean the struggle. The struggle we were once making?"

Rob wasn't sure if it was good to bring this up or not. A little ray of hope held somewhere in the depths of your mind is better to hold onto than for it be destroyed by realising you're stuck pedalling for the rest of your life and the only good days will be the odd bottle of Beardy and Weirdy's cabbage wine.

"I don't think we've been here long enough yet to know." Rob looked at Sam, she was looking avidly at Sal. They'd obviously talked about this, but when? The other night when he fell asleep after dinner or when he was in the shower? Remembering her fragile state the other night, he didn't want to bring that back again. He thought a lot for Sal and didn't want her feelings hurt.

"I know, Rob, I'm talking general terms here. We don't know what's happening outside, I know that, but there must be something we can do in here to help?"

Rob thought it'd be just their luck that the Consortium had resigned, everyone was partying and they'd forgotten to tell the Isle of Wight.

"Someone here must be doing something," said Quiety. "I'd be surprised if there weren't loads of little groups trying to find ways to help. After all, it's the reason we're here. You don't stop believing after you've been caught."

"I still like Sam's canned horse of Troy idea," said Richard. He'd obviously meant to lighten the mood, not to be flippant. Either way, he was ignored.

"We need to find other groups," said Yorkie. "Join together."

Rob expected him to add, 'Unity is powerful,' but he didn't.

The conversation fizzled out. It was too soon to plan anything, and they were too tired anyway. They'd barely got their bearings here. What it had done, which may have been Sal's intent, was to keep the spark alive. To make them look at everything and everyone differently. To believe again.

Chapter 32

Another week rolled by, the days much like the first. Sal earned her first can of stew from the power plant on her fifth attempt, though Rob thought the bearded dungaree assessing her tachograph had recognised and pitied her. Sal was also getting closer to Ralf, if they hadn't already been close at some time before. Rabbit Boy John had finally accepted they had nothing and was starting to show a friendlier side.

The now thin Richard and Rob had become good digging buddies, and were ploughing at a good pace three fields away. Rob himself had noticed his muscles were bulging, both legs and arms, and the work was becoming easier each day.

Sam was also growing muscles, though she still retained her petite figure. Through sheer nosiness and persistence, her friendship grew with Sharon, the guard's cleaner. It turned out Sharon had only been on the Island a month herself. She'd been bought over on her own from Beaulieu and had drawn the shortest straw by meeting Frank the guard on her own. Unaware of what was going on, and with only the less than pure morals of Frank for guidance, she'd become his live-in cleaner. Sharon insisted nothing had happened between them, he repulsed her, but as she was in his spare room, she knew one day it would come to a head.

Yorkie and Quiety were getting on with it in their own steadfast way. Moaning about each other's snoring and sleepwalking had become regular jokes.

Beardy and Weirdy had become occasional evening visitors to the cottage. Their own sense of humour and Beardy's tales of the telephone system and his views on the collapse of the nation had become popular evening stories.

John's procurement of bits and bobs continued with a battery for the radio. Although the lack of unbiased Consortium radio channels was a problem, they did find a Swiss station broadcast on long wave. This was welcome in, what they thought was, unbiased news of world events. The only problem was it was broadcast in French. Though they all knew a smattering of words, Richard, Ralf and Sal seemed to be able to follow parts of the whistling transmission and translate it. It seemed Europe had descending further into chaos. Spain and Portugal had embraced the Consortium. Rob wondered if they had chicken stew or some canned version of Paella.

The week's highlight was John's find of three disposable razors. Obviously all the men, except Beardy, wanted one of the two spare razors. Bartering had got to the giddy heights of ten cans of stew before Richard suggested they could employ some form of futures arrangement.

The promising of future vegetables grown in the garden, or Cabbage Futures as Sam had named them, looked set to become a valuable and well used trading method until Quiety pointed out that Richard's last attempt at monetising future commodities had caused all this shit anyway. Sam continued with a dogged, almost Rottweiler persistence until Quiety and Richard gave up. Rob got one of the spare blades, Yorkie the other.

Midweek produced a memorable evening as Beardy attempted to answer Sam's question of, "We've got nothing to offer the world now. Just how did we become so crap at making stuff?"

"Globalisation." His huge beard bobbed up and down with each syllable.

"But why? That's what I never got. Why did we ever let them make all our stuff for us abroad?"

"Short-termism?" said Rob, though he really wasn't sure if he'd missed the point.

"Supposedly it was specialisation. That's what Adam Smith said," Beardy continued. "But you have to go back to the seventies to see the problem."

No one else butted in so he continued. "Strikes, ever increasing wage demands and the start of competition from overseas goods. Massive inflation by a spike in the oil price left us pretty clear then that living standards weren't going to rise for a long time. That, in my opinion is where it started to go wrong."

He ran a finger through his beard, almost losing it. "What we were looking at then was chaos. Wages couldn't carry on increasing if we were to make everything ourselves. The unions were almost running the country, but we were heading downhill fast. It was a real crunch moment. Luckily, a bit too luckily in my opinion, North Sea oil and gas were discovered. We gained some protection from future spikes, but only until it runs out."

"Wages and the unions were still a problem, but the milk snatcher sorted that out."

Yorkie murmured something in disgust. Beardy nodded his head. "She went too far too quickly, that's without a doubt. We started selling our assets. The company silver. All those flotations. Again, that was just short term gain to hide where we were really going."

"This is where we get to globalisation. All through the eighties, more and more things were getting cheaper. Household goods: tellys, washing machines. Personal goods too, clothes, shoes. Everything was cheaper to import than to make ourselves. The reason, labour costs. We were priced too high and out of the world economy. Cheaper to pay some poor Chinese sod a bowl of rice a day to make a pair of shoes and sail it over here, than to make them ourselves."

He sighed and stared at the fire.

"But why," said Sam. "Why let it happen?"

"Living standards." He looked lost in the fire. "If we'd have been self-sufficient, white goods would have cost a higher and higher amount of our take home pay. Living standards would have dropped gradually and noticeably. There's a huge rebalancing going on. West to the East. We're lowering our standard of living, they're increasing theirs. Being self-sufficient would have made it too obvious. It would have happened too quickly. No politician would have wanted that on their watch. As Rob said, short termism all the way."

Rob nodded, though he guessed everyone knew it was a lucky guess.

"The real criminal thing," Beardy continued. "Was the few that got super rich over the past few decades. Billionaires never existed twenty years ago, now there's loads of them. Like an elite, they are. They're not eating stew and drinking cabbage wine, that's for sure."

He looked back at the fire, lost in thought.

"Of course," Richard continued where Beardy left off. "The other unspoken thing is the expected life of white goods." He paused. "Years ago, you'd buy a telly or hoover. It'd last ten, maybe fifteen years. But, when China and the Far East specialised in making them, they could chuck out enough units to sell the entire world one every two years. All that investment and labour they used to do it, they had to make sure we needed a telly every other year."

"Cheap parts?" asked Rob.

Richard nodded. "They probably only saved a few quid a unit, but they made stuff almost guaranteed to break down before it was five years old. They knew exactly when repeat customers would be buying again."

"We've all been conned. Selling our companies to foreign investors and States and using that money to buy goods off them that were not only guaranteed to put our own workers out of jobs, but also to keep theirs in constant employment. And then, when the nation couldn't balance its books anymore, we'd borrow more money off them to keep buying their tat. Every year a larger percentage of our tax went in paying interest on the borrowed money we'd never be able to repay. The circle was complete. Gradual shift from West to East. The only winners here were the rich who planned it."

It went on. Rob wasn't sure how much of it was the truth but, despite his physical exhaustion, it did keep him awake a few hours thinking about it.

Their day off was spent walking and gathering fire wood, which was now rapidly running out as summer faded into autumn. They spent most of the afternoon devising a way of turning piles of leaves into something burnable, though the practicalities kept floundering.

Eating dinner, stew plus a bonus runner bean each, at the lads' house, Beardy, Weirdy and Sharon joined them and were in good spirits until the conversation turned to the struggle.

"I still think we don't know what pot we're pissing in yet," said Yorkie. "Excuse my French, ladies," he added.

"Maybe," said Sal. "But from what I can see, everyone on the island has organised themselves into little groups. Without any definite plans, we're going to end up just competing with each other, even fighting each other."

"But," said Ralf. "The point is they're expecting some kind of action or reaction from us. Chuck a load of rebels together and they're going to rebel. About three months ago, there was a riot in a village on the west side. The guards and army seemed to come from nowhere. Helicopters, trucks of troops, they even scrambled a jet. Blew a whole street back to the Stone Age. Fifty dead."

Everyone sighed. Rob had heard rumours that something had happened, but no one had so far wanted to talk about it.

"Everyone must be doing something though," said Richard. "All those people peddling every day? We can't be the only people sitting around like this. We need to find others and join together. Rioting's out of the question, I know, but there must be something we can do?"

"As I said lads and lasses, bide our time," said Yorkie. "We've only been here two weeks. Something will happen. We'll think of something. If we rush into a half-cocked plan, we risk losing everything."

Rob saw most of them nod agreement. "Suppose it wouldn't hurt if we tried to make friendships though. I don't mean ask openly or admit to anything, just try and get to know others outside of the group?"

No one disagreed with him, though they advised caution and discretion. They decided not to discuss it again until next weekend. Beardy reckoned one of his cabbages would be ready by then, if the guards or the slugs didn't get it first. Sharon had the last words of the evening by wondering aloud if there was a difference between the two.

Chapter 33

Sal pedalled her way to two more cans of stew over the week as the gang fitted into their routine. John procured a bottle of 'Two-in-one' shampoo and conditioner, for which the four women were forever in his debt. Richard was now as slim as Rob, though he did point out his large mass of loose skin would never make him a pin up. Sharon had moved into Ralf's spare room, which highly annoyed Frank the guard. After some deliberation, Frank decided he no longer needed a cleaner and sent her to work the fields with Richard and Rob. Sharon and Richard seemed to hit it off, despite the age gap, and spent much of the day talking while digging.

Sharon wasn't the only one to find alternative sleeping arrangements. On the fourth day of the week, Sal failed to come home, leaving Rob and Sam to speculate that Sal and Ralf had rekindled what they reckoned was once there.

Their day off spent again in Shanklin, they returned with a small can of spam and five tiny potatoes, it having cost them twenty cans of stew, two metres of electrical cable and one of Beardy's small cabbages.

Their two course dinner of spam, potato and cabbage, followed by a stew desert, felt like a banquet. With the large amount of cabbages coming to fruition over the Island, Rob did wonder if the Consortium were missing a trick by not harnessing wind power instead of pedal power.

The conversation turned as darkness fell. Continuing where they'd left off the previous week. Though they'd all met people over the week, most were coy about getting close. Rob himself had talked at length with another digger called Brian about the system and the island. Brian seemed defeated, resigned to end his days here digging and peddling.

Despite them trying, only John seemed to be allowed into the other, small groups in the village. Of course his job as a power station technician was the cause. Everyone wanted to be his friend. So far he'd gleaned no information.

They decided to subtly keep at it. Someone somewhere must be doing something.

"Any ideas over the past week?" asked Sal. Her face and the way she'd changed the topic showed she had at least one idea herself.

"Still think it's too early," said Yorkie. "Contacts and lay of the land, that's what we got to find."

"Funnily enough," said Ralf, "That was our idea too, well, in a different way to how you mean it."

Rob knew wasn't the only one confused by that.

"We feel that no matter who we meet here, if a big change is going to happen, we need to be on the other side of the fence."

"You've probably got a point, but getting over that fence is the problem," said Sam.

"I think I might have found a way," said Ralf. Beside him, Sal looked very excited; too excited.

"Go on," said Yorkie.

"We can forget tunnelling, cutting the fence or swimming, it's what they're expecting. Their weak point is the place they haven't thought of."

Rob thought he was milking this for every bit.

"It was actually Sam who put the idea in my head the other night, when she pointed out the dual meaning of the word underground?"

Sam smiled then looked confused. "The underground? Is there tube trains here then?"

"No, actually yes there were, but they used to run overland. Old Central Line trains. That's not what I meant though. What connects the two halves of the Island?"

Rob really wished he'd just get on with it.

Smugly, he continued, "Drains."

"Drains?" said Sam. "Are you serious? You mean sewer pipes go under the fence?"

She wasn't the only one with a disgusted look on her face, Sal looked surprisingly happy with the idea. Rob guessed the plan didn't actually involve her wading through shitty sewers during peak cabbage season.

"Yes, I'm deadly serious. The first trek would be purely for getting directions and seeing what's at the other end. After all, we don't know where it ends, do we?"

"What then though?" said Quiety. "How do we get to the mainland? I'm pretty sure we can't just get on the hovercraft anymore."

"Well," Ralf said, "as I say the plan isn't finalised, but when we crossed in the bus, there were Lorries carrying stew, troop movements and a lot of other vehicles. There's a lot coming in and out. It looked chaotic."

Looking chaotic and being chaotic were two different things. The Consortium prided itself on efficiency and paperwork. "Surely a gang of sewage covered dungaree wearers couldn't just get on a ferry?"

"As I said, early days. There's a lot to think about. We'd need clothes and somewhere to freshen up obviously. There are empty houses on the other side of the fence. It's just an idea at the moment, remember. We're just kicking it through."

Almost all of them turned up their noses at the buzzword Ralf churned out.

"It's the only way I can see of getting over, or rather under, the fence."

They were all quiet, pondering the idea while Richard and Sharon put a fresh pot of tea on.

Finally, Beardy broke the silence. "Did anyone else have any ideas? His beard, which Rob swore was growing faster than ever, swung nearly six inches each way as his mouth opened and closed.

The evening ended earlier than normal, but they all had plenty to think about.

Chapter 34

Another week, another gallon of stew. Rob's carrots were just starting to poke through the earth, as were his cabbages. Beardy seemed to have an EEC sized mountain of cabbages he was only too glad to share. His wine was fermenting well, underneath the stairs, though Rob still had mixed feelings about it.

On the day before their day off, something happened that set curtains wagging: the arrival of a minibus. Sat outside the guard's house overnight, everyone wondered what it was there for.

Everything became clear at four in the morning as an armed guard burst into Rob and Sam's room. His assault rifle had a light attachment fixed, nearly blinding Rob in the murky darkness. "Get dressed and be downstairs in two minutes," was all the guard said.

Instantly the dread Rob thought had gone returned. He'd got used to expecting the early morning call, but after everything they'd been through, he thought it was over. Life was just pedalling and stew with some freedom. The armed guard bought back the fear held deep down.

He wasn't alone in thinking that. Sam was visibly shaking as she pulled on her paint splattered dungarees. He pulled her close before they went downstairs.

Leaving the house first, with Sam behind, Rob noticed the van was now parked opposite the cottage. Rubbing sleep from his eyes, he took in the three armed guards standing opposite and the queue of people in front of them. The four lads were there and beside them Ralf, Sal and Sharon from three doors down. They looked as terrified as he felt.

His heart dropped. Just when they'd got in a routine. Just when they'd started to plan escape, though admittedly it was a crap plan. Just as it was their day off too. Rob's only good thought was at least Beardy and Weirdy weren't here. They'd escaped whatever was happening.

The guards were in full combats and heavily armed, but most worryingly, they wore balaclavas. Another guard stepped out of the minibus. Though suited and gun totting, it was Frank with that annoying grin that badly needed wiping off. "Good morning. I'm

212

sorry to get you up so early, but needs must. We needed some volunteers to pick some vegetables and, as it's your day off I knew you'd all volunteer. Of course, you'll be paid in stew. You can consider it overtime, can't you?"

He paced up and down in front of the other guards, adopting his most upright posture. Any minute Rob was expecting him to say, "Vee have orders that must be obeyed."

Stopping in front of Sharon, he moved nearer. Sharon tried to back off, and Ralf moved slightly in front of her.

Staring straight in Sharon's terrified eyes, he whispered, "Of course, maybe I could get other people to work today instead? What do you think, Sharon? Is there anything else you'd prefer to do today?"

Rob grabbed Sam's arm. The guards in front were still aiming their weapons at them. He'd no idea how this was going to end, but giving them a reason to fire would be too easy a way out.

Sharon was about to speak when Ralf stepped to his left, completely in front of her. "We don't mind overtime." Though his voice was croaky, Rob was impressed with his bottle. Since they'd met, Rob had his card marked as a spineless television producer. He came from a world of three hour lunches, procedure meetings and seminars about feelings. When the day and time had come though, he'd shown up.

Turning round, Frank said, "Ah, the spirit of comradeship. The Consortium will approve of this." He walked back to the other guards then turned. "All of you, on the bus now."

Cramped into a fifteen-seater minibus, with two guards on the back seat and the other up front, Frank drove them through the dark and windy roads. With only the misfiring chug of the engine to fill their ears, they remained silent, wondering where the hell they were going.

Seated beside Rob was Sam, with Sharon on the other side of her. He could almost feel Sharon shaking through Sam. Sam was holding her hand, occasionally they'd give each other looks and smiles. Unsurprisingly, Sharon looked sorry for the trouble she'd caused. Rob knew she shouldn't be. If it wasn't this, it would have been something else.

The road widened. Rob presumed it was the main circular road round the island. With the first rays of morning light in the sky, the fence loomed ahead. Lit up, it could be seen for miles, even at night. Snaking across the countryside, the fence's watchtowers could be seen but their guards couldn't. Approaching the gate, where the road was partially blocked by concrete posts, guards lined the fence. All of them were armed. None of them looked afraid to use their weapons.

The gate opened as they approached. Frank parked on the other side and guards lined the side of the van. Opening the driver's door, Frank got out and handed over a bunch of papers, saluting afterwards.

Acknowledging the salute, the guard checked the papers closely then thrust them back into Frank's dirty hands. Re-entering the minibus, he sat down. "Exciting isn't it boys and girls? Nearly there now, nearly there."

Rob felt Sam's fist curl up. Although seated two rows back, he knew she could still reach him. He also knew that, although one punch might make her, Sharon and the rest of them feel better, it wouldn't end this. He grabbed her fist and looked her in the eyes. Those pleading, doey eyes that could make him do anything she wanted tried to plead with him. Just one slap, they said, please. Somehow, Rob shook his head. This wasn't the time.

Setting off again, the rapidly rising sun bathed the northern part of the Island. The sea met a beach in the distance; though unguarded by the mesh-like barbs of Shanklin, it still had a guard tower in the middle.

This part of the island seemed deserted; no man's land. Driving through, they looked through the windows obscured by condensation. In the distance, some yachts and boats lay in a harbour. Rob guessed they were nearing Ryde.

Slowing, the minibus spluttered as it halted in a lay by. Beside them, the field was full of ripe runner beans, carefully grown on cane supports.

"Here we are, bean pickers," said Frank. "Okay two rules. One, don't try to escape. Two, we'll shoot if you try. Clear?"

The rear doors were opened by the two balaclava'd guards. They gestured with their guns, and the gang departed the van. The morning was still fresh. Only Sal had had the foresight to bring her jumper while the rest of them shivered in the damp morning air.

"In the field, move. As I said, don't try and escape, these bullets are valuable you know."

Sal led them through the gate and into the field beyond. The ground damp underfoot, they plodded round the side of the field, the ripe beans filling their eyes. Birds and occasional seagulls fled at their approach, Rob wondered how much of the produce was lost to birds; the scarecrows weren't doing anything like their proper job.

"Stop," Frank ordered.

They halted by a wooden shed and turned. Lined up, the four guards stood in front, rifles in hand. Rob wondered just how easy it would be for Frank and co to end it here. Maybe that was the intent? True, there's nothing like a woman spurned, but a spurned guard-cum-mayor of a village? He reached for Sam's hand and squeezed it. He could feel her trembling. He was shaking too. This could be the end. Shot dead and buried in a shallow grave. That twat would probably make them dig their own grave, too. He was just that kind of bastard.

"What I'm going to say is going to come as a shock, but please listen until the end. It's unavoidable that I had to do things this way, I hope you'll realise this soon."

Shit, thought Rob. This was it. End of the line. Under his breath his whispered, "I love you," to Sam. She squeezed his hand.

"We really haven't got much time, so I'll be quick," he continued. "Firstly, I apologise for being an arse at times. Especially to you, Sharon, but you know why."

She nodded. She didn't look as scared now, not half as scared as in the minibus. In fact she was almost smiling.

"There are cameras everywhere on the island, you see. Very little privacy. Every conversation gets recorded, every piece of dissent seen and crushed."

So that was it, thought Rob. They'd heard a meeting. They know we're thinking of escaping through the sewer. He thought of running towards the guards. Though armed, they'd maybe never fired one before. It was pointing down too, Rob was sure he could reach him before he could shoot.

"Sorry, rambling aren't I." He smiled that smug arsed smile that still needed wiping from his face. "Basically, you're all free."

"What?" they replied as one, apart from Sharon.

The two faceless guards pulled off their balaclavas. Rob couldn't believe his eyes. Beardy and Weirdy dressed in full army combats. Weirdy looked so unbelievably manlike inside her flak jacket, Rob couldn't help but shudder. Beardy had shaved most of his beard so he could fit the remains inside his balaclava. They looked apologetic, so sorry for deceiving them.

"We're escaping in about half an hour," said Frank. He looked at Sharon. She smiled. The other guard, thus far nameless unloaded his gun to show they were safe, no hard feelings.

"Our guns weren't loaded," said Beardy.

Rob noticed Richard was smiling too. He'd not appeared too nervous during the journey. Either he'd gone rock hard overnight, or he knew about this.

"Sorry we couldn't tell you," said Frank. "It really had to be kept a secret. I'm as much a prisoner here as you are. I can't leave, go out, I work seven day weeks and the food I get is not much better than yours. Okay, so it's not stew every day, but as I say, I'm as much as prisoner here as you. Anyway, while listening to one of your chats, we've got cameras recording in all the houses you see, that was when I heard about Richard's gold in Switzerland."

Richard was smiling. He was in on it. Sam looked furious, Rob was glad he'd let go of her hand, she looked ready to hurt someone. Turning at Rob, her eyes bulging, fists waiting, she shouted, "Did you know?"

"No, course not, sorry. No I didn't."

"Sam," said Frank. Though still a little slimy, he'd lost some of his grease ball quality. "Jim and Brenda came to me four months ago. They knew I was unhappy. We've been waiting for the right moment. This is the only time of year it's possible for me to leave the fence as well as you."

"I got hold of some extra uniforms. The original plan was for me and Dougie here." The other guard nodded. "To take a work party out with Jim and Brenda, then we'd escape. There are loads of boats down there." He pointed at the harbour. "With the right pass, you just take one out and pretend you're on patrol round the Island."

"Then," said Weirdy, "young Sharon turned up on her own. Well we couldn't leave her could we?"

"Look," said Frank. "We can carry this on later, but we need to get changed now, before we're spotted. He opened the shed door and pulled a tarpaulin from the floor. "Ladies first," he said. "Can you go inside and get changed. Sorry Sam but they didn't do uniforms your size, you're a nurse I'm afraid, best we could do."

Shrugging her shoulders she joined Sal and Sharon inside the shed. "You could have told me," Sam said to Sharon.

"Why?" asked Yorkie. Rob noticed him staring with pure hatred at Frank. He looked more than ready to knock his block off.

"Why what? Why are you coming with us? As I said, Richard's gold. Our original plan was to sail to Spain, sell the boat and make a new life, but things kept changing. First Sharon arrived. Brenda made me promise to take her under my wing, which I did until we overheard Richard talking about gold in a Swiss bank."

"A little gold buys a lot in this new world. And the sort of size Richard was talking about buys enough for all of us. So Sharon moved out and into Ralf's place and popped the question to Richard during their digging."

Richard shrugged his shoulders. "It was a no brainer, wasn't it?"

"But that's your gold," said Quiety, "not ours. Your life's earnings, you can't give that up for us. For him." He looked at the smooth Frank.

Richard shrugged his shoulders. "You can't take it with you, can you? This is my only chance of using some of it."

Sam opened the shed door and emerged in a nurse's uniform. "Shoes are a bit tarty and me legs are in a shocking state," she said.

Rob couldn't disagree. Though gorgeous in the blue uniform, the white stilettos on her feet and the hairs poking through her tights ruined the effect.

Sal came out looking like she was about to rouse the troops with a weather forecast in the way Vera Lynn might once have, while Sharon looked lost inside a large uniform.

"In you go, lads," said Frank. "One of you is going to have to be the doctor."

Rob thought it only fitting that he should take that job.

Chapter 35

Back in the minibus, heading for the harbour, the group of guards, soldiers, and the doctor and nurse kept quiet. Rob had so many questions running round his head he didn't know where to start.

"You could have told us, Richard," said Quiety.

"I couldn't," he said. "As Frank said, there's cameras everywhere. I found one in our house, just above the corner you sit in, Pat. These past few days have been a nightmare. Sorry, Sharon, but I half wondered if you were mad at first, it was only when I saw Frank and he winked at me that I realised this was for real."

Rob was pretty sure there was more to the story. Why would Frank be bothered with the rest of them? He only needed Richard to get the gold. Rob reckoned Richard must have insisted they all go along, everyone, including Rabbit Boy.

"What happens next is important, guys," said Frank. Though he'd become almost human recently, using the word 'guy' reminded Rob of what he really was: the sort of man who makes you buy freedom. "When we get to the harbour, me & Dougie will get on a boat and head for France, then Switzerland. Sharon, you're welcome to join us if you want?"

Rob guessed that was Frank's last chance chat up line for hooking Sharon. She stayed silent.

"You have to drive and get on the ferry. The paperwork's here." He held up a wadge of official forms, all stamped in triplicate. "Your story is, the Heart Surgeon, that's you, has been working at the Island's Hospital but is needed in London. His wife is a nurse and the rest of you, all nine, are guards being redeployed to London. As I said, the paperwork's there." He turned round and shoved it into Richard's hands.

"Where's the guarantee we won't be arrested?" said Quiety.

"There's no guarantee in life, pal. Don't forget it'll take you as long to get to London as it will us to cross the channel. We're risking our lives here too. We might get blown up a mile from Portsmouth."

Rob could only hope that Frank couldn't swim.

Approaching the harbour, that was probably once called a marina by an over-enthusiastic council, Frank and Dougie pulled over and got out of the van. Opening the back door, they pulled out two of the ten army kitbags. Daybreak was now lighting the sky and with it, the chill lifting from the air.

"Remember," said Frank, "First ferry's in about quarter of an hour. You should have plenty of time to get there. Be lucky."

He waited, possibly for thanks or acknowledgement.

"See you then," Richard said.

"Okay. Remember what I said, Richard, if there's a problem when I get to Switzerland, I'll find you."

"There won't be a problem. All those details I gave you are correct. You know the gold's there, we checked it online."

"Okay. See you folks."

Quiety climbed into the driving seat, rammed the gearstick into first and pulled away. Rob turned to Sam and shook his head. Her headshake in return said she was as puzzled as himself.

A minute up the road, Yorkie turned to Richard. "Did you give him the right details?"

"Yeah. I had to prove it was there so we used his computer to go online. Due to the blocks and restrictions, it was hard work connecting overseas, I had to use two proxies and almost rewrite the browser. Eventually, we connected and the online statement showed the amount of allocated gold in the account. It's not a secret box in a vault or anything. It's allocated gold, you like share it with hundreds of others. You can still withdraw it though. So I gave him the username and password."

"Why though," said Sal. "Why give it all to him. Why didn't you go with him?"

"Well." His eyes twinkled. "When my mate first saw this coming and told me that banks, currencies and even governments might fail, he told me to get out of cash and into Swiss gold, which I did." He paused, the smile growing. "He also advised me not to leave it all in one bank. Spread it around three or four, he said, it'll avoid the risk and hassle if one of them fail. Also, it's useful in case you need to pay a ransom or have to divulge the details. So, I set up four accounts. One of them had hardly anything in, just ten grams of gold. An almost worthless amount."

"I think I get where this is going," said Sal.

"Yeah." He smiled further. "When I said I had to rewrite the browser, what I meant to say was, I hijacked the script and told it that when it displayed grams it would put the word kilo in front of it. That's kind of why I didn't want to go with them. They're going to be a bit disappointed when they find out there's ten grams and not ten kilograms."

With the ferry port approaching, Quiety slowed down so they could run through their stories again.

Though the northern part of the island was devoid of the fences and gates the southern had, the port was different. Entering the complex, the road narrowed as concrete blocks lined the path, coming to a head at a checkpoint. As the minibus stopped, Rob wasn't the only one taking a deep breath.

Not trusting Frank one bit, he wondered just how genuine the forms, transfer notes and ration books were. The only benefit was the three guns they had aboard and the small amount of ammo inside. Not enough to hijack the ferry, but enough to get them away from the port and back onto the island.

"Papers," the guard said.

Quiety handed them over, his hands shaking. Rob tried hard to look like a stern doctor, he could see how hard the others were trying to relax.

"What's this, fancy dress?" The guard gestured at Rob.

Quiety forced a laugh. "Wanted in the big city. Heart Surgeon."

The guard nodded and rifled through the papers. Looking at each of them in turn. His eyes stopped on Sal. She'd tied her hair back and rolled her collars up. Without make up and in a soldier's uniform, she looked little like the nation's favourite that everyone knew. She did however, look familiar. Familiar enough to warrant a second look.

"I'm sure I've seen you before."

Sal shrugged.

"You look familiar?"

"I was on Crackerjack when I was younger?" She tried to laugh.

The guard laughed. "Crackerjack, eh? You still got your pencil?"

Sal smiled. "Oh no, I lost that years ago."

Banging on the roof, the guard handed back the paperwork. "Go on."

Quiety thanked him and drove onto the ferry.

Only one car and a lorry shared their voyage. Guards stood along the top of the ferry, though they were concerned with the outside, not inside. The car, a rare sight in itself, was a Jaguar with a single occupant in the back and a guard in the driving seat. However much Rob tried not to stare, he kept looking at the passenger, trying to work out who he was. The lorry resembled the one they'd travelled in a few weeks ago, no doubt it was returning to pick up more dissenters.

Half way across the water, Quiety said, "We're not going to make London, there's less than a quarter in this tank. Doubt we'll get as far as Winchester."

"Bastard," said Yorkie.

"That wasn't the agreement," said Beardy. "It was supposed to be a full tank. Are you sure the needle's working right."

"Don't know," said Quiety. "There's one way to find out and I don't fancy trying."

"That kind of ruins the plan," said Weirdy. Beardy put his arm round her shoulders, Rob shivered.

"We'll have to find somewhere in Southampton," said Sam. "There's loads of unused and empty flats. We'll find somewhere."

"Good idea," said Rob. This had happened so quickly he'd not had chance to think if Sam would want to even continue. Sure, they'd got close, but Southampton was her home. A million other unanswered questions were still knocking on his door. What do we do for food? How long can we survive on the run again?

"Did you make any sort of plan, Richard?" asked Yorkie, who seemed to be on the same thought pattern.

"Not really, I just presumed we'd, well, do something."

As the ferry pulled into Southampton, Yorkie said, "Southampton sounds good. For now at least."

Exiting the ferry and onto the car-less streets of Southampton, Sam showed Quiety the way to the unfinished housing estate. Dressed in combats, they stood out a mile. Driving any sort of vehicle stood them out further. It was clear they needed to dump the minibus and change into the civvies hidden in the kitbags. Though early, the city was just waking: the odd person walked to work and a half filled bus passed. Driving past once thriving shops and markets, the City had lost something Rob couldn't put his finger on.

Pulling into a side street, Quiety said, "We got to be quick, it's mainly the trousers that are giving us away."

Beardy, at the back next to Weirdy, threw the kit bags down the minibus. Richard took them one by one, tossing them in various directions. Within minutes they were stripping down and re-clothing. Some of the sizes were wrong and needed to be swapped, Richard in particular appeared to have ended up with Weirdy's clothes.

Leaving the van, carrying a kit bag each, they walked at a good pace. Sam said they were two miles from the flats, but they made the walk in less than twenty minutes. The newly half-built flats towered over the city. Once offering a luxury lifestyle and views across the Solent, they now offered only pigeons and seagulls somewhere to sleep. Though the front entrance was still sheeted and padlocked, the grille was off its hinges. Twisting it, they gained entrance and climbed the stairs.

The first three floors were empty and had been stripped of anything sellable. Moving up, the fourth floor was inhabited. A group of young men came out of the first flat on hearing their entry.

"Who are you?" one of them said. Maybe eighteen, his features were taut and his clothes fairly clean. A pleasant smile wasn't shared by one of his mates, who was built in a way Rob could only term a knuckle scraper.

"Like you, I think," said Ralf.

As the rest of them climbed the stairs behind Rob, and with just Ralf in front, he could see the three faces drop as they realised the sheer number arriving. He sensed they weren't the first to seek shelter here. Maybe people had tried to burgle it? Perhaps guards made visits, searching for people like them. Whatever it was, the three young lads were scared, but they also looked like they'd stand their ground.

"What's in your bags?"

Rob knew that carrying army kit bags wasn't the best idea. They were so obvious. They'd wanted to keep the uniforms and paperwork, it might come in handy.

"Long story," said Ralf. "Look, we err, we're just looking for somewhere to hide out. Just until we find somewhere. Are there any free flats?"

The three lads were the oddest estate agents Rob had ever seen, but they were bouncers of a sort. They'd made this their home and were choosy about their neighbours.

"Suppose." He looked at the others for agreement. The knuckle scraper stared straight ahead, while the other nodded reluctantly. "Follow me."

Leading them up the stairs, he introduced himself as Johnny. They'd come from the West Midlands, looking for passage across the channel. Struggling to raise the money needed, they ended up in the flats. They weren't the only occupants, whole families who couldn't find work lived on the fifth floor, the only other option being the work camps.

Though Ralf said they were on the run, he didn't say where from. The lad seemed genuine enough, but some things were on a need to know basis, and he didn't need to know.

"Still got water here, don't know for how much longer." He pointed to the four flats on the sixth floor. This was the last finished floor, the two above were partially finished and above that a wire mesh grew uncompleted into the sky.

"Thanks," said Ralf. "What do you do for food?"

"Beg, borrow and steal. Mainly steal."

"I think we've got some ration books somewhere. Not sure how legit they are, but if we get some food, we'll repay you."

"Thanks. You don't need to, but thanks anyway."

Splitting the four flats was time consuming. By midday, Rob, Sam and Richard were at number one, Beardy, Weirdy and Rabbity, number two, Quiety and Yorkie took three with Ralf, Sal and Sharon in the last one.

Number one was bare. Just the essentials in the bathroom and kitchen remained. No beds or bedding, not even carpets, just bare concrete floors. Further inspections on the kitbags revealed a Doctors ration book and more travel papers.

With mid-afternoon came a feeling of boredom and hunger. Speaking to the lads downstairs, Ralf discovered there was a shop nearby which didn't ask too many questions over ration books.

Convening a quick meeting, they decided Rob and Sam should check it out. After all, they were the only ones with paperwork that listed their jobs as something other than guard.

The lads told them to be careful as they left. You never know who's watching, they said. Nervously, Rob pushed the door open, looking out and around the fenced off ex-building site. The late afternoon rain had kept most people who weren't working indoors. The streets were deserted as they walked towards the shop. Sam gave Rob a walking commentary on the streets of Southampton, pointing out old haunts and good pubs before they'd closed forever.

Her spirits were good, Rob supposed his would be if they'd ended up in Basingstoke, but it was clear there was something she wanted to do. He thought he knew what. "Do you want to visit your mum?"

"Have you become a mind reader? I was just thinking that."

"Where does she live?"

"A few miles from here. I'd like to, maybe not today, we need food don't we. Tomorrow?"

"It's a date," he said.

The shop, an old warehouse style cash and carry, resembled a stew depot. Very few questions were asked as Rob and Sam filled their baskets with stew and handed over the six forged ration books.

Leaving, they returned via backstreets to the flats. Borrowing a saucepan and an old brazier from a family on the floor below, Sam and Sal heated the stew in the corridor. The smoke quickly filled the stairs and empty lift shaft. With no electricity or fireplaces in their flats, they soon realised that cooking and keeping warm would be a problem.

The evening was spent talking and joking about their escape. Richard in particular was on great form as he tried to explain what the look on Frank's face would be when he discovered the lack of gold in Switzerland.

Ralf meanwhile explained the flats did have electricity connected, but the power cables terminated the floor beneath. The other flats were using small electric hobs and ovens for heating and one of the rooms had even rigged up a water boiler. Rabbit Boy offered to take a look the following day. With the help of Richard and Ralf he reckoned he could get them power although cable was needed. Rob reckoned if they wore the guard uniforms, they could get anything.

As night fell, Rob and Sam watched the stars flicker and the moon cast its light over Southampton. From their vantage point, the darkened city lay beneath. Occasional lights from the port and various police stations and guard houses were offset by the haze of smoke rolling over the town.

"I used to go to school over there." She pointed to a darkened building.

Rob nodded. Something felt missing. Despite freedom, and all the friends he'd made, something didn't feel right. It was obvious Sam felt the same, even though she'd be visiting her mum the next day. Putting his finger on that something wasn't easy. After all they'd escaped the labour camp. They were free.

Free to do what though?

"Come on," she said, "let's get some sleep."

Chapter 36

Stew for breakfast was followed by a walk to the other side of town. Beside him, Sam was giddy beyond belief at the thought of visiting her mum. Chances are, she kept saying, she'll be out. She had to visit though. If she wasn't there, she could leave a note.

Rob's initial fears over the Consortium searching for them had been quelled by Ralf. He was right of course, they had no order, no real chain of command. Just a bunch of disparate agencies trying to act as one. It would be days before they even realised people were missing. It would be weeks before they worked out exactly who was missing. Months before they checked their nearest and dearest for contact.

Sam's mother was younger than Rob had imagined. Early forties, with similar good looks and the same powerful hair Sam possessed. She too could certainly handle herself in a fight. Rob gave them some privacy in the living room as he sat in the kitchen with her stepdad.

"Escaped from the Island, eh?" he said. A not unlikeable late-forties man, his balding hairline was covered as best he could. An electrician working for the department of electricity, it was his day off.

"Yeah. Just drove straight out. Scared sh..." He paused. "Scared witless we were."

"Not many come back you know. Get the occasional swimmer turn up, but most get arrested."

Rob nodded. "I know it's a bit rude to ask, but can you get your hands on any wire?"

"Course. The shed's full of borrowed stuff. I'll show you later."

"Thanks. There's power in the floor below, you see."

Sam's stepdad took another sip of his weak tea. "How is she? Her mother's been out of her mind the past two months."

"As well as you can be. Still feels like a dream. All of it. Not just being captured, but escaping too."

"Take care of her, won't you?"

Rob nodded.

The shed was full of every borrowed item Rob could imagine. Fifty metres of cable on a reel, several switches and an electric water heater were packed into a box. Her stepdad said pilfering was rife. A whole new bartering economy had emerged and government workers seemed to be doing well from it.

Sam's mum insisted on cooking them lunch as well as giving them sleeping bags, jumpers and some of Sam's old clothes she'd dumped years ago. They'd got on very well. A spark he hadn't seen before filled her eyes as they talked about old times and family.

A bowl of stew and potatoes later and the afternoon had dragged on. On the fifth offer of a bed for the night, Sam relented.

"They'll come for us eventually," she said. "Sorry, but they will. I'm sure tonight will be okay though."

"You can stay as long as you want, you know that," her mum said, filling four glasses with wine that had been obtained from somewhere.

"It's not fair on you two. They'll take you away for helping us."

A look flashed between her mum and stepdad. Rob reckoned they'd been round the first time they took Sam. Luckily Sam missed the look. Rob instinctively thought of his own parents. He wondered if they had been visited and what had happened to them.

"You alright, hun?" she said.

"Fine yeah." He smiled, but doubted it was convincing.

"You're both welcome to stay as long as you want. Plus any other of your friends."

Rob could tell her mum didn't really mean it, but she had to say it.

The bedroom was just as she'd left it three years ago. Stained wallpaper hid where a Boyzone poster had been ripped from the walls, possibly as she turned from a girl into a teen. Sitting on the edge of her bed, Rob felt more than awkward. Her mum and stepdad were next door. He half expected her mum to come through any minute and give him a good talking to.

"That bath was great," said Sam, walking back in. Her pink fluffy slippers and nightgown from a different age.

Rob nodded. He too had had his first hot bath in months. Showers just weren't the same, especially the holding centre ones.

Despite their many discussions on the island, the time in the holding centre had never been discussed. They all wanted to forget about it. Especially that guard and the interview.

"You alright?" Sam asked.

"Fine." He nodded. "I think that brandy went to my head." Sam's stepdad had produced a bottle of brandy when the wine ran out. It had been a long time without alcohol and he felt wobbly.

She blew out the candle and moved towards him. "If you're drunk, I'd better take advantage."

Rob woke early the next morning. Despite the comfort and friendliness her mum displayed, he sensed he wasn't alone in wanting to join the others. The last of her bits were packed away, along with a few clothes for Rob and the others before they left.

Another bonus of working for the government was the van her stepdad used to take them back. Avoiding all the roadblocks was a time consuming and long winded drive, but it saved a long walk with heavy bags.

Saying goodbye, they entered the flat and quickly caught up on what had happened the night before.

John was over the moon with the cable and other lifted goods. He'd been working on a cable scam from a depot using the guard uniforms, which made having it fall into his lap even better. With the help of Rob and Richard, he spent the day re-wiring most of the building. Having working power and even a grill in one of the flats made it just that bit more comfortable.

"Funny isn't it," said John.

"What?" replied Rob.

"This power, where it comes from. All those people peddling. Two days ago, that was us, well you."

Rob agreed it was funny in a way. If anything could make you conserve energy, the thought of thousands of people pedalling in giant warehouses was possibly the best.

Evening dinner of stew was followed by the usual get together. After the previous day's joy at being free, they were now coming to terms with just what they'd been freed into. A life on the run. Once Rob got his head around what it involved, it lost its romantic qualities. It felt like the New Forest again. Every twig snapping or gust of wind brought with it the thought of capture.

Rob fell asleep hours before Sam, who once again, struggled to comprehend just what was going to happen next. Meeting her mum again had forced a lot of emotions to the surface, but there was something deeper making her unhappy, something much deeper.

Chapter 37

A week quickly passed. Sam met up with her mum on pre-planned days and they went shopping for stew and generally just swapped gossip on park benches

Mattresses, clothing, electric cookers and even kettles were liberated from various places. Evening meetings had once again become regular, usually in Sal's flat, but occasionally Yorkie and Quiety played host.

The conversation had grown from the initial, aren't we lucky to escape and I wonder what Frank's doing now, through to, I found a great wood stash earlier, ending with what happens next?

Of course, Rob and Sam had been wondering this since the first day; perhaps the others had too but it'd been unspoken. Gradually it was being skirted around, each time they'd get nearer and nearer to saying it aloud.

Finally, the day came. Sam came straight out with it. "What do we actually do then?"

"How do you mean?" said Quiety.

"I mean now. The reason we're here is because we were fighting. That's why we got captured and plonked on that island. What happens next? We can't just live here forever and hope other people will save us."

"I've been wondering that too," said Richard. Sitting next to Sharon, he looked happier this past week than Rob had seen him. They were spending more time with each other, and when Quiety found an old laptop computer four days ago, Richard barely flinched an eyebrow. He did however, take it back to his room and Rob suspected he was burning the midnight oil, trying to make it work.

"Take the fight to them, you mean?" said Ralf.

"Yeah," said Sam. "Obviously try not to get caught this time."

Rob laughed expecting others too, but only Beardy joined him.

"What can we do though?" said Sal. "I mean what can we really do to make a difference?"

"There must be something," said Rob. "I think, going over it in every detail isn't going to help. We just have to put our heads together and eventually, something will come up. Some decent plan."

Heading off to bed, Rob didn't have a clue what that plan could possibly be.

When Sal spread the word the next morning that she'd had an idea, Rob doubted he was the only one with reservations. He'd figured it could take weeks or months for a workable idea to take shape, if it ever did. Obviously, it would involve protest or direct action, but the thought that Sal had come up with a plan so quickly, and without losing any sleep, just seemed unbelievable.

"My plan," Sal explained at that evening's meeting, "is to start a revolution. Get the whole country involved. If everyone protests, we can retake power. It's the only way. Piddling about doing the odd thing here and there isn't going to work. It has to be everyone together."

As Rob had suspected, it wasn't well enough thought through, if at all. "A revolution means mobilising everyone onto the streets together. It's not possible for just us to get that kind of support."

Sal's eyes twinkled. "But, you don't have to actually have a revolution to make people believe it's happening."

They all paused, trying to understand what she'd actually just said.

"Propaganda," said Ralf who obviously knew her plan.

Smiling at him, she continued, "Exactly. You only have to look at what's happening now to see that. Fear is the biggest weapon. And food. Food is maybe a bigger weapon if used correctly. To most people, the Consortium's some all seeing eye, a highly efficient organisation that tracks every movement and logs it. Break any rule and you're off to the Isle of Wight."

"We've seen the reality though," said Ralf.

"Precisely. They're a shambles, ruling on terror and lack of food. The reality is a disorganised mess that has nowhere near enough resources or support to actually put in place the things people think they have."

Okay, so maybe she had thought it through, but Rob still wondered how the hell they could use this to their advantage. "Let's face it. We're just a bunch of old uns, except you three of course." He nodded at Sam, Sal and Sharon. He later realised he should have included Weirdy. "What can eleven people do?"

"We had about fifteen," said Sam. "It was a disaster. There's not enough of us to even start a supermarket stew riot."

"We need to think on a bigger scale," said Sal. Her smile showed she was only halfway through explaining her plan. "We need to mimic what they're doing. Information, or rather disinformation, is power."

Standing up, she went over to the television that Rabbit Boy had got working and turned it on. Flicking through the four remaining channels, two of them showed news programmes that everyone knew was propaganda, another showed a wildlife documentary and the last, a soap repeat.

"Whoever controls this controls the country."

Rob knew his jaw had hit the floor and his mouth was bobbing like a trout. She was right. About the only thing you could rely on to actually work was the television. People had once believed everything the respectable news programs transmitted. Was that belief now lost, or just temporarily suspended?

"Are you seriously suggesting we take over the television stations? Then what? Seriously, what then? Plus, how?"

"I'm not sure if we'd even need to take them over. Just redirect the signals. I have to admit, I'm no expert in how it's run or broadcast, but there must be some way to hijack or replace the signals. If only for an hour or so. Richard knows everything about computers, Ralf was a producer, Rob was a reporter and well, Sam's got a lovely face for telly."

Rob felt Sam's blushes coming from beside him. "Stop it," she said.

"Seriously. I'm sort of known too, that can only add authenticity." She blushed through her modesty.

The flat fell silent as nine people pondered Sal's idea, while Sal and Ralf beamed smiles.

Yorkie was the first to break it. "I know nowt about owt technical, but it can't be that easy, can it?"

Rob looked at Ralf, along with everyone else.

"Well, yes, I think it is possible. But there are variables and things that can go wrong. A lot of planning would be needed."

"How does it actually work though?" asked Sam. "I mean, how does the signal get to the box?"

"Radio waves, but I'm sure that's not what you meant. Starting at the beginning, a signal of audio and picture is transmitted from the main transmission sites. I'll come back to how that picture arrives there later. These transmitters, there's about a hundred, cover Britain. There's also little feeder or booster stations in hard to reach areas."

"If you can intercept or redirect where these transmitters look to for the signal, then, yes, I'm sure it can be done. Never been done before, but I don't see why not. I can instantly think of many problems. Taking over the transmitters by force won't be easy for a start. Not with eleven of us. But as I say, I think this has a chance. I also think we'll find the answers."

"Supposing though," said Sal, "we can feed a new signal through it. How long would we get before they take down the system?"

"However long it takes them to notice, drive to the transmitters and pull the plug."

Rob suspected they'd rehearsed that question and reply.

"How about," said Quiety, "if you just did the ones covering the largest population. Big cities, you know. How many would you have to man then?"

Ralf nodded. "Low double digit should catch more than half the population. I'm thinking along the lines of what happens with an outside broadcast. You bounce the signal off one of the redundant satellites up there, you don't have to go anywhere near the TV centres then. That's the first place anyone would look if the TV gets taken over. They'd go straight to television centre and find they're still drinking tea and showing EastEnders. That might buy us an hour or so while they tear the TV centre apart looking for where the signal's coming from."

Despite the amount of wide eyes round the room, Rob remained sceptical. Richard looked like he was too. "Even if that works," said Rob, "Would it really be enough time to pull off a coup? There's not enough of us is there?"

"But Rob," said Sal, getting quite excited. "We'd get help wouldn't we? As soon as everyone thinks a coup is happening, they'll get off their arses and join in, creating the actual coup we can't."

Rob nodded his head slowly. These past two years had been like a dream or a nightmare, but it showed that anything could happen.

"What about the Army and Police," said Quiety. "First sign of serious disorder and they'll be on the streets?"

"He's got a point," said Beardy, who hadn't shaved despite the haul of razors they'd got. "Even if individual soldiers or units have mixed loyalties, their job is to protect the country."

"We could knock out their phone lines," Richard pondered aloud. "I'm not sure how, but it's all electronic now. A bit of hacking could probably do it. I'm certain they'd have more than one back-up and emergency system though." He shook his head.

Quiety, who'd been listening intently, scratched his head. "Though he's a puppet, the prime minister still has control over the army. An order would have to come from him through senior Generals to give up fighting the riot or revolt or whatever it's called. The police uphold the law. Whether they like the law or not, that's their jobs. The prime minister has no direct control, as such."

Ralf scratched his chin. "Can we, I'm just guessing here, but is it possible to confuse the army into thinking the order's come not to attack people? This is still new territory, remember. Rightfully the Queen should be appointing a prime minister to run her government, not the current charade. But what if the Army thought she'd be re-throned, if that's a word."

"If we get hold of Helen Mirren, we could pretend," said Richard.

"Richard," snapped Sharon, "this is serious."

"Sorry," he replied. "This just seems too big. I can see it's possible. I can reprogram anything if I've got the right bit of kit. Possible and probable are two different things. They're not just going to sit there watching while we take over the country. We're outnumbered and relying on people hitting the streets. Oh, I don't know."

"We need hope, Richard," said Sal. "Out of small acorns and all that. We have to do something."

"Just supposing," said Rob, "that we did manage to take over the TV. Would people really take to the streets? We're not exactly known for complaining and rioting are we? Okay so the riots over food were prolific. But everyone's got food now. Well, stew is sort

234

of food. We're not going to starve is what I'm getting at. Will anyone risk life and limb to take to the streets just because the telly's been hijacked for an hour?"

Sal scrunched her nose up. "We can't give up. We have to do something. Where's the future otherwise? Not just for us, but for everyone else. We're being ground down into second rate citizens. We need to fight to at least control our destiny."

"Rob's right," said Richard, "as a nation we haven't got a fighting spirit, have we? The French have, it's like some inbuilt rioting thing they're born with. Expecting the public to take to the streets is risky, I think. Protesting isn't something we're good at. The only things we are good at are sarcasm and teenage pregnancies."

"Look," said Ralf. "It's getting late. What say we sleep on the idea? We're not going to get anywhere here and now."

"Sounds like a plan," said Sam.

The others agreed.

Slipping back into their flat, Sam and Rob hit the sack. Sleep took a long time to come. Sam's questions of could it work and what they'd have to do and should she have a haircut before going on the telly were answered as best he could.

Rob was close to not caring whether it could or would work; making the stand was the point. With good planning and a lot of luck, it had promise. It was the stand, though, that was important. Not just rolling over and accepting a foregone conclusion. Showing everyone out there that people were trying to help.

Something's were worth fighting for.

Chapter 38

Waking just after ten to an empty bed, Rob walked through to the kitchen. Sam was in her dressing gown warming up chicken stew. Shuffling behind, he placed his hands on her shoulders.

"Morning,"

"Morning. Thought I'd make you breakfast in bed."

Kissing the top of her head, he wrapped his arms round her. "You are good to me."

"I know. Go back to bed, I'll bring it through."

He did as told.

Five minutes later, with a cold Sam next to him, Rob ate with renewed vigour. He sensed her spirits were high too. This could work. It could also fail, but it was that little ray of hope that made the chicken stew taste like bacon and eggs.

The breakfast eaten, they showered and got ready for what they knew would be an important meeting.

When the knock on their door came, they were more than ready. A million ideas, questions and different television-hairstyles filled Sam's mind.

"Ready?" asked Richard.

"Course," replied Sam. "How long you been up?"

"Oh, I didn't sleep too well, so I got up early."

Judging by what he was wearing and the glint in his eye, Rob reckoned he hadn't slept at all. If he had, it certainly wasn't in his own bed. As much as Rob liked Sharon, he couldn't help but wonder if she was just after his gold. Time would tell.

Leaving, they made for Sal's flat. Inside, Rob noticed that only Ralf was missing. Within a minute he came out of the bedroom, armed with a notepad.

As usual, Sal started. "Well? What do we reckon?"

Most of the heads in the room nodded, a few even said yes. The only real dissenter, Richard, said, "I'm not against it..."

"But?" asked Sam.

"Yeah, there's a but, I just wonder if there's a better way. I don't know what, I'll be the first to admit that, but if we're going to go into the dragon's lair fighting, then we at least need to be sure which dragon we're going for."

Despite the muddle of metaphors, Rob knew what he meant. If you've only got one shot, make it the best. Whether this was their best attempt or not, who could tell. Richard's ability to think clearly despite the obvious haze of Sharon, possibly his first ever relationship, impressed Rob.

"Unless we have other ideas," said Quiety. "I think we have to work at this one."

Richard shrugged his shoulders. "I'm in, don't get me wrong, I'll do whatever I can, but. Well just, but."

"Butt out," said Sam. "Anyway, Sal, what do you reckon?"

"I thought long and hard last night. I'm sure we all did, but the thing I explained before? When I read the weather? Well, I need to get in contact with that handler, or contact or whatever he was."

Her bright red colour after saying handler gave Rob a clue as to who was involved: the Secret Service.

"They'll either be able to help, or suggest something else we can do or point us towards other people. The problem is, he's in London and we're not."

As easy as travelling had once been, Rob knew trying to get to London would be like flying to the moon. Sal would have no chance. There were at least fifty checkpoints on the road between Southampton and there, and the minibus, if it hadn't been stolen, was low on diesel. Trains were now non-existent for passenger travel. Some coaches existed, a few a week to the big city, but Sal would have no chance of getting the paperwork needed to travel.

"There are other ways of getting in touch with someone," said Richard.

"Carrier pigeon?" replied Sam.

"Similar but more secure. Short wave radio. You can use it like the internet. You transmit secure packages of data that only the receiver knows how to decode."

"Can you do that?" asked Sal.

"Yeah. Me and a friend tried it when this all started. There are two problems though. One, I don't know if my friend will be looking for the signal and two, you can tell where it's been transmitted from."

"So we need to get a message to him to tell him to listen out for a message from you to give to someone else?" asked Quiety.

"Mmmm. It has a few flaws, doesn't it?"

237

"Can't you just ring this spy bloke?" Sam asked Sal.

"He's not a spy, no, nothing like that." Her face blushed. "I could ring from a callbox I suppose. Can't guarantee it'd be a secure line, but at least he'll know I'm alive and need help."

"Don't you have code words or a secret language or nothing?" No one could mistake Sam's look of awe.

"I think," said Yorkie. "We shouldn't get bogged down in all this now. One of us will think of a way. For now, we need to start planning. If this does happen, we're going to need stuff. Technical bits I wouldn't even begin to know the names of. I suggest we start planning that. The rest will come."

Of course Yorkie was right, he usually was.

For the rest of the day, Sal and Ralf explained a TV studio set up and the very basics that were needed to operate one. Transmitting to a satellite seemed to be the tricky part, but Richard and Quiety both had ideas on fixing a dish to the top of the flats. Richard also reckoned the wire frame of the building reaching into the sky would make a good aerial in itself.

The list of equipment needed grew by the minute. Richard needed a whole raft of computer equipment, though he suggested reusing old computers. Walkie-talkies would be needed to keep in touch, and maybe even a shortwave radio receiver and transmitter would come in handy. By the time they'd finished, the list resembled a Christmas list for a mid-life crisis gadget freak.

Though still feeling they were biting off more than they could chew, Rob suggested a few places to liberate equipment. The old BBC studio, redundant since regional television stations were abolished could possibly have some equipment. Everyone once had gadgets and electronics equipment throughout their homes, but when the food ran out, these were soon bartered away. They were easy and cheap enough to find, if you had food to swap.

After a rushed dinner of chicken stew, the day had gone. Returning to their flat, Rob felt talked out. Switching on the television, the mix of rehashed old programs and biased news washed over him.

Rob could just see the television news, taken over by the bunch of misfits that they were. He could see it working. A light was starting to shine at the end of a distant tunnel.

Chapter 39

The next two days were full of chicken stew and planning. The actual planning was difficult as it still wasn't clear exactly what was being planned. Bits of old computers borrowed and bartered lay in Richard's room. He'd stripped them and saved anything of value. Quiety helped him rebuild some type of hybrid, multi-processored computer. With a bank of three screens, plus two other PCs next to it, it already resembled something NASA would use.

A heavily made up and disguised Sal had made it past two checkpoints with the forged papers and reached the far side of Southampton. Her heart in her mouth in a public phone box, she picked up the phone she knew would be tapped and dialled a London number. Taking over twenty seconds just to get a dial tone, she realised the tappers must be busy. In some ways, a busy tapper is the best sort. With too much to do, the chances of missing something covert was higher.

That was what Sal hoped as the phone started ringing.

"Hello?" someone answered.

Sal had not been expecting her contact to answer. The phone number she'd memorised was just a normal office in Islington. Its occupants were normal people. With one exception: they were sleepers. They had a day job and went about it normally with no sign of their involvement with the Secret Service.

After the bailout, the Consortium was given access to the Secret Service, supposedly to show there was nothing to hide. As the police state grew, parts of the Secret service grew with it while others were disbanded. Other parts, including some previously hidden from the Consortium, withdrew and became Secret-Secret Services. Hidden from all view, their aim was only to achieve the best for their country. It was this latter group that first recruited Sal.

"Oh hello," said Sal. "Is that Masons and Masons solicitors?"

"No," the woman replied. "Sorry, this is Masons, Fordhams and Masons."

"Oh. I think I've been given the wrong number. I don't suppose you happen to know their number do you?"

"I think I might," the woman replied. "We do get calls for them occasionally. Yes it's here, are you ready?"

"Uh huh."

"London, that's zero one, then eight one one eight zero five five."

"Five five," repeated Sal. "Okay, thank you very much for your help."

"No problem," the woman replied. "Have a nice day."

I will, thought Sal as she hung up.

Determined not to arouse suspicion, she made the lonely and long winded journey back to the flats. Stopping at a near empty supermarket on the way, she queued for nearly an hour for some soft potatoes and two cans of stew.

Handing over the forged ration card for Glenda Brown, Sal noticed the till operator look closely at her. Twisting her head as she looked, the operator seemed to either recognise her or be looking at something. The hobnailed and well fed security guard behind the tills was maybe seconds from noticing something amiss. The checkout operator, a young girl herself, smiled. In fact, Sal was later convinced the girl subtly winked. Retrieving her ration card and food, Sal walked past the security guard, her heart in her mouth, and walked the final mile home.

The third day brought another long walk from Sal, this time to the Southern tip of Southampton. Her aching legs a constant reminder that more than enough walking had been done this past month.

Reaching another phone box, she dialled not the number she'd be given yesterday, 01 811 8055, but the number she thought it decoded to. Again, a long wait for a dial tone, was followed by ringing. After a minute of ringing, she was sure she'd decoded it wrong until the phone answered.

"Hello, Rothman's TV repairs."

"Oh hello. I've got an old set that's on the blink I wonder if you would be able to fix it. It's a twenty inch LCD. The picture keeps breaking and, well, we can't afford a new one." Sal spoke very clearly and slowly.

"We're a bit full this week," the answerer said.

"Oh, okay. Well, maybe I'll try a few other places. If I don't have any luck would you be able to fix it next week?"

"Yes," he said. "I think I'll be able to next week. Can I take your number?"

"We haven't got a house phone. I'll ring you again tomorrow if I can't get any other help."

"Okay," he said. "Good luck."

"Thanks."

Leaving the phone box, she walked back towards the flat. Trying not to smile as she walked, she thought of next Monday and the meeting she'd just arranged with her handler.

Back at the flat, Rob, Sam, Ralf and John had spent the morning planning. Not just any planning, this actually had an immediate purpose. The old BBC building less than a mile away, the target. Stealing a large camera and carrying it a mile, was not part of the plan. But there had to be other things in there. Ralf was most interested in a mixing desk and outside production equipment.

Ralf's ideas for the broadcast involved small hand-held camcorders with a line fed through. The quality would be worse than normal television, but not really noticeable to the casual viewer. All of them had no idea if the television studios had been cleaned out of everything already. They may be guarded, too. A quick scout round would prove that.

Waiting until the curfew was underway, the four, dressed in guard uniforms, Sam and Rob having borrowed theirs, left the flats and kept to the shadows as they walked.

The sight of patrolling guards wasn't unusual, though as fewer people openly rebelled, it became rarer. Walking through the city in two groups, Rob and Sam just behind the others, they soon reached the building's perimeter. The guardhouse by the front gate empty, the entire entrance had been given an additional fence to ward off burglars.

Skirting the fence, they found an opening; someone had obviously had the idea of looting the building before them. Though the site was large, the main studio complex was only the size of a small terrace of houses. Heavily padlocked and gated, they realised they'd little chance of entrance.

Abandoning the plan, they instead looked for a stores building. Ralf insisted every television centre would have one. With most of the signs torn down or rotted away, finding it proved difficult, but eventually they came across an outbuilding that had already been broken into.

Inside, it had been ransacked. Only a few leads, microphones and rolls of gaffa tape remained. Settling on just them, they left. Ralf was sure there'd be equipment inside the ex-studios, but devoid of something to tear down the walls with, they had no way of getting in.

Chapter 40

The next day brought more progress. Richard was getting further in his hacking of various computers and systems. Finding a backdoor into the old satellite TV network, he slowly and methodically went through their satellites. It seemed two older ones were now unused, digital television having succeeded them. These interested him the most: no one would be monitoring them. Well, he hoped no one would be monitoring them.

Weirdy, Sam, Sharon, the three lads from downstairs and a few others in the flats were busy decorating the abandoned last floor. Only partially built, it had television studio written all over it. Part of it was cordoned off: Ralf had suggested another use for that which surprised them all.

Beardy, with his telecommunication skills, had spent days in the sewer system, rerouting telephone cables. He'd connected a telephone line the first day, which Richard was using, but he was also intent on rerouting nearly every phone line in Southampton to set an untraceable trail.

Sal, ahead of her meeting, was nervous. Though convinced she'd planned every eventuality, she knew things could still go wrong.

When the day came, she walked to the city centre and stood outside the old Woolworths shop. Though lunchtime it was quiet. Some office workers and the few retail shops left were doing a business of sorts, but she was concerned at standing out in such a public place. Her false glasses and dyed hair weren't enough for her to feel comfortable.

Her contact, known only to her as Seventy Two showed up fifteen minutes late. Smiling when he saw her, he looked lost in his big trench coat.

Smiling back, she wondered again how the man in front of her had ever made a secret agent. A sinewy, eczema ridden man with clammy hands, he was the most anti-spy she could imagine. She had of course thought time and time again that he was an imposter, a charlatan. But he'd proved he knew things. He was able to pass on information and could be trusted.

"I didn't think I'd see you again," he said.

She smiled. "Bit of a long story."

"Good idea to stay in Southampton. They're looking in London for you."

She nodded. No doubt Frank had left behind something pointing that way. "A group of us have got a plan."

"Oh yeah." He started walking beside her, keeping up the pretence of a dinner break walk.

"I'll start at the beginning."

The next week saw the television studio take shape. Sal's mysterious handler popped round a few times with some camcorders, a small mixing desk and a few dates and times that would be ideal. There were, he explained, a few sympathetic army generals, but they wouldn't show their hand until it was clear this wasn't just a normal riot.

Beardy's sewer diving took on more twists. The more the actual event was planned, the more they realised he'd need to be in London to cut off phone communications. Apparently temporarily cutting the lines wasn't as hard as they thought; getting to London would be much harder.

Rob's chosen job, to be the reporter on the ground, required him to go to London too. Sam, in between trying out new hairstyles, really wasn't happy about it. It took both Rob and Sal a lot of persuading before she came round.

Richard continued to soup up his computer to the power of a rocket launching mainframe. He'd tapped into the satellite and re-routed its trajectory so it could be used. With the help of Sharon, he was arguably doing most of the work: leaving snippets of code inside the transmitters so he could re-route them, working on code that Beardy could use to crash and reprogram the phone network, and also working on software to enhance Sam's hair colour and complexion while on camera.

Yorkie, Quiety, Rabbity, Weirdy, the three lads, and some other volunteers had one clear job: protect the transmitters. Given the biggest transmitters by size of population, they were split into pairs and when the time came, they would make their way to those sites and protect them from assault. They filled these jobs with a certain amount of trepidation. They realised they could easily be outnumbered and killed, despite the arms shipment the secret agent was working on. Protecting it from a distance became the chosen method. But even so, it was the riskiest job.

As the day grew nearer, Ralf's plan for the other half of the studio became clear. The brick walls of the shell had been converted into two street scenes. One, the outside of a police station, the other a town hall. Though close up it looked like a block of flats crudely painted to look like something else, Ralf insisted that TV magic would make it look realistic.

With cameras set up at a distance. Rob filmed the carefully organised mini riot inside the flats. Using the three lads from downstairs and some other volunteers, Rob filmed them breaking down the police station door and entering the building. For added effect, Yorkie, Quiety and Ralf dressed up in guard uniforms and quickly surrendered to the ensuing revolters. Near the end of the filming, Sharon had the inspired idea of having some of the guards fighting alongside the rioters. If the guards swapped affinity, Ralf agreed it would make the perfect newsflash item.

Adlibbing, Rob introduced the item. "Well, the revolution seems to be gathering pace here in London. The guards, once loyal to the Consortium, have swapped sides and are fighting arm in arm with protesters. He spun the camera around to Richard, dressed as a guard, who was helping Weirdy break a window with a concrete block. "With the guards changing sides, it can surely only be a matter of hours before the Consortium throws in the towel."

Editing the film removed the obvious flimsy sets and visible fire exit signs, leaving three, two minute, very believable outside broadcasts.

"Fancy a pop at doing a moon landing tomorrow?" said Richard.

Chapter 41

With two days to go, the transmitter protectors left after saying long goodbyes. With forged documents and guard uniforms, they began their treks to the major television transmitters.

Meanwhile Doctor Rob, after a tearful night with Sam, made his way to London by coach. Also on the coach was Telecom engineer Jim the Beard, who had been persuaded to trim his forest to a more respectable size. The secret agent had come up trumps with the travel plans, documents and also a place for each of them to stay. It seemed odd for Rob to ignore Beardy on the coach after all they'd been through, but he had to. Besides, Rob was worried enough about the contents of his suitcase: a handheld camcorder, tiny LCD television, a small electronic box of tricks that Richard had invented and a shortwave radio that Richard had also doctored. With each checkpoint passed, Rob gave a sigh of relief but also another bout of anxiety over the next.

Eventually, they arrived without incident. One final nod between Rob and Beardy as they split could be the end of their friendship. Rob never had tried out his cabbage wine. Maybe one day in the future, when all this was just a memory, they could share a bottle of Chateau de Sprout 2013?

The room, a second floor flat in the heart of the city, was bare but had the necessities. Emptying his bag, Rob hid the shortwave receiver and other electronic bits under a floorboard and placed his spare clothes in the wardrobe.

Wandering around in late afternoon to get his bearings, Rob still couldn't believe this was actually happening. All that planning and risk taking had resulted in this: a crazy attempt to fool people into rebelling.

The streets of London were unlike anything he remembered from his infrequent visits over the years. Whether he was out clubbing or shopping, the city always had an unmistakeable bustle. Like some busy, living organism. The city had lost it. It had died. People walked with their heads down. The streets, now nearly deserted, were full of closed shops and empty parking spaces. The roads once impossible to cross, empty.

It took less than ten minutes for Rob to know everything they were trying was worth the risk. The heart ripped from the country needed urgent surgery to reconnect and revive it. And, he was the doctor that could do it.

After an evening meal of cold stew in his new flat, Rob slept poorly on the double bed. Crunched up in a corner, he spent half the night sure something was missing. He'd only known Sam a few weeks, but the closeness of their situation had made him utterly smitten. Being without her was like being without an arm.

Next morning he headed for the hospital. A bag containing his doctor's uniform and the box of tricks filled with wires, resistors and other components Rob had never seen before was carried by his side. Alongside the morning walkers to work, he blended in well. The streets were busy this time of day, but were still no comparison to the old days. Arriving at the hospital, he checked into reception as the renowned heart surgeon who'd been transferred from Southampton General.

"I'll show you to your office, Doctor," said the Nurse.

Containing a desk, pot plant and coffee machine, Rob couldn't help but allow himself the briefest of smiles. Within ten minutes, freshly brewed coffee filled the air as he changed into his surgeon's outfit. Though not scheduled to do any operations that day, which Rob was very relieved about, his purpose at the hospital became clear after a few cups of heavenly tasting coffee.

Sneaking to the roof, he attached Richard's electronic box of tricks to an old satellite dish, unused since the hospital's television system failed. The box in place, Rob's short wave radio could directly communicate with it and in turn, the satellites being used by Richard to feed the television transmitters. If necessary, Rob would be able to run a live feed through his camcorder; a real outside broadcast.

Back in his office, and two coffees later, he told his new secretary he'd take the rest of the day off as there were no operations. Giving them a false contact address, Rob hoped to hell there weren't any actual emergencies needing heart surgery as he left.

Returning to the flat, Rob settled down for a long and sleepless night as he waited for the next day and the revolution it would bring.

Chapter 42

Barry, Sheila and Lloyd were settling down in front of the television for the evening's entertainment. Barry and Sheila had been together for over ten years, but had nothing to celebrate. They'd had it all once. The good life. A house with more bedrooms than they'd ever need, different car every year, holidays in the sun. All on tick. All on the never-never. The crash hit them hard. Everything they had became worthless while their debts remained. Losing their house, they accepted the only lifeline on offer: Lloyd's spare room.

Lloyd, an habitually single man and Barry's best mate from old, was only happy to have them. A dustbin man, or recycling controller as he called it, he saw how times were hard. The council had let many go, but they'd kept Barry and a few others on to collect and recycle the mountains of empty stew cans.

Barry and Sheila, now unemployed from their previous expendable jobs, spent their days walking the streets trying to find work, money and food. They usually came back empty handed. The evenings were spent eating stew, drinking weak tea and watching the box, dreaming of better times.

"Come the revolution," Lloyd had always said. "We'll be there. We might be a bit late, but we'll be there."

Sheila had always laughed at this. The pair were less revolutionary than a non-bagless vacuum cleaner. Not that she'd let either of them revolt anyway. After losing so much the past few years, how could she lose Barry as well? And Lloyd, the best friend who'd always been a bit annoying and got in the way, when the crunch came he'd stuck by them, given them somewhere to live. She wouldn't want to lose him either.

Walking to the kitchen to finish making the tea, she heard the pair squabble over some minor thing on the television. She sighed. Just like every night.

Chapter 43

Though worse than expected, Yorkie was confident this was going to work. The transmission tower was hidden behind a perimeter fence. They'd expected that. Security guards had been half expected too. But six of them? That wasn't expected.

Turning to Rabbit John, who, in his commando gear looked like he was enjoying himself too much, Yorkie shrugged.

"What now, chief?" asked John.

"I wish you wouldn't keep calling me that."

"Sorry. What are we gonna do?"

"Just watch a minute."

The guards didn't look particularly interested in guarding. They were more concerned with the contents of the car boot they were looking in. Their discussion and occasional laughter was only side-tracked by the sight of the sub-machine guns hanging loosely round their shoulders.

As the minutes passed, their conversations died down. Two of the guards removed some boxes from the boot and carried them inside the opened mesh fence, towards the portacabin next to the tower.

"Looks like they're just visiting," Yorkie whispered.

"Still half an hour 'til d-day."

"Plenty of time, plenty."

"Don't like the look of their guns, though."

"To be honest, neither do I lad."

"You think they know we're here? There's so many of us, wouldn't be surprised if someone at the flat's a grass."

"Keep it down," said Yorkie. "You're being paranoid for the sake of it. Everyone's alright. No one's a grass."

"I'll remain unconvinced."

"You do that."

In less than thirty minutes, they knew Richard was going to knock out the alarm system, with Beardy covering the phone lines. John grunted something, but Yorkie either didn't hear or didn't want to hear.

Finally, two guards re-entered their cabin with the last of their boxes. The car started, its rough engine taking a few bites before the tell-tale smog of biomass diesel left its exhaust. Three guards got in the car and as it chugged away, Yorkie turned to John.

"That's more like it, one on one. Fairer now."

Waiting in his second floor flat, Rob couldn't believe this was going to happen. His heart raced. The biggest crunch time ever.

The call would come from Jim, over the short wave radio, telling him when to ring the government and try to speak to the Prime Minister. In this new world, in his new cover, he was just passing on a message, but what a message it was. Soon, most of the phone lines wouldn't work, every television would be showing four channels of Sam, and he, Rob from the Basingstoke Bugle, would be ringing up Downing Street for an exclusive Consortium resignation.

His heart skipped more beats as he thought about it. 'It's all over the television, Prime Minister. They've taken over the country. Now I'm not a spokesman for them, but they've asked me to meet you.'

How risky? He'd be in Downing Street, setting out what the Prime Minister had to say and then film it. He'd be there, telling him what to say. The puppet would still be a puppet, but he'd be Rob's puppet.

They were all taking risks, Yorkie, Quiety, John and the others were risking death from the guards and Army. The flats with Sam, Ralf and Sal inside would eventually be traced, and the mock studio raided. And Jim, in the sewer near the telephone tower, they'd try to trace the source as soon as the phone and emergency network went down.

But this? Going into the lion's den of ten Downing Street? If any part of it went wrong, there was nowhere to run. Thank god Sam didn't know what he was really doing.

Trudging through the sewer, Jim wondered how he'd chosen the shortest straw. Yesterday had been the hardest day of his life. Walking into the Telecom Tower in the heart of London, hoping to god his phoney pass would let him through. It had of course, and after he'd entered restricted area after restricted area, he logged into the exchange and carefully followed the procedure that Richard and the spy had worked out.

Of course, they all knew with regional exchanges this was only going to temporarily shut down London's phones. All they had to do was reboot the system and they'd spot where the problem was. That hour or so it would give, that hour of complete chaos, he hoped it would be long enough to disorientate them. Long enough for panic to set in and fuel the riot.

Reaching the junction just under Telecom Tower, Jim scratched at his rapidly re-growing beard. In front of him, the secure lines that made up London's other, secret telephone network. Secure fixed lines between Downing Street, the Palace and army bases around the country terminated here. How easy had they made it for him? The remarkable thing was no one had thought of this before.

His cable testers and re-wiring jig in hand, Jim set to work on the switch that would deaden all lines except one: the line through to Number Ten that Rob would ring.

Finishing quicker than he thought, Jim made for the sewer exit to send a message to Richard, telling him all systems were go.

Sat at his bank of PCs, Richard surveyed the screens. Looking and seeing all, his mind running at many miles an hour.

The so-called secure networks had been easier to crack than his wildest dreams would suggest. And he'd had some pretty wild dreams in his previous, computer obsessed life. The old satellite, now in position was just waiting to receive Sam's transmission. The existing satellite that broadcast to the many relay stations over Britain was also just a key press away from being diverted. That one had been a bonus find, though how long it would last before being terminated was anyone's guess.

Though most of his life had been spent worrying, worrying about life, doing the wrong thing, getting caught, a curious sense of power had removed that terror. The phone lines Jim had diverted, reconnected and hidden many times that linked him to the internet would be traced. But that didn't worry him; he'd been assured it would take at least two days. They would have to dig up the street to trace part of it, and by then they'd have stopped looking. Frank the guard with his poxy ten grams of gold didn't worry him either. He'd gained a huge inner strength the past month, his life seemed to have found its purpose. Everything had led this way.

He knew in less than two days, the country would be theirs. No, not theirs. The country would belong back where it should: the people.

Picking up his walkie-talkie, he pressed button three and waited for Ralf to answer.

"We're ready to go. The satellite link's ready. The only part left is to reprogram the servers. My finger's hovering over run. Let me know when."

Chapter 44

"Sam," said Ralf. "We're ready to go. Give us a final check for levels."

"Shit, shit, shit, fuck, shit."

"Okay in five, four, three, two, one, go." Ralf flicked the switch.

Good luck Rob, she thought. See you soon.

The lights flashed as the extra current drawn by the satellite transmitter drained everything else. Sam stared at four TVs in front of her.

They still showed the normal channels.

After three seconds, Sam was convinced it'd failed. Then, very slowly, the pictures broke up. Ghost lines formed over the monitors, slowly but surely revealing the picture of her, Sam, with her new hairstyle, sitting in a chair with a REVOL TV banner behind her.

Looking at Ralf, he clearly mouthed the words, "You're on, don't swear."

Plucking the last of her courage from somewhere deep, she smiled.

"Good evening," she said. "Welcome to REVOL TV. Please don't be alarmed but our country is in the process of being saved from the Consortium by brave freedom fighters."

She tilted her head to one side before continuing, "Up and down the country, millions of people, just like you, who've had enough of chicken stew and this police state are taking to the streets."

"Please do what you can to help. If we act as one, we can reclaim our country. The Queen fully supports this action and has instructed the Army to assist us. Please, we implore you, help regain our country, take to the streets. Take over council and municipal buildings. Take over police stations. Only if we all act together can we overcome this."

"Wass all this about?" asked Barry.

"Dunno," replied Sheila.

"Is it an advert?" said Lloyd.

"Nah, looks real to me. Quality's a bit poor though. Do you think they're really revolting?" asked Sheila.

"Well, she's no looker," said Barry.

Sheila whacked his arm. "Baz, you know what I mean. Anyway, she's quite pretty. I had hair like that when I was younger."

Watching in silence as Sam continued her speech, the trio were engrossed.

"Maybe we ought to go out, see what's going on?" said Barry.

"You ain't going nowhere," Sheila replied. "You're not getting involved in that."

"But, you know, if we do our bit, we might help." Lloyd was ever the optimist.

"He's got a point. You said yourself you're fed up with chicken stew and the power cuts."

Sheila pondered this. Surely it was obvious she wanted freedom. But she'd lost so much already. She'd take a life of stew and oppression over losing him. He'd never understand that though. Never.

Sam continued, "The cities of Bath and Manchester have already been taken. We're also close to having a hold on Bristol and Southampton. Please stay tuned for further announcements."

"In time we'll be producing our own programmes detailing the struggle and how we'll change the nation back to how it used to be. However coming up next, it's the Morecambe and Wise Christmas Special from nineteen seventy seven."

Barry's eyes lit up. "Hmmm. Maybe give it an hour or so, you know, then see what's happening? No point rushing out."

"Yeah," agreed Lloyd. "Nineteen seventy seven, that's the one with the dancing newsreaders isn't it?"

"Is it?" lied Barry. "I really wouldn't know."

Sam continued, "Before Morecambe and Wise, here's the weather." She turned her head right. "Hi Sal. What's the weather like, is it revolting too?"

Camera switches to Sal, facing to her left.

"Thanks Sam. Well this evening we've got a high pressure coming in from..."

"That's Sal," said Sheila. "Look it's Sal. I wondered what had happened to her. Well, if they've got Sal involved, it must be good, whatever it is."

"I'll put the kettle on," said Lloyd. "This could be a long night."

Epilogue

Rob knew it could have been so different.

As the lorry picked up speed, he swayed from side to side, his wrists handcuffed to the roof.

It wasn't that it hadn't worked. It wasn't even that he'd been caught. The worst thing, the truly bad thing, was what they'd caused.

People had taken the streets. Instead of the millions needed, just a few thousand bothered to get off their arses and help. He'd blamed it on many things this past week since it'd failed. Lethargy, fear, Sam's low cut top, and even showing Morecambe and Wise, but whatever it was, only a fraction of the people needed had hit the streets. The ones that had revolted had been hardcore too. The sort that'd been plotting away, trying to change things in the background. They were the sort that were needed if the country could ever be saved.

Unfortunately, they were all rounded up by the police and army within hours. Everyone with enough rebellion in them to help was now locked up and on their way to the Isle of Wight.

They hadn't just messed up this chance: they'd fucked up every chance ever.

As the lorry continued droning through the New Forest, Rob wondered again if Sam had made it or had she been captured too.

Would she be waiting for him on the Isle of Wight?

Part of him hoped she'd escaped. It really did. But the other part of him...

The End

Printed in Great Britain
by Amazon

84229837R00148